The cobra's hood flared. It hissed.

Anok concentrated on the Scale of Set, but something seemed wrong—

The snake drew back.

It struck.

Anok gasped as he felt the needle fangs sink into his neck, felt the hot gush of poison into the wounds.

Something liquid trickled down his neck. Blood or venom, he could not be sure.

He gasped for breath, feeling the poison pumping with each surge of his heart, into his chest, into his brain.

His body seemed to go limp, the priests holding him up as his legs failed him.

His vision dimmed. His mind seemed to float away into the night air, looking down upon the scene.

He heard Ramsa Aál's voice, as though from far away. "By this venom he shall be changed! By this venom he shall be judged! Let him wake an instrument of our god, or let him not wake at all!"

As the blackness surrounded him, he could still hear the chanting: *"Set, Set, Set, munificent Set! Set, Set, Set munificent Set!"*

Look for the first adventures of Anok,
Heretic of Stygia . . .

SCION OF THE SERPENT

HERETIC OF SET

And don't miss the Legends of Kern . . .

BLOOD OF WOLVES

CIMMERIAN RAGE

SONGS OF VICTORY

AGE OF CONAN™
HYBORIAN ADVENTURES

ANOK, HERETIC OF STYGIA
Volume III

VENOM OF LUXUR

J. Steven York

ACE BOOKS, NEW YORK

THE BERKLEY PUBLISHING GROUP
Published by the Penguin Group
Penguin Group (USA) Inc.
375 Hudson Street, New York, New York 10014, USA
Penguin Group (Canada), 90 Eglinton Avenue East, Suite 700, Toronto, Ontario M4P 2Y3, Canada
(a division of Pearson Penguin Canada Inc.)
Penguin Books Ltd., 80 Strand, London WC2R 0RL, England
Penguin Group Ireland, 25 St. Stephen's Green, Dublin 2, Ireland (a division of Penguin Books Ltd.)
Penguin Group (Australia), 250 Camberwell Road, Camberwell, Victoria 3124, Australia
(a division of Pearson Australia Group Pty. Ltd.)
Penguin Books India Pvt. Ltd., 11 Community Centre, Panchsheel Park, New Delhi—110 017, India
Penguin Group (NZ), Cnr. Airborne and Rosedale Roads, Albany, Auckland 1310, New Zealand
(a division of Pearson New Zealand Ltd.)
Penguin Books (South Africa) (Pty.) Ltd., 24 Sturdee Avenue, Rosebank, Johannesburg 2196, South
Africa

Penguin Books Ltd., Registered Offices: 80 Strand, London WC2R 0RL, England

This is a work of fiction. Names, characters, places, and incidents either are the product of the author's
imagination or are used fictitiously, and any resemblance to actual persons, living or dead, business es-
tablishments, events, or locales is entirely coincidental. The publisher does not have any control over
and does not assume any responsibility for author or third-party websites or their content.

THE VENOM OF LUXUR

An Ace Book / published by arrangement with Conan Properties International, LLC.

PRINTING HISTORY
Ace edition / December 2005

Copyright © 2005 by Conan Properties International, LLC.
Cover art by Justin Sweet.
Interior text design by Stacy Irwin.

ISBN: 0-441-01354-6

ACE
Ace Books are published by The Berkley Publishing Group,
a division of Penguin Group (USA) Inc.,
375 Hudson Street, New York, New York 10014.
ACE and the "A" design are trademarks belonging to Penguin Group (USA) Inc.

PRINTED IN THE UNITED STATES OF AMERICA

10 9 8 7 6 5 4 3 2 1

Acknowledgments

This trilogy is the most massive undertaking I've ever been involved with, and it could not have happened without the assistance, support, and occasionally the patience of many wonderful people.

First I'd like to thank my agent, Jodi Reamer, for her able support and council.

As always, my deepest thanks to my wife, Chris, whose huge assistance proved not merely to be invaluable, but indispensable. Also for her eternal understanding and support. I hope I'm up to returning the favor as she faces her own deadlines.

My thanks to all the great folks at Conan Properties International who have participated in the project and guided it through its various stages, including Fredrik Malmberg, Matt Forbeck (with special thanks to Matt for tolerating my frazzled nerves, all the way to the end), Theo Bergquist, and Jeff Conner.

Special thanks to Ginjer Buchanan at Ace, who has stood with me through five novels now.

My thanks to all the friends who have offered encouragement, support, advice and offered feedback through the project, including Sean Prescott, Dean Wesley Smith (yes, Dean, you told me so), Kristine Kathryn Rusch, Loren Coleman, Rose Prescott, the entire Sunday Lunch Gang, and my buds from the Sandbox who helped keep me sane when I ceased to have a life.

Thanks to my family, especially my father, Jim York, my mother, Martha York (secret sleuth of the Internet), and my brother, Tim, who help keep me anchored through all the rough spots. Thanks to my kids, Shane and Lynette, for actually thinking something I do is cool.

Finally, my gratitude to Justin Sweet for some of the most breathtaking covers I've ever seen.

And of course, my appreciation to Robert E. Howard. Without him, we are nothing.

And so, on my hundred and third, and last, year in the Stygian city of Kheshatta, came to me the young wizard and warrior Anok Wati. He came to me as an acolyte of the hated snake god, Set, who has poisoned this land, and my very soul, with his evil.

Before I could send him away, I learned that he was a heretic of Set, secretly plotting against the cult. Though his goals seemed hopeless, I could not help but identify with his anger, and agreed to aid him. Yet I did not realize that he was a man of many secrets, some dark and terrible.

As I innocently tempted him with the terrible sorcerous secrets of my ancient texts, little did I know that he shared with me one other thing: the awful curse of the Mark of Set, a brand of power almost certain to lead its bearer to corruption and doom.

Only after he was on the brink of madness did I learn the truth, and he and his companions sought out the Band of Neska, the one object that might balance out the Mark of Set and help him fight his way back to sanity.

He returned, victorious, having plucked his prize from an ancient tomb and certain that he had destroyed a traitorous companion from his past.

Yet overconfidence is a terrible thing for a sorcerer. For just when he believes he has mastered the magic is often the moment that he discovers that the magic has mastered him.

—THE 287th TABLET OF SABÉ THE WISE

1

THE HOT WIND blasted sand against his face, and Anok pulled the cloth covering over his mouth and nose, squinting against the dust. His camel rocked gently under him as it made its surefooted way across the Stygian wilderness.

Then the wind passed. He wiped the sand from his dry, burning eyes, and gazed out past the other camels in the caravan, across the rolling red rock of the plain, at the distant mountains. His eyes felt like they were full of boulders, and they were long out of tears.

The Mark of Set tingled on his left wrist, and he was reminded of its healing powers. Until now, he had resisted using its power for anything other than matters of life and death, yet, now he had the Band of Neska to control its power.

What harm could it do?

He closed his eyes and concentrated. "Heal," he whispered.

There was an electric sensation that started with the mark, flowed up his arm, his neck, across his face, and into his eyes. As the tingling faded, the relief was immediate and dramatic.

He opened his eyes, which troubled him no more. The sand was gone, and he saw the distant mountains with crystal, almost supernatural, clarity. Even more, he had the feeling that no matter how much the sand blew for the rest of the day, he would not have a vision problem again. It was as though his eyes were made of glass, their lids of rugged yet supple leather.

He smiled, until he remembered his friend Sabé, with whom he shared the curse of the Mark of Set. Sabé, who was known to all in Kheshatta as the "blind scholar," was not blind at all.

Rather, in his youth, the magic of Set had so corrupted him that his eyes became like those of a snake, seeing the world only in shades of hate. Finally, to save his sanity, he had been forced to bind them shut and live out his life in darkness.

Yet Sabé had never had the advantage of the Band of Neska, which was now bound around the bones inside Anok's right wrist, nor had he been warned of the terrible danger the Mark of Set represented.

It won't happen to me. It can't. I have other things to do.

One of the other camels in the caravan fell back beside him. The man riding it wore the scarlet robes and yoke of office of a priest of Set. And not just any priest, but a *Priest of Needs,* one of the most powerful in all the cult.

He was a tall man, thin but muscular, with pearl-white skin, white hair and dark eyes, which marked him as belonging to one of the oldest and most powerful of Stygian noble families. His name was Ramsa Aál. He was Anok's sponsor in the cult, his trainer, his master.

He was also secretly Anok's hated enemy, whom he would gladly kill with his own hands. By at least one account, Ramsa Aál had murdered Sheriti, Anok's first love and oldest friend. Without doubt, he was complicit in her murder, and for that alone he would have to die.

But not today.

There were still many secrets to learn from Ramsa Aál, and as the priest rose in power he took Anok with him into the highest reaches of the Cult of Set. Anok knew well that the only sure way to kill a snake was to cut off its head.

Ramsa looked at him with a familiar grin. "The Tomb of the Lost King is just over the next hill." He pointed to a rise, where a caravan from the west, loaded with white-robed travelers, wound its way along the crest of a hill. "Pilgrims from Khemi, wealthy elders and patrons of the cult come bearing tributes of gold for the shrine."

His grin turned into a wide smile as he gazed off at the travelers. "It amuses us to let them think that the Lost King was a chosen of Set, taken up to join him in his Realm Eternal beyond the stars."

Anok raised an eyebrow. "The stories are not true?"

Ramsa Aál laughed. "The temple is empty, and always has been. It is so pristine and undisturbed by vandals or tomb robbers precisely because it was never used."

They topped the rise and looked down into a small valley occupied by a complex of ancient but beautiful stone buildings, the most splendid and ornate being the tomb itself.

"Within those splendid walls, there is no golden sarcophagus, no treasures for the afterlife, save those brought as offerings by pilgrims, which are quickly taken to our troves in Khemi or Luxur." He laughed again. "These fools will never know that within the burial chamber are only unfinished walls of unadorned stone."

Though he suspected that Ramsa Aál only laughed at the foolishness of Set's followers, he decided to see if that was all. "I don't see the joke, master."

Ramsa Aál glanced at him, eyebrow raised quizzically. They'd engaged in much verbal jousting since the priest had first arrived in Kheshatta, and it ran both ways. "The idiocy of these fools trying to buy their way to eternal life is obvious, but the richest jest is far less apparent. The nameless king who built this tomb was murdered by his own brother, his heirs slaughtered in their beds, his riches divided among his scheming relatives, his body burned, his ashes scattered. If there is indeed a Realm Eternal, he shall never go there."

"You don't believe in eternal life, master? The Scrolls of Set . . ."

"There are scrolls and there are scrolls, acolyte. Much of what you read in your early training is but the pabulum we give to the sheep you see here." He cocked his head strangely. "And the path to eternal life lies not in the bribing of fickle gods, but in the attainment of earthly power!" He chuckled, and looked back at the pilgrims. "If you learn nothing else, learn that lesson well."

Anok had other questions about their mysterious mission to this seemingly pointless shrine, but he kept silent for now. The more questions he asked, the more questions Ramsa Aál asked in return. There were few questions that Anok wished to answer right now. Especially about what had happened at the tomb of the lost Atlantean sorcerer, Neska, weeks before, and the death of Anok's turncoat friend and fellow acolyte, Dejal.

On returning to Kheshatta, Anok had provided Ramsa Aál and Kaman Awi, the High Priest of the Kheshatta temple of Set, with a version of those events that stayed as close to truth as possible without giving away Anok's secrets.

Anok reasoned that it might be easier to keep a lie straight when it contained large stretches of truth.

This had proven to be a wise decision, as Ramsa Aál seemed to want to hear the story again and again, each time pressing for some new detail, challenging each small inconsistency. In this altered version of events, they had gone to the tomb seeking not the magic-controlling band of Neska, but objects of magical power. As in reality, he told of how Dejal found the Rings of Neska, turned on his companions, and nearly killed them. He had also told them how he'd been able to defeat Dejal by attacking and destroying the rings rather than Dejal personally, and that Dejal had been buried when the tomb collapsed.

What Anok had neglected to mention was that the Band of Neska was now sealed within his right wrist, and that it gave him the ability to wield great magic while resisting its corrupting and maddening influence. With it, Anok had restored his fragile sanity, and now felt equipped to continue his infiltration of the cult, hoping to destroy it from within.

But he also found himself wondering, what was the Cult of Set? He had expected a tightly knit army of evil, united under, and controlled by, one supernatural god. What he found was a loose group of men drawn together by their lust for wealth and power, each with his own agenda, each building his own power base, each seeking some advantage over the others.

The Temple of Set at Khemi was as different as could be from the temple in Kheshatta. The former was a grand center of power, wealth, and intrigue, wrapped in the great trappings of Set. The latter was a more modest structure, devoted to Kaman Awi's study of sorcery and "natural law." His lust for knowledge was as total, and just as corrupting, as the more common lusts for power or wealth. It was knowledge that he truly worshiped, not Set.

Even the cult's high priest, Thoth-Amon, secretly conspired against his own god. What little loyalty existed within the cult could turn into treachery in a moment, and every priest knew it.

Anok suspected Ramsa Aál was well aware that Anok intended to betray him when the opportunity arose. But in that, Anok was no different than any other acolyte within the temple.

He had joined the cult expecting to be a lone heretic, but it seemed he had joined a cult of heretics, bowing to their snake god even as they plotted to use and steal his power. Was he that different than the others?

Yes, I am.

He still had his family secrets. He still had the rage over the cult's role in the killing of two of the most important people in his life: his father, and Sheriti, his oldest friend and first lover. He still had the Mark of Set on his left wrist, a brand of frightful mystical power that he had only barely learned to tap, and one of the mysterious Scales of Set, a mystic artifact much desired by Ramsa Aál.

He had many reasons to hate Ramsa Aál and the cult, and he had resources with which he might yet do them great harm.

As he looked toward the sun, low in the horizon, he caught a glimpse of a large camel silhouetted against the horizon, a camel with two familiar riders. He saw them only a moment before they passed behind a hill, out of sight, and was careful not to draw attention to them. Still, he smiled a secret smile at the sight.

I have one other thing as well. I have friends!

TEFERI SAT BACKWARD in the white camel's over-sized saddle, his long, dark legs contrasting with the pale hair on the big animal's flank. He toyed idly with his bow, pulling back the string, sighting on imaginary targets in the landscape that slid away into the distance behind them, and the occasional lizard scurrying between hiding places.

He could feel the naked skin of the woman's muscular back pressed against his, but he found the sensation more annoying than erotic. He tried to catch some whiff of her scent, but the camel's stench overpowered everything else. He squirmed, trying to put a little distance between them.

Fallon brushed back her long, black hair and glanced back over her shoulder. "You have something to say, Teferi?"

He considered a dozen alternatives, abandoning each in the name of diplomacy. "I was just looking for a more comfortable position. I do not like riding on the back of this camel like a child."

"White camels are large, Teferi, born to carry heavy loads. Fenola does not mind."

"*I* mind. We should have hired a second camel."

"Why waste silver when the camel I already own will suffice?"

He grunted.

"You don't care for me, Teferi?"

"You are adequate company."

She smirked at him. "Flattery! Do all men from the plains of Kush have this gift?"

Her remark made him twitch, and he almost didn't reply at all. "I was born in a city. I remember the plains of my ancestral land only in my dreams."

She was quiet for a moment, and he felt her shift nervously. When she did speak, her voice was apologetic. "I meant no offense, Teferi. It's been a long ride, and you've hardly spoken. If you do not care for me, I would like to know why."

He chuckled incredulously. "You've made it clear you don't care for me as a man." The words sounded surprisingly bitter, even to his own ears. "Why do you care at all? I am entrusted with my friend's, my *brother's,* safety as a matter of honor. It's but a job to you. Can you not do it in silence?"

"Anok doesn't pay me enough for silence, Teferi, and he pays you as well as a matter of his own honor, though I know you would be here anyway. But perhaps you don't understand me nearly as well as you think."

"Are you saying you would still be here if there were not silver to be made?"

"I'm a Cimmerian, Teferi. We live as Crom made us to live: to struggle, to fight, to club life over the head, throw it to the ground, and steal its purse. But a purseful of silver is worth nothing. A purse *emptied* well is another matter, and a purse *filled* well is better yet. In these past weeks I have battled ancient monsters, survived supernatural evil, and untold treachery. I have seen things to make hard men tremble, and have tales to tell my grandchildren, if by some accident I should live long enough to have any." She looked off at the horizon and nodded, seemingly more to herself than to him. "That is better than silver."

He sighed. "For silver or glory, there's little difference."

"You think so poorly of me? Anok is your friend, but he has been more to me than that."

Teferi laughed. "You shared his bed! And how much does that mean to you?"

"You think that because I'm a forward woman I lie with a man the way a dog scratches an itch? It's a man's way to think with his loins, and I'll wager you've let yours think for you more than once."

Teferi winced at the truth of it, but said nothing.

"For what it matters, Teferi, you are a fine figure of a man, and were that my only concern, I would happily test your skill in the darkness. But I am not the woman you think I am, and my heart and mind are much confused these days."

He licked his dry lips. "Then perhaps if you did not add to that confusion with wine—"

She spun her head around and glared at him, those dark Cimmerian eyes filled with blood and fire. "Is that what this is about?"

"When Anok needed you, when he faced the devil Thoth-Amon alone, you were holed up in a bar."

"And you were holed up in a library with Sabé! Neither of us was there for him, Teferi. We must both live with our failure. Yet much as we might try, we can't always protect Anok from the danger of the path he has chosen for himself. He has put himself against the Cult of Set itself."

He sighed. "Then why are you here shadowing Anok? Why even bother to answer his summons?"

She was silent for a time. "There was no summons. I overheard Anok talk of this journey and thought of following him myself. Then I lied to you about his instructions. I did not want to hire another camel because Anok did not give me the silver to hire one with."

Teferi blinked in surprise. Then he laughed. "You tricked me, woman! I have wronged you greatly, doubting your goodwill and courage. I humble myself before you."

She grinned. "I won't forget it."

"A fine figure of a man?"

Her smile vanished. She pushed his head down and quietly ordered the big camel to kush. It dropped quickly to its knees, then belly down in the dirt.

Following Fallon's lead, Teferi rolled off the camel and
crawled along the ground to peer over the top of a reddish-
orange boulder. They watched a pair of lightly armored
soldiers on horseback ride along a path below. Teferi instantly recognized the scarlet sash and the scarlet ruffles on
the reins.

He slid down, his back against the rock, and listened as
the hoofbeats faded into the distance. Then he glanced
over at Fallon. "Guardians of Set. Are we close to this
shrine you told me about?"

"Without doubt. From what I learned on the streets back
in Kheshatta, the cult keeps an entire garrison of troops
here to guard the shrine and its treasures."

"You could have warned me."

"I did not know there would be patrols. I thought they
would stay close to the treasure."

Teferi peered over the rock again. Off to the west, he
could see a caravan of pilgrims cresting a ridge. The riders
were richly dressed, and there were many pack camels, all
heavily burdened with *something*.

He slid back behind the rock. "Perhaps," he said, "the
treasure is not where we think it is."

2

ANOK HAD EXPECTED the shrine to be little more than the ruins of an ancient tomb alone in this desolate desert. But as their caravan wound its way down the hillside, he saw something quite different.

The tomb itself, a large, flat-roofed stone building topped with a low, central dome, was in excellent repair, its many columns cleaned, polished, and decorated with freshly painted pictograms in the ancient style.

Nor did it stand alone. It was surrounded by what amounted to a small village of buildings, some restored from ruins, others more recently built. There were small cottages where pilgrims could stay, apartments for workers, a large and elaborate building that probably housed the resident priesthood, kitchens surrounded by smoking ovens that smelled of bread, a long communal dining hall, warehouses for supplies, corrals for camels and horses, a large well and a covered cistern for water, and barracks for a very visible contingent of guardian troops.

It all spoke of the great wealth the cult was able to collect here from its followers.

All this for an empty tomb!

The caravan made its way along streets of packed stone to the corrals. Servants waited to help the riders from their mounts and unload the pack camels. A priest of high rank waited just outside the stone fence, watching them intently.

Anok watched the other riders dismount, several acolytes from the temple at Kheshatta, all loyal to Ramsa Aál, and several of Kaman Awi's "scholars of natural law." They were only passing familiar to Anok, but he believed that they were alchemists by specialty.

What business can alchemists have in a place like this?

"Anok!" Ramsa Aál gestured him over. "Come with me!"

They went to greet the waiting priest, an elderly man, thin, his dark skin made leathery by long exposure to the desert. The man bowed his head as they approached. Though his rank was considerable, Ramsa Aál's title as Priest of Needs still exceeded it.

"Lord Ramsa Aál, I presume. I am Suten Rasui, Priest of the Shrine, at your service." He raised his head and smiled insincerely. "How is our Lord-master Thoth-Amon? Well, I hope."

"Well enough to turn you inside out with a wave of his hand!"

Suten Rasui's smile faded. "Lord?"

"I've heard you opposed my mission here, that you appealed to Thoth-Amon himself to stop it."

Rasui made an expression like that of a stubborn child caught stealing a fig. "Very well then." He kept his voice low and looked from side to side to see who might be nearby. "I did oppose it, yes. You know the wealth that this shrine generates for the cult. You would endanger that for some foolish quest? The tomb is empty!"

"Not totally empty, and you know it. It has *guardians,* still, and it is they that I seek, that our *master* seeks."

Suten Rasui scowled. "You bring nothing but trouble on yourselves. Never have the mystic guards of this temple been felled."

Ramsa Aál smiled slightly. "They will fall today!" He looked toward the barracks. "Is the garrison at the ready, as you were instructed?"

"Yes."

"Then have them form up by the back of the tomb, ready to fight. As for your gold, keep the pilgrims away from the tomb for a few hours, and they will never know what transpires inside."

Suten Rasui looked confused. "What shall I tell them?"

Ramsa Aál looked annoyed. "You are a priest! Tell them some lie!"

He walked back toward the camels, and Anok followed.

"I don't understand, master. Why would an empty tomb have guardians, and if the guardians have never been bested, how can you be sure the tomb is empty?"

Ramsa Aál smiled. "The cult long ago drilled a tunnel through the rock into the rear of the tomb and found it empty. The guardians wait at the entrance of the tomb, and do not trouble those who remain within its depths. As for the purpose of the guardians, they were created by the Lost King before his murder. Learning of his family's treachery, he set them to their timeless task before he could be killed. If he was not to be buried in his tomb, then he was determined that no man would be, most especially his turncoat brother. In that, his guardians have ever been successful."

"Then we will enter the temple through the secret tunnel?"

"Indeed, and we will go through the temple almost to its entrance, where the guardians wait. We will go with soldiers enough to engage them while I work my magics."

"But why, master? Of what value can these guardians be to you, especially if you have already defeated them?"

The priest was momentarily distracted as two servants clumsily unloaded a large pottery cask and nearly dropped it. "Careful! That contains the blood of virgins, treated with holy herbs and the rare Elixir of Orkideh. Break it, and I will have to try my spell using your blood instead! It likely won't work, but you'll be dead anyway!"

Anok's ears perked at the mention of the Elixir of Orkideh. Anok had, at great peril to himself, helped Kaman Awi obtain the rare potion from Lord Poisoner Sattar back in Kheshatta. He had won the elixir in a trial of combat against an acolyte of the Cult of the Jade Spider, an enemy of Set.

Anok realized now that his efforts had been driven by pride rather than reason, and in obtaining the elixir, he had, to his regret, aided the very people he had sworn to destroy. Whatever their mission today, it would clearly have been impossible. It was also clear that Kaman Awi had wanted the stuff quite badly.

But why? It made no sense. What could Ramsa Aál want from an empty tomb?

WHILE FALLON REMAINED behind to hold the camel, Teferi crawled to the edge of the cliff on his belly and peered over. He watched the scene below for several minutes, then crawled away from the edge before trotting back to her side, a frown of concern on his face.

"What did you see?"

"They are mustering the soldiers. They are armored and prepared for a foot battle, though I see no one for them to fight."

She smiled. "Perhaps they have heard that a Cimmerian warrior and her fearsome Kush companion are nearby."

"Do not joke. There is danger about, though I cannot tell you from which way it comes. From whatever direction, our friend Anok is in the heart of it. But that I could stand by his side. This secrecy torments me!"

"I have little love of skulking about either, Teferi, yet we would do no good rushing in there. We must be patient."

"You be patient. I will gnash my teeth."

She chuckled. "As you would have it."

He glanced at her with annoyance. "You make fun of me."

"You fuss like a nanny goat. Anok is a man. He does not need you as his nursemaid."

"You don't know him as I do. We were boys together, fought side by side a hundred battles in the alleys of the Odji slums. He is a good man, a strong man, but a troubled man, with secrets that, even after all these years, I suspect he does not share with me. He has dabbled in dark magic and thinks now he has beaten it. I do not think it is done with him yet."

Fallon frowned. "There are some devils you cannot fight for another. They can ask for aid, but it cannot be given."

"Devils like drink?"

Her eyes narrowed. "Perhaps."

He considered for a moment. "Then perhaps my greatest devil is that I do not know my place. I have no wish to be a nursemaid, and this is not the way I would have taken my life, but for my concern for my friend. I feel there is some reason for me to be here, if I can but find it."

She raised her eyebrow. "What, then, is my purpose?"

He chuckled. "If you care, you are the hired help, and perhaps not the best available."

But she frowned, as though she didn't appreciate the joke.

THREE DOZEN SOLDIERS lined up in front of a small building behind the tomb. The building was windowless, and a substantial wooden door protected by heavy locks blocked the entrance. It could easily be mistaken for a storehouse, but Anok was sure it hid the tunnel entrance to the tomb.

The soldiers were uniformly equipped with polished steel helmets, chain mail, light plate armor, and armed with swords and painted rectangular shields bearing the seal of Set. Ten men at the head of the formation also carried short pikes with points of fine steel.

One of the soldiers was older than the other, and his helmet was topped by a red horsehair crest marking him as an officer. Anok watched as Ramsa Aál approached him.

"You are the officer in charge of this garrison?"

The man's face was expressionless, seemingly chiseled from stone. "Yes, my lord!"

"Then for the next hour you are demoted."

That got the officer to blink, but nothing more. "May I ask why, my lord?"

"If we are to survive, these men must follow my every order, directly and without hesitation."

The officer frowned ever so slightly.

"Forgive me, my lord, no disrespect intended, but I do not believe the men will follow you as you wish. Such loyalty must be won through hardship and blood."

"You have won this loyalty?"

The officer looked just slightly smug at having made his point. "Yes, my lord, I believe I have."

Ramsa Aál considered for but a moment. "Then you will order your men to follow me as they would you, on pain of your death."

The officer's rigid facade finally cracked. "My lord? Even for one of your station, this is outrageous!"

"*I* will not be the one who kills you. It will be what awaits us," he pointed at the door, "in there."

The officer looked at the door nervously.

Anok wondered if the officer knew what awaited them. The keepers of this place would have no reason to go inside, and the temple had been entered centuries before.

Ramsa Aál continued. "But you will not die alone, for your men will die, too, as will I, and"—he pointed at Anok—"my student as well. If they follow me, you will have your command back in an hour and a promotion as well. If they fail me, we will die as one."

The officer regained his composure, clenching his jaw, puffing his chest, holding his chin high. "We will not fail you, my lord." He turned sharply to face his men.

"Hear me, guardians! We face today an enemy unlike any we have ever faced before, unlike any we have ever trained to fight. As such, I temporarily hand my authority to this High Priest of Set, whose knowledge of our foe exceeds my own. He and his acolyte have committed to stand by us in battle and share our danger as their own. Are you with us?"

The men shouted as one, *"Yes, my lord!"*

Ramsa Aál stepped in front of the men, standing tall before them, as Anok had often seen him do before his acolytes. The priest was not unfamiliar with command.

"Make no mistake," he said. "This is war. It will be brief, but it will be fierce, and deadly. Each man who stands with us today will earn five pieces of gold in combat pay. To the family of each who falls, seven pieces." He watched the men's reaction to his last comment closely, seeking, Anok imagined, some weak member who needed to be culled. He found none, through there were some unhappy murmurs when he mentioned the survivor's payment.

That, Ramsa Aál seemed to be expecting. He smiled. "It does not sound like much for your families, but I do not believe in bribing a man to fall on the enemy's sword! Live to collect your five pieces, and we will all be happy!"

That brought chuckles from the troops.

Anok had to admire the smooth way the priest had won them over. If Ramsa Aál was ultimately his enemy, there was still much to be learned from the man.

Behind them, a workman carrying a lighted torch unlocked the door and swung it open. "There are torches inside the door," he said.

"Every sixth man take a torch and light it from this man's," announced the officer. Then he looked sheepishly at Ramsa Aál. "If it suits my lord, of course."

Ramsa Aál nodded. He pointed at the cask of blood, which sat just outside the door. "Have two of your men take this down—*carefully.* I have studied maps of the tomb. There is a large chamber at the end of the tunnel. Have your men form up there. We will be along presently."

He saw the look of disapproval on the officer's face. "There is no danger until we reach the front chamber of the tomb. Go!"

He turned to Anok. "Tell me, acolyte, do you remember how to use those swords of yours?"

Anok's eyes narrowed, almost wondering if this were a trick. Ramsa Aál had always treated Anok's attachment to his conventional weaponry as a weakness. Still, there would be little point in lying. "I've kept in practice, master."

Ramsa Aál nodded. "That is good. Your magic will do you no good in the temple. Our foes are immune to all spells, save one, which is why they have remained untouched until this day. Now, give me your hand."

With the almost unthinking obedience that had been drilled into him back at the temple at Khemi, Anok extended his right hand.

Ramsa Aál held his fingers for a moment, then Anok saw a dagger flash in his other hand. Quick as the serpents their cult worshiped, the point of the dagger was drawn lightly across the back of his hand, drawing a line of blood drops.

Ramsa Aál then sheathed the dagger and removed from a belt pouch a small, oval crystal sized to fit in the hand. He drew it across the blood, leaving a smear. As he did, the crystal began to glow from within. In the sunlight, it was barely visible, but in the dark, Anok knew the illumination it provided was considerable.

Ramsa Aál released Anok's fingers, and Anok shook them. They felt like they'd been trapped under a heavy stone.

"You have your Jewel of the Moon?"

Anok nodded. He removed a similar crystal from his shoulder bag and rubbed it in the blood, then sucked the wound, the blood coppery in his mouth. Though it was a small indignity, it angered him to be used so. *He couldn't be bothered to shed a single drop of his own precious blood!*

He had other reasons to feel used as well. As they climbed down the stairs into the gloom below, Anok realized that he was feeling disappointed. It had not been long since he had sealed the ancient Band of Neska to his right wrist, an anchor against sorcerous corruption that he believed gave him control over the evil Mark of Set on his left wrist.

But since that day, there had been little opportunity to test that theory, and he thought it foolish to risk great magic for the sake of doing great magic. *Here,* he thought, *there may be a foe worthy of its use.* But he had just been told that even great magic would not serve. Never before had he resented the opportunity to use his swords.

If I am nothing but a strong sword arm to him, then I shall prove myself a mighty one! He'll give me respect one way or another.

Yet even as he thought that, he knew it was wrong. If he faltered at the right moment, allowed Ramsa Aál to be struck down by the temple guardians, then the priest's conspiracy plans might be thwarted. Even if he only allowed the contents of the flask being carried down the steps behind them to be spilled, it could delay them for months, or years, until more of the elixir that was its most important ingredient could be brewed.

Then they would still have to secure it. After their last encounter, Lord Poisoner Sattar would not hold the Cult of Set in high favor. Anok had seen the way Sattar had looked at him when they'd faced each other down.

Something in Anok's eyes, in his voice, something he didn't yet understand, had given one of the most feared men in Kheshatta a taste of his own medicine, so to speak. Sattar had known fear, and for those few moments, he had been willing to give Anok anything he asked. Sattar would never allow that humiliation to happen again.

They found the guardians waiting in formation for them in the chamber below. In the flickering light of the torches and the cool blue light of their jewels, the stone walls of the chamber were revealed as rough and unfinished. Elegant, tapered columns supported the ceiling, but they had no carvings, no decorations. Some stones even bore the chalk marks of the stonecutters and masons who had ages before built the tomb.

The laborers, eyes wide with fear, set the cask upon the floor at the base of the stair. Ramsa Aál looked at it, then the captain. "These cattle lack the courage to carry the cask where it needs to go. Assign two of your men to the task. They should be strong of limb and steady of nerve. Only the most courageous will do."

The captain nodded and selected two men from his ranks. They reluctantly sheathed their weapons and took up the cask by its rope handles.

In the center of the room sat a waist-high block of stone. Ramsa Aál walked over and brushed his fingers over the top, examining it.

"This," he said, "is the burial chamber of the Lost King, where his sarcophagus would have preserved his mortal form and all his worldly riches, so they could reclaim them in the afterlife. Now, it holds nothing but the dust of shattered dreams." He glanced at a tall, narrow doorway near the far end of the chamber. "We must go this way."

A stone seal that clearly had once covered the opening lay on the floor just inside the chamber, and they stepped over it on their way out.

They filed through a long, narrow, tunnel, triangular in cross section, wide at the floor, just wide enough for a man's head at the top. All but the smallest men had to duck their heads and turn their shoulders to make passage. Anok could not see the men with the cask, but he could only imagine the difficulty they faced.

"There was another, larger, entrance," said Ramsa Aál, "where the king's body and treasures would have been brought into the temple. But it was sealed shut by his traitorous family after his murder. This was to have been used by the last workers leaving the temple as it was sealed, those responsible for securing the burial chamber itself."

Anok looked over the shoulders of the men in front of him, and was surprised to see what appeared to be a dead end. In fact, the tunnel turned and doubled back on itself. Perhaps the intent was to hinder tomb robbers in their ability to quickly remove the king's treasures.

Ramsa Aál leaned close to him. "I am not ready to share the full nature of our plan, acolyte. Have faith that it will unfold as a wonderment before your eyes, and that in time all will be clear. But know that what we do will transform the Cult of Set, and that is but the beginning. The lost glory of the Stygian Empire will soon be restored, then surpassed. Our master Thoth-Amon will sit on the immortal throne of this empire, and those of us who have served him well shall be his lords of power. Ours will be an empire such as never has been seen." His voice grew cold as ice. "Let the world tremble before it."

Anok shuddered. The words were madness, of course, though said with such conviction that Anok could not dismiss them. He had met Thoth-Amon, and the man's thirst for power was such that he would dare aspire to such a thing.

Yet what, in this empty tomb, could lead to such power? Perhaps nothing, directly, but there were many elements in play here that he still didn't understand. There were the three Scales of Set, one of which he still held in his possession. He had seen hints that the three Scales, if ever combined, were somehow far greater than the sum of their parts.

There were still the bones of Parath, the lost god of Stygia, which Ramsa Aál and Dejal had recently brought to Kheshatta. Yet Parath was a declared enemy of Set.

There were also still the secrets of his own past, which seemed in some unknown way to be part of this puzzle: the reason for his father's murder, where he'd gotten the Scale, what his relationship to Parath had been, and to the Cult of Ibis. And what about his mysterious sister, of whom his father had spoken only in his dying moments?

Anok was tormented by the thought that, by striking at Set too soon, he might destroy his only chance to unravel his past. If Ramsa Aál died here, what secrets would die with him?

No, things had come too far for him to become clouded with uncertainty. He had acted once too often in the true

cause of Set's service. Today he would hinder the path of
the serpent, not aid it. Opportunity would choose which, but
this day he swore, either their quest would fail, or Ramsa
Aál would die!

The tunnel doubled back on itself once more. Upon the
unfinished walls, Anok occasionally saw graffiti, written in
old Stygian, left by someone, possibly workers who had
built the tomb. Most of it was meaningless to him. He
could read the words, but without any context, they meant
nothing.

> A pox on Sebishai, for he is unjust

> The mother of Sokkiw lies with a donkey

> The stonework of Nebie is without craft or skill

It was a sobering reminder that the concerns of men
rarely outlived them, if they mattered even that long. Anok
wondered it he should take a lesson from this and forget his
obsession with the past. He resolved that if Ramsa Aál
died, taking the secrets of Anok's past with him, so be it.

They passed though an archway into a wide, shallow
room. Pedestals lined the wall behind them, spaced roughly
an arm's spread apart. Anok imagined they were intended to
hold statues, perhaps even of the king's traitorous family, but
they stood empty.

On the wall ahead of them, a series of arched doorways,
one in front of each pedestal, opened into what seemed to
be an even larger chamber beyond.

"This chamber," announced Ramsa Aál loudly, "is
where our adversary awaits."

The guardians stared at him in alarm.

"They cannot hear us, or sense us, until we walk through
these portals and cross a line defined by a certain spell. By
my studies, that line will lie five paces within. Once we
step beyond that line, we shall not be allowed to depart
alive unless they are stopped by my spell. Protect me, and

protect the cask, with your lives, for they depend on these two things."

Anok drew his two swords from the scabbards on his back. He wondered how much of Ramsa Aál's speech was to be believed. He had no doubt that the priest would sacrifice the lives of all these men, and Anok's as well, if it served his purposes.

No, if the spell were interrupted, there would be another way out, and perhaps a better chance of survival if their only purpose were to escape.

"Two lines to the fore," ordered Ramsa Aál. "Strongest swordsmen first, torches second. The rest shall stay back to protect the cask and me."

Anok caught Ramsa Aál's eye. "I should stay close to you."

The corner of Ramsa Aál's mouth twitched up. "Have your skills fallen so?" He studied Anok's face for a moment. "I thought not. You shall be front and center to lead our advance."

And where I won't be tempted to stab you in the back.

Anok tried not to frown, but he did as the priest instructed, shouldering his way between two broad guardians, arms hard as tree trunks, each carrying a sword almost twice the size of Anok's twin blades.

Anok stepped through the center archway, and the line followed. He stopped three short paces inside, careful to remain behind the five paces that Ramsa Aál had identified as the point of no return.

Anok stared into the darkness ahead. He could just make out *something* there, an even row of shapes just a little lighter than the rest of the gloom, that stretched across the room in front of him and away in either direction.

Anok glanced back, and as he did, something on the wall next to the arch caught his eye. At first he thought it was simply more graffiti, but then he noticed the brown, crusted appearance of the ancient Stygian symbols and realized it had been written in blood.

> To the thin blood of usurpers
> I leave only this curse
> To all those whose greed
> Leads them to aspire
> Live as kings
> Die as kings
> Sleep eternal in the tombs of kings
> With the blood of the true king
> To decorate their daggers
> Curse your undying spirits
> Guard this empty tomb forever
> While our king feasts in paradise

As he read the words, Anok felt a tingle that made him shudder. These were no idle words. They had the taste of magic, most dark and terrible. He felt the Mark of Set stir, as though hungry for a share of that blackness, but there was none to share.

Those cursed were long dead. But as Anok considered the blackness ahead, he wondered if they were truly gone.

One more step into the darkness, perhaps to see what danger waited there.

He could just see the yellow glitter of polished metal armor, identical back plates engraved with arcane symbols, and helmets adorned with unique decorations.

There was a creaking, as, in one identical motion, all the hunched figures stood straight up, dust cascading from their shoulders and helmets.

He had caught Ramsa Aál in his first lie. Four steps in, and there would be no turning back.

Again, as though driven by an identical clockwork, the row of armored figures spun, swords and spears and shields at the ready, booted feet landing upon the ancient stone of the floor in perfect unison.

Though their armor was only dimly visible in the torch-light, beneath the helmets, faces could be seen.

Green, slightly luminous, gaunt faces of the dead, mouths drawn open, teeth bared, eyes vacant orbs of green fire. They were phantoms of a sort, spectral and translu-cent, but from their movements, from the way the heavy armor rested upon them, they had some kind of weight and substance.

One of the men recoiled in terror, dropped his torch, and turned to run.

A dead knight stepped forward with a clanking of chains and threw a metal hook. The hook struck the man between the shoulder blades with a wet *chunk*. The man made a gur-gling scream, and the chain attached to the hook was in-stantly pulled tight, yanking him off his feet.

He was dragged away across the floor so rapidly that there might have been a galloping horse at the other end of the chain, so fast he had no time to scream before the ar-mored undead surrounded him, and their weapons began to fall again and again. Steel ringing against armor, bone, and stone.

When they parted, their weapons dripping red with gore, there was nothing like a man there, only a pile of ar-mor, chopped meat, and bone amid a pool of blood.

Now, thought Anok grimly, *I've caught Ramsa Aál in a truth.*

There was only one thing to do.

He dashed ahead of the larger men flanking him. "Get them!"

With a cry the men came after him, though he could hear the fear in their voices. They were fighting for their own lives, not for the glory of the cult.

Anok locked his crossed swords with the short sword phantom wearing a hawk's-head crest. The phantom's open mouth gaped at him in a silent scream, the black, dried tongue curled within like a piece of charcoal.

From that undead mouth, and dozens of others, the bat-tle cry of the undead came. Not a wail or a scream, but a deep moan, so low in pitch that Anok could feel it in his chest.

He struggled against the thing's sword arm. For crea-tures lacking flesh and substance, they were strong as a man, though mercifully slower. Around him, Anok could see the others holding their own against the undead knights.

Faster than his opponent could respond, Anok swept the thing's sword to one side, drew back his left sword, and jabbed it into the thing's neck.

There was a crunch, and a weak resistance, like plunging a sword through a melon. The thing flailed its arms, dropping its sword.

They can be hurt!

His greatest fear had been that the things couldn't be harmed at all by physical means. But as he had suspected, they had at least some substance, some physicality, that could be cut and pierced with a blade. Now he knew that they could also fight.

He yanked the sword to one side with a rapid motion, rotating it through the phantom neck, and the head popped off cleanly, helmet clanking as it struck stone.

He heard a crunch of bone on stone behind him, and whirled in time to slice the sword arm off a knight that had been creeping up behind him. From behind it, a guardian's broadsword took the thing's head and finished the job.

Anok nodded in thanks to the guardian and turned to engage another knight. Out of the corner of his eye, he could see Ramsa Aál and the two guardians carrying the cask advancing slowly into room, surrounded by fighting.

The tomb's protectors seemed to sense that they were the real threat and were attacking their circle of guardians intensely. But still, the phantom knights fell rapidly, and Anok had an uneasy feeling.

Something moved by his boot. He looked down to see a beheaded knight reach slowly out, grab the helm of a nearby helmet, and place helmet and head back on its shoulders. Glowing, spectral flesh almost instantly healed itself, and the knight began to climb to its feet.

He was so transfixed, he didn't notice the sword clutched in its other hand until it was almost too late.

Steel flashed toward him. He leapt backward, gasping as the sword nicked his right arm. He grunted in pain and brought his left sword down on the thing, chopping its arm off at the elbow.

Still it moved, rolling over, looking for its lost arm.

He glanced around. Everywhere, fallen knights were restoring themselves. "Watch the fallen," he cried at the top of his lungs, trying to be heard over the din of crashing swords and armor.

The warning came too late for one guardian. A restored knight came up on one knee and thrust its sword under his chest plate straight up into his heart. He coughed a gout of blood and fell over facefirst. There would be no restoration for him.

It was then Anok understood the terrible nature of these protectors. They were tireless, relentless, and no matter how many times they fell, they always came back.

If they fell easily now, the men would tire, they would make more mistakes, be caught unaware by their fallen foes, and one by one, they would die.

Anok fell back, slipping into the circle of protectors around Ramsa Aál. The priest was paying little attention to his surroundings. Instead, he was reading from an ancient book of magic, his lips moving, but the words barely audible.

Anok knew from experience that it was not the volume with which a spell was spoken that gave it power, it was the conviction and concentration with which the sorcerer read the words. He suspected Ramsa Aál's concentration was very deep. He couldn't help but admire the priest's ability to screen out the noise and danger around him.

Anok's eyes narrowed.

He's vulnerable!

Anok fought on, but with less fervor than he might have, waiting to see if fate would effect the priest's downfall.

Slowly, at a pace that would have made a tortoise impatient, they moved toward the center of the room, a constant clatter of blades and armor, and occasionally the cry of a wounded or dying man.

The guardians were tiring. He could see the fear in their eyes. When they stopped believing in their own survival, they were as good as dead.

He hacked away at a knight's arm, his first blow glancing off armor, the second slicing the hand off at the wrist, even as it was falling toward him.

The blade spun past him, the point slashing across the face of the guardian next to him, hot blood spraying across Anok's left arm. He felt the Mark of Set surge with energy on contact with the blood, heard its cry of joy in his head.

The wounded man shrieked in pain, half-blinded by his own flying blood, caught totally unaware as another sword found his gut.

Anok watched him fall, trying to focus on the Band of Neska around his right wrist, to use its unyielding strength to push the Mark of Set's evil back into hiding.

Then another man fell beyond him, and another.

Suddenly their lines crumbled.

Many torches fell or went out, plunging them into gloom.

An undead knight slipped past Anok, headed for Ramsa Aál.

The priest looked up just in time to see his impending doom, eyes wide, not with fear, but with rage.

This is it!

A blade plunged into the phantom knight's armpit, twisting it half-around, delaying it long enough that a nearby guardian could chop the thing's legs off at the knees.

It took Anok a moment to realize that the sword which had saved Ramsa Aál's life had been his own.

He yanked his blade free of the thing with a wet, sucking sound, then chopped its head off with one smooth motion.

Why did I do that?

He glanced at Ramsa Aál. If he had expected gratitude from the priest, he was to be disappointed. The priest's attention was on the cask, which was being dragged across the floor by one of the guardians assigned to carry it. The other lay on the floor a few paces behind, his lifeblood spurting out through his open neck.

An axe flashed out of the gloom splitting the other guardian's head.

Anok stared at the cask for a moment.

Ramsa Aál continued to read, men crowded in around him trying to fight off the undead. But the priest kept glancing nervously at the cask.

Anok took a deep breath.

The cask!

Without it the spell would fail, as would Ramsa Aál's plan.

It was suicide, of course, unless Ramsa Aál had some secret plan to escape and took Anok with him. But when Ramsa Aál saw what was about to happen, Anok doubted he would have the priest's favor any longer.

He gritted his teeth, then stepped toward the cask.

Two knights stepped into his way. He spun, slicing the arm off one, kicking the other in the stomach, shoving it backward out of the way.

Spun again, plunged his right sword into another knight.

Kicked again, hitting the cask, high up on the neck, sending it falling to its side.

Clay shattered.

Anok smelled the metallic stench of old blood, the exotic tang of magic herbs, and something like ocean air, which might have been the salts in the Elixir of Orkideh.

The blood gushed out across the dark floor in a wide fan.

Ramsa Aál's voice instantly became louder, the words clear.

"—by this river of blood, wash away this ancient curse, so these spirits may fly free!"

There was a whoosh, the blood flashed into reddish vapor, a knee-high fog that spread across the floor of the room, boiling and churning.

A knight charged toward Anok, sword held high.

Then it hesitated, its glowing green eyes seeming to grow wider.

The moaning grew louder, all around them, until Anok's ears twinged in pain, and he felt his skull might crack open.

The attacking knight's armor suddenly slumped and started to fall, but the glowing phantom inside did not fall with it. Instead, he seemed to elongate as he was drawn upward, features distorting until he was drawn up through the stone ceiling and vanished.

Anok looked around in wonder, as one after another, the phantoms were drawn up and away, leaving their armor and weapons to clatter to the floor.

The cloud of red vapor was sucked into the center of the room, where it twisted for a moment like a dust devil, then swirled up into the ceiling and vanished with a clap of thunder.

Anok held his swords high, looking for something to fight, but the temple's protectors were gone. They were alone, the living, the dying, the dead, and mounds of empty armor, glowing gold in the remaining torchlight.

Ramsa Aál pointed at an uninjured guardian. "Run! Get help to move the injured and wounded! Tell them there is no danger here now!"

Ramsa Aál turned and stared at Anok, who waiting for the reprimand and punishment that must now come.

"Acolyte," his voice was low and serious. "Excellent work. Your mystic instincts must have told you exactly the right moment to spill the blood and complete the spell. When those guardians carrying the cask fell, I feared the spell was doomed to fail."

The right moment! He had not averted the spell. He had completed it!

Ramsa Aál chuckled. "You should know, you have also done a great service to the usurpers of the Lost King. That was the spell we just broke. As they died, their spirits were drawn here, into this enchanted armor, to spend eternity guarding the empty tomb of the man they had killed. We set their spirits free to pass on."

Anok looked around at the fallen armor that lay all around them. The spirits of the undead seemed to have held it together, given it form. Now the disassociated plates, helmets, boots, and gauntlets lay everywhere.

Anok knelt to examine the inscriptions of the back of a gauntlet lying at his feet. As he reached for it, he started as the glove twitched, nearly tumbling over on his backside.

Ramsa Aál laughed. "That, talented acolyte, is the *real* reason we are here. The ectoplasm of the undead held this armor together, gave it direction, and allowed it to re-assemble when cut asunder, but those spirits had little enough power of motion. They could not have, without aid, taken a single step, much less lifted a sword. It is the armor itself, or more specifically, the mystic alloy from which it is constructed, that has the true power of motion. Our spell did not change that."

Anok looked up. "You're here for the armor?"

"For the *metal,* and its power of motion."

"But why?"

Ramsa Aál chuckled knowingly. "In time, that will be revealed." He looked toward the front of the chamber, the side farthest from where they'd entered. "Our business here is almost done. Now that the temple's protectors are gone, there is no need for us to leave by the torturous path through which we entered. You see that arched outline in the wall? It is a door, long sealed. Make yourself useful, acolyte. Open it!"

Anok stood. The Mark of Set on his left arm still tingled and burned from the touch of fresh blood. Blood, he knew, was among the most powerful ingredients of dark magic and one to which the Mark of Set seemed most responsive.

He rubbed his wrist as he considered the bricked-over opening. It was twice as tall as a man and five paces wide. Certainly a small hole would have done, large enough for a man to walk through. But he had power that *ached* to be used.

"So be it," he said.

He focused on the doorway, then drew back his left arm as though about to throw an invisible stone.

"Shatter!"

He felt the power move up his hand, though his fingers, as he threw his invisible stone at the center of the sealed door.

Bricks shattered, forming a hole the size of a man through which the orange light of sunset flooded. From outside, he heard countless gasps and cries of alarm.

It did not end there.

It was as though a crack had opened in a dam, and the waters had begun to rip through. Bricks peeled away from the edge of the opening, flying out into the glare of daylight, rapidly expanding the hole, until the entire doorway was opened.

Through the door, he could see throngs of pilgrims, priests, and acolytes, staring up at wonder at the hundreds of bricks that hovered, spinning silently in the air a dozen feet above their heads. He had not expected them to be waiting there, and if he dropped the bricks now, dozens would be injured.

His left hand still held high to levitate the bricks, he drew it back, then slammed his open hand forward.

"Dust!"

With a deafening crack like thunder, the bricks blew apart into fine yellow sand that rained down upon the startled crowd.

There was a moment of fear that turned to cheers, and even laughter as they collectively realized that they were in no danger.

Seizing the opportunity, Ramsa Aál stepped through the door, urging Anok along with him.

They stepped through the doorway, onto a raised landing at the top of a broad marble stair, sheltered by an overhanging roof and framed by colorfully painted columns. Ramsa Aál raised his arms dramatically.

The crowd responded with a cheer at the sight of the priest. He yelled to them, "Witness the power of Set! The spirit of the Lost King is risen this day, his treasures gone with him to paradise!"

The pilgrims seemed to go mad with joy. They began to chant, "Set! Set! Set! Glory to Set! Set! Set!" Over and over.

Ramsa continued to play to the audience, his arms still held high. He leaned toward Anok, and said just loud enough that only Anok could hear, "Well played, acolyte. Word of this day will spread throughout Stygia, and the pilgrims will flock here with endless tribute in order to tour this empty tomb!"

The priest seemed to consider something for a moment, then leaned toward Anok again. "There is only one way this day could be improved, acolyte. Tonight in celebration, we shall hold a ceremony. It is time for you to begin your initiation as a full priest of Set!"

3

TEFERI CRAWLED THROUGH the darkness, guided more by his ears than his eyes. In the tomb site just over the rise, it sounded like a party was going on, though of a subdued and well-behaved variety. He could hear temple music, played on harps, horns, pipes, flutes, and drums, and the sound of many excited voices.

As he reached the edge and peered over, he could see many torches burning in front of the now-opened tomb, warming fires burning in assorted stone caldrons, and scores of people, standing or seated in front of the temple steps, seemingly awaiting some event.

Many guardian soldiers stood at attention around the edge of the tomb's forecourt. Many more mingled with the assembled crowd, forming easily the loudest and most boisterous part of the assembly, as though celebrating some event to which the others were not privy.

What happened in that tomb today?

That was a puzzle. Teferi had seen Anok, the priest Ramsa Aál, many soldiers, and others, enter a small building far behind the temple. Most of the others had later

emerged. Some carried out wounded or dead, but Anok and
Ramsa Aál had somehow emerged through the front of the
temple, and in a most spectacular fashion.

None of it quite made sense, and a great deal about it
Teferi found bothersome. Much dark sorcery had been
done here this day. He could feel it in his bones. And it did
not bode well for Anok.

He rolled back into the darkness, crawling for a bit before trotting the rest of the way back to their camp. He
found Fallon huddled under a blanket, her face a pale oval
barely visible in the starlight. "What news?" she asked,
keeping her voice low.

"I can't guess. They seem to be waiting for something, a
speech, or a ceremony of some sort. I don't see Anok or
that cursed priest anywhere."

She looked up at him, and he paused to wonder if she
could really see his much darker skin in the gloom. He had
heard that Cimmerians were gifted with particularly keen
senses.

"Since this afternoon, you seem especially worried about
our absent friend, yet you haven't told me why."

"You didn't see what happened when they emerged
from the temple."

"I heard it."

"They probably heard it in Khemi. It was powerful
magic, done for little more than show so far as I could see."

"Yes, and you said the priest emerged from the opened
doorway, with Anok behind him."

"The priest acted as though it were his doing, yes, but
that is the nature of priests: to take credit wherever it is
worth taking. I fear that may have been Anok's doing."

He heard her blanket rustle and suspected she had
shrugged. "What of it if he did? He told me that he now
masters the sorcery, that it no longer masters him."

"So he says," Teferi answered skeptically.

"Then did we all risk our lives for nothing, to help Anok
obtain that bracelet thing?"

"The Band of Neska."

"Yes, that. We did risk our lives for a reason, did we not? For if it was without cause, then I should have spent more time helping myself to Neska's treasures and less helping Anok and Dejal plunder his corpse for trinkets!"

Teferi frowned at the mention of Dejal, his traitorous and now-dead childhood companion. He was a victim of his own lust for power. Let him stay dead and never be spoken of again.

"For nothing? No, it brought Anok back from the edge of magical corruption and madness, but he now acts as though it gives him mastery over the evil Mark of Set. I fear it is not so. If anything, it has increased his thirst for magical power, with all the danger that comes with it."

She snorted derisively. "If you hate magic so, why do you study those dusty tablets and scrolls with Sabé?"

"For many reasons. To honor my dead friend Sheriti, who studied to be a scribe, to aid Anok in his quest to bring down the Cult of Set, but mostly—" He sighed. "Mostly because you cannot fight what you do not know. If sorcery is my enemy, I will know it well."

"And be corrupted by it yourself? Better to know nothing. Better to fight by skill and instinct, like the true warrior I know you to be! You were not made for libraries or dusty tomes, any more than I.

"We are different, you and I, but we are also alike. Barbarians by blood, raised in exile from the lands that are our birthright. How then did we come to this place, far from our homelands, freezing in the dark because we dare not light a fire?"

She growled, slammed her fist into her own leg. "Fine Cimmerian I am, too long away from the northern lands of my birth, to shiver in such little cold as this! I wager Conan would not shiver under blankets on a night like this!"

Teferi chuckled. "The great Conan is a king, now. Doubtless he sleeps this night in front of a great fire in his castle, with a dozen Aquilonian concubines to keep him warm. You need not slight yourself on his account."

Suddenly from over the rise, cheering could be heard, and large drums sounded a steady rhythm.

Teferi listened for a moment, then jumped to his feet. "Something is happening!" He started for his hidden vantage point.

Fallon hesitated but a moment before throwing off her blanket. "Wait for me!"

ANOK HAD ONLY been gone from the Tomb of the Lost King a few hours before he returned, once again by the secret tunnel in the back. To his surprise, the chamber at the bottom of the stairs had been transformed in his absence. It was well illuminated with oil lamps, furnishings had been brought in, and curtained screens had been set up to create a series of makeshift rooms and dressing areas.

As he entered, he had seen bearers removing the last of the Armor of Mocioun, as he now knew it to be called, out through the tunnel entrance, still twitching and moving, even tied in bundles for transport. Most of it had already been lashed to camels when he had reentered the tomb, and by now the caravan might already be taking it back to Kheshatta.

The Armor of Mocioun. The irony of it struck him. The Lost King's name was long forgotten, but Mocioun, the wizard who had created the armor, his name was still known. There was a kind of immortality in sorcery, Anok supposed. A king's power died with him, but a sorcerer's power could live on thousands of years after his flesh had turned to dust.

Servants, priests, and acolytes swarmed about, preparing for what was obviously going to be quite an elaborate ceremony.

Anok looked around skeptically.

This can't all be for me.

No, likely it was for the benefit of the pilgrims massed outside the tomb. Ramsa Aál and the local priests saw an opportunity to increase the power and influence of the cult over the wealthy classes, and they were taking full advantage of it.

Uncertain where he was expected to go, he looked around for someone, anyone, familiar. So intent was he that he neglected to watch where he was walking and stumbled into a large, round basket tended by a leathery little Stygian man dressed in only a loincloth.

Anok heard an angry hissing from inside the basket and quickly stepped back. The little man glared at him. Eyes half-mad, thin as though starved, the man's skin was wrinkled and nearly black. "Take care," he growled, "you do not anger my babies."

Anok quickly turned away and found himself looking at a tall, bald male servant of, judging by his rank and silver temple yoke, high rank. "You are to be prepared for the ceremony. Follow me."

Anok was led into one of the dressing rooms, where several servants waited. A curtain was drawn, and they quickly went to work, washing the dust from his feet, face, and hands, and removing his regular robes. They also, despite his protests, unbuckled his swords and hung them on a chair with his discarded clothing.

As he was dressed by servants in an elaborate black, gold, and scarlet ceremonial robe, Anok tried to sort out the day's events. Once again, he had come to the unwitting aid of his sworn enemies. He had saved Ramsa Aál's life and completed the spell that had obtained for the priest the enchanted metal he needed for his mysterious plan. Finally, Anok had provided a show of magic that would doubtless greatly benefit the cult.

How had he failed so miserably in his efforts to foil the priest?

Anok found himself disoriented and overwhelmed by the situation. Things were happening so fast.

A priest!

Becoming a priest had never been part of his plan. Of course, the presumed ambition of every acolyte of Set was to become a priest in the cult, to gain access to the power and sorcerous resources that only priests possessed. Yet most never advanced to that rank, and for those that did, it often required years of service to the cult in order for them to be considered for advancement.

Anok had been with the cult scant months.

His promotion should not be happening, and as such, he was ill prepared for it. He knew almost nothing about what to expect from the initiation ceremony, or what would happen to him afterward. He had a vague idea that this might only be the first of many ceremonies, but of even that he was not sure.

A servant stood before him holding a new yoke of Set, trimmed in gold, with a large, bloodred stone set into the front. Another servant, an old, hawk-nosed Stygian who had been supervising Anok's preparations, grabbed his father's iron medallion, which hung around Anok's neck. Anok tried to pull it away from him, but only succeeded in choking himself on the chain.

There was almost no chance the man would accidentally find the hidden catch that would reveal the Scale of Set hidden inside, but Anok did not like anyone else touching it.

The servant looked up at him, frowning, a look of disapproval in his eyes. "What is this ugly piece of rubbish? I should take it."

Anok finally succeeded in yanking it back. "It is a keepsake, nothing more."

The servant raised an eyebrow. "I will keep it for you then. One of your station should not be seen wearing such trash, especially not during such an important ceremony."

"No one will see it! The yoke of Set will hide it, and I wish to keep it near me."

The man scowled, his dark eyes narrowing. "What is it to be of such importance to you?"

He stared directly into the man's eyes. "It contains the dried testicle of the first servant I killed for insolence. I like to keep it near my heart."

The servant blinked in surprise and took a small step backward. "Well, yes then. Certainly nobody will see! We will leave it where it is."

"That," said Anok, dryly, "would be good."

He suppressed a smile. If he had learned one thing of value from Ramsa Aál, it was that fear was the way a priest of Set maintained the devotion of his lessers. The servants here were used to dealing with spoiled, rich pilgrims from Khemi and Luxur, who in turn expected to be humbled by the keepers of the holy shrine. It was part of the show, part of the pretense of suffering for their god.

But Anok was no pilgrim to be pushed around. He might not be able to control what Ramsa Aál and the other priests did to him, but there were still many in the cult over whom he could wield his own authority.

A female servant appeared with a palette of colored pastes and powders. She carefully painted dark outlines around his eyes and applied rouge to his cheeks and lips in the ancient style. Anok had occasionally seen priests made up this way for some of the oldest and most sacred of ceremonies. His finery was finished off as she covered his head with an embroidered black headcloth, trimmed with roping made of gold thread.

Ramsa Aál appeared, wearing an even more elaborate robe, with a long sash that draped over his neck and extended almost to the floor on either side. It was embroidered to resemble a great snake, with the head hanging down the left side of his body. He also wore a tall headdress with a golden serpent crest. Like Anok, he wore ceremonial face paint, including a squirming serpent, painted in gold across his forehead.

He glanced down, carefully so as not to unbalance his tall headgear, and brushed a bit of dust off his sash. "The shrines always have the best finery, even better than the Great Temple in Khemi."

"Master, I don't know what is to happen here tonight."

He raised an eyebrow. "You know what you need to know. To place yourself unquestioningly in the hands of the higher powers of the cult, that is part of the trial." His expression seemed to soften slightly. "Know this acolyte, today you will take an important step on the road to priesthood, though only the first of many."

He stepped to a basket in the corner, containing a number of ceremonial scepters and staffs. He extracted a long golden staff with a cobra's head on top, mouth opened wide exposing silver fangs, and with red rubies for eyes. He examined it for a moment, then, seemingly satisfied, removed it and took it for himself.

He turned back to Anok. "Let that be your lesson here, one I have learned through trial and experience. Great things are achieved through steps, through building one thing, one action, one piece of knowledge upon another. This, I have learned, is where most great sorcerers fail. They seek one great object of power, one great spell, that will give them all they desire. But from Kaman Awi, I have learned the value of studying how things may be combined. Through a series of steps, studied and planned, anything can be achieved. No power is above the power our cult will soon possess."

He smiled at Anok. "You are part of the plan, acolyte, though you do not yet know how. Have faith that you will serve your purpose, and it will be *glorious!*"

4

DRUMS POUNDED, AND the assembled pilgrims cheered as Anok and Ramsa Aál emerged from the newly opened front door of the tomb. Half a dozen priests in full ceremonial regalia already stood on the wide, columned, portico of the building, along with many servants, also in elaborate ceremonial costumes.

Anok couldn't help noticing, though, the dark, wrinkled little man crouched behind one of the pillars, hidden from the assembly, clutching his dangerous-sounding basket. He still wore only his simple kilt, and his eyes glared up at Anok from the shadow that was his face.

Anok turned his attention to the hundred or so assembled pilgrims looking up at him expectantly. He was uncomfortable being in front of so many people. He had lived most of his life as little more than an anonymous face in a crowded city, and he found this kind of attention disturbing.

What was he seeing in their faces? Did they view him as some hero to be celebrated, or were they merely looking at him as they would the main course at a banquet? He wasn't sure.

Ramsa Aál stepped to the front and center of the portico
and stood at the edge of the top step, flanked by a pair of
guardians in brightly polished armor holding golden ceremonial spears.

He lifted his arms, and the crowd swiftly fell silent.
"Hear me, followers of Set!" He yelled the words, but
with the trained voice of a skilled orator. "You have traveled far to pay your respects to Set at this most sacred
shrine. Yet you have been blessed with far more! You have
been fortunate enough to arrive here on a great day! A
great day indeed!"

A cheer rose up in response, and he allowed it to continue for a few moments before again signaling for silence.

He continued. "You have been witness to a great thing.
It is your duty to Set to return to your hometowns and temples and spread word of what has happened. On this day,
the Lost King has summoned his earthly treasures from his
tomb to the Realm Eternal, where he sits at the left hand of
Set, as one of his most beloved servants. All now can witness that his temple stands empty, stripped of all its riches
and decoration, proof of the reward for *all* those who serve
our master Set! Life, power, and wealth eternal shall be
yours!"

Again cheering, even more energetic this time. Ramsa
Aál had some difficulty getting them back under control,
finally waving the golden staff he carried in the air to get
their attention.

"Beginning tomorrow, the Tomb of the Lost King will
be opened to all pilgrims so that they can see what has
transpired here. You who are assembled here shall be the
first to see it with your own eyes!"

Again cheering. Anok couldn't believe the audacity of it
all. They would be shown an empty tomb that had always
been empty, and told it was proof of an afterlife that Ramsa
Aál assured him was a sham.

When finally they quieted again, Ramsa Aál glanced
over at Anok. "Yet there is more to this tale. It begins
months ago in the Great Temple of Set in Khemi, where a

young acolyte was granted a special gift, a brand of power not seen for generations!"

Two of the local priests stepped up on either side of Anok. One lifted his left arm over his head and pulled back the sleeve so all could see.

Ramsa Aál glanced back at Anok, then announced, "The Mark of Set!"

The pilgrims spontaneous began chanting, "Set, Set, Set!"

"He heard the summons of Set and was drawn here to use the power granted him to open the tomb so the Lost King might reclaim his treasures."

The crowd murmured. Someone shouted, "The hand of Set!"

Ramsa Aál went on. "This was his mission, just as *you* have been summoned here to make offerings to Set. We are *all* offerings to Set. Our blood, our flesh, our very lives. Believe in him, serve him, and you shall be rewarded in the Realm Eternal!"

More chanting. "Set, Set, Set, munificent Set!"

"Hear me, pilgrims! You are once again blessed with good fortune this night. As reward for his excellent service to Set, this acolyte, Anok Wati, shall begin the trials and ceremonies of ascension to become a priest of Set!"

There were cheers. Someone again shouted, "The hand of Set! The hand of Set!"

"Normally, these ceremonies and trials are held in secret, shrouded in mystery from all but the innermost circles of the cult. But today, we wish you to know what we know, that we priests stand above you for a reason. We have earned our titles, through service, sacrifice, and peril. Watch, go forth, and tell what you have seen today. Tell what it means to be a priest of our god!"

He glanced casually back at Anok, then at the priests on either side. "Seize him," he said quietly.

Before Anok could react, each of the priests at his side had grabbed an arm and twisted it behind him so that he could not move. He stared accusingly at Ramsa Aál, but the man's face was an unreadable mask of detachment. Again, his voice rose for the benefit of the assembled. "Anok Wati, you have been chosen by your god for the rites of ascension, to become his instrument on earth! Your god asks not your pledge of fealty. He has no need of your promises or pledges. He has *chosen* you, and he will own your soul! Through these trials, you will become one with your god!"

He walked briskly to where the little man and his basket awaited. He paused for a moment, placing his fist over his heart, where the second Scale of Set, and perhaps even the third, was likely hidden.

Then the little man removed the lid from the basket and reached inside. A loud hissing commenced from the interior, and Ramsa Aál came up holding a huge, black cobra behind its head.

He turned and stepped out from behind the pillar, and the pilgrims gasped in both fear and wonder.

The snake was as long as a man was tall, thick as a woman's wrist, the shiny black scales iridescent in the torchlight. It did not struggle or attempt to bite the priest, only looked around curiously, its flicking red tongue tasting the air.

Ramsa Aál walked back to Anok, who tried to draw back from the snake. As he did, the priests twisted his arms, pushing him forward.

He tried to call on the power of the Mark of Set, but he realized why he was restrained by priests, not guardians. He was also restrained on a mystic level, the two of them united in a binding spell that could, for a time anyway, keep even the power of the Mark of Set impotent.

The snake turned toward him, eyes shining in the darkness, then suddenly reared up, hissing, flaring its hood.

The crowd gasped, and even the priests holding him tried to draw back. Only Ramsa Aál remained calm, untouched by fear.

Anok's heart pounded. He had but one hope. If Ramsa Aál commanded the snake by using the power of the Scale of Set around his neck, he didn't know that Anok possessed one as well. Neither would the priest binding him, so their spell would have been cast without consideration of the Scale's power.

There was the chance, of course, that he would reveal its existence to Ramsa Aál. But as he watched the poison drip down one of the serpent's fangs, he decided that was the lesser of his problems.

He reached out for the amulet with his mind. It was difficult even to sense, hidden within the cold iron of his father's medallion, even knowing it was there. Even though he had mingled its powers with his own. Months earlier, it wouldn't have been possible at all, but Anok's skills in sorcerous matters had grown considerably of late.

There! He dimly felt the Scale of Set awaken from it slumber.

"It is time, acolyte of Set, for the essence of our god to flow through your veins! I give you the gift of venom!"

Anok watched the snake, saw it draw back as though to strike.

He tried to put aside his fear, focus only on the power of the Scale of Set.

The snake's head darted forward.

Then stopped.

The hood relaxed ever so slightly. The snake seemed confused.

Ramsa Aál frowned, his brow knitted in concentration.

The cobra's hood flared wide. It hissed.

Anok concentrated on the Scale of Set, but something seemed wrong—

The snake drew back.

It struck.

Anok gasped as he felt the needle fangs sink into his neck, felt the hot gush of poison into the wounds.

Something liquid trickled down his neck. Blood or venom, he could not be sure.

He gasped for breath, feeling the poison pumping with each surge of his heart, into his chest, into his brain.

His body seemed to go limp, the priests holding him up as his legs failed him.

His vision dimmed. His mind seemed to float away into the night air, looking down upon the scene.

He heard Ramsa Aál's voice, as though from far away. "By this venom he shall be changed! By this venom he shall be judged! Let him wake an instrument of our god, or let him not wake at all!"

As the blackness surrounded him, he could still hear the chanting: *"Set, Set, Set, munificent Set! Set, Set, Set, munificent Set!"*

TEFERI WATCHED IN horror as the priests seized his friend, and the cobra was lifted before Anok's face. Fallon reached over, squeezing his wrist until he felt as if the bones would snap.

Never before had he wished for Anok to use magic, but he wished now.

He was to be disappointed.

Nothing happened, no reprieve came. He watched helplessly as the snake plunged its fangs into Anok's neck, hesitating an eternity that might have been the span of a single heartbeat, before drawing back, folding its hood, and curling calmly around the priest's arm.

He watched his friend slump between the two priests, who carried him by either arm, as Ramsa made his speech to the followers assembled in front of the tomb.

They began to chant and cheer as Anok was dragged back through the arched doorway into the tomb.

Teferi's mouth was dry. Tomb. The implications of that were too terrible to consider.

"Butchers," said Fallon, her voice a strained whisper.

Teferi pulled his wrist from her grasp and rose to his knees. "I have to go to him."

"Are you insane? That is one of the cult's most sacred places. No person without clear Stygian blood will be tolerated there, much less a full-blooded Kushite."

"Then," said Teferi, as he scrambled to his feet and headed back to the camel, "I will not go in the front door."

Fallon scrambled up and chased after him. "You can't do anything. He may already be dead!" She seemed to choke on those words.

Teferi gathered his weapons. "We can't know that."

She reached out and put her hand on his shoulder. "Teferi, if I have lost one friend this night, I would not lose two. It is the warrior's wish to die in glorious battle, but not without cause or profit." She paused a long moment. "We can still give him vengeance, but only if we seek a time when the odds are more in our favor."

He turned and looked at her, her eyes glinting in the starlight. "I must go to my brother, no matter the cost. I must hope that Jangwa, the god of empty places, holds sway here and will stand at my side." He picked up his bow. "You are wise to stay behind. If I do not return, you can serve vengeance for us both. But if I do return, I will need you to stand ready for our escape."

He heard her swallow hard in the darkness. "I will make Fenola ready to travel then, and I will take up your spare bow and wait. I am not half the bowman you are, but perhaps I can shoot well enough to cover your escape if I must."

He chuckled grimly. "You will be lucky if you can even pull my bow, but it is as good a plan as any."

ANOK STOOD ATOP a tall, wind-sculpted dune and surveyed his surroundings, an endless sea of towering dunes extending to every horizon. A constant wind blew, lifting a fog of sand that softened everything. Yet the fine, blowing granules did not sting his eyes or clog his nose as they should have.

His surroundings were as bright as noon, but there was no sun, and the sky was pink. He cast no shadow. It was as though the light came from everywhere, and nowhere.

The air smelled like honeysuckle in bloom.

He looked down, and realized he was dressed in a simple kilt, sleeveless tunic, and coconut fiber sandals, a type of clothing he had favored during the time he lived in the slums of Odji. His swords were there, too, worn at his belt as had once been his fashion.

He had no temple robes, no yoke of Set, and even his father's iron medallion was gone. Remembering what had happened before, he brought his fingers to the place on his neck where the cobra's fangs had struck. There was no wound, no scar, only a strange heat under the skin.

"Am I dead?" He asked the desert.

The answer was a dry rustling from over the crest of the next dune. A flat, skeletal head appeared, empty eye sockets set as wide as his shoulders, jaws bristled with needle teeth, followed by a sinuous body, a spine lined with curved ribs.

He had seen it before.

Parath!

The last time he had seen the self-professed lost god of Stygia, the skeleton had been immobile, trapped in the desert, so it said, by the ancient treachery of the gods Set and Ibis.

Now it moved with the graceful power of a real snake.

"This is a dream," he said.

The great snake reared up before him, sand running off its white bones in rivulets. The voice came at both a booming rumble and a dry hiss, so his ears strained to hear both its high notes and its low. "This is the shadowland between life and death. I have been trapped here, in this serpent form, since before the time of true-men, when great beasts walked the world!"

"Then if I am not dead, I soon will be."

"No! I have brought you here so that we may speak. You have lost faith in me, Anok Wati! You have lost faith in the mission on which I sent you! You have lost faith in the beliefs of your father!"

Anok twitched at the mention of his father. His memory was drawn back to his Usafiri into the Sea of Sand, a spiritual quest where he had first encountered Parath. Parath claimed that his father, indeed Anok's entire male family line, had served the fallen god.

But Anok had since learned things that made him think otherwise. "I have doubts. I have concerns. I have seen evidence that my father was secretly an agent of your declared enemy Ibis, not your servant, as you claim."

"I *claim,* nothing, little human! I speak truth! Both Ibis and Set are my enemies! As you pose as an acolyte of Set, to strike at him for me, so your father posed as a servant of Ibis for the same reason! Are you so simple that you cannot see this?"

Anok blinked in surprise. It made sense. His father might have pretended to be a follower of Ibis in order to strike at the Moon god for Parath. "What then, of my sister?"

"Sister?" Parath's voice was incredulous. "You have no sister!"

Anok was confused. What was the truth here? His father told him he had a sister, that he had to find her, and give her the Scale of Set that his father had entrusted to him. Yet ever in that task, he failed. Even here, on the edge of death, he had failed.

What was the truth? Only one person could tell him for sure, and that person was long gone from the world of men, murdered before young Anok's eyes.

He missed his father so.

He felt empty and cold. The warm spot on his neck began to throb painfully. He noticed a part of the sky, darker than the rest, where the pink sky and yellow swirls of sand gave way to deepest indigo. It called to him.

"I have failed. I cannot free you from this place, any more than I can free myself." He began to walk down the dune, headed for the dark spot on the horizon. "Perhaps my father's spirit waits for me, beyond that next dune. Let me go to him."

With startling speed the skeletal snake slithered down the dune after him, passing him, blocking his way with its massive coil, curved ribs surrounding him like a fence.

"Your father is gone. Nothing waits for you there but cold, darkness, and oblivion. Life is not done with you, and neither am I! You are destined to play an important role in the destiny of gods!"

"I have no destiny. I cannot bring you back to life. I am a poor sorcerer."

"You are more powerful than you know, but you resist that power at every turn. Your efforts to fight it are pointless and pathetic, but you cannot resist forever. You will let the power claim you!"

"I am my own man."

"You are an instrument of powers you cannot even begin to understand!"

"I still can't bring you back."

"You do not need to. Such is the task of others. It is only afterward, that your time of greatness will come. When it does, remember who your *true* master is and bring the Golden Scales to me!"

The sand beneath his feet seemed to move, to draw him back, faster and faster.

The Parath faded into the distance.

"Remember your master," the voice faded in the distance. "Bring the Scales to me!"

The sand seemed to run out from under Anok's feet, as though he stood in an hourglass, and he fell, swallowed into blackness.

The darkness enfolded him, and he welcomed oblivion.

TEFERI TROTTED AWAY along the ridgeline, ducking low so he wouldn't be seen silhouetted against the night sky from below. It was difficult to see much by starlight, but that was all to his advantage.

He'd spent the better part of the day lying at his vantage point above the shrine, studying the surroundings and committing it all to memory. He carried in his mind's eye a map, and he already knew his exact route into the temple.

He worked his way around to the west side before heading down the slope through a narrow wash in the embankment he had spotted earlier.

Though it was even darker in its depths, he didn't need to see. He could reach out and touch the steep walls on either side. He also didn't have to keep watch for attack from all directions, only front, behind, and above.

He moved with an emphasis on speed rather than stealth. More than once he stumbled, or started a cascade of pebbles sliding noisily down the slope, but it couldn't be helped. With the venom in Anok's blood, every moment counted.

Teferi had seen Anok heal himself magically from major wounds, but he was far less confident of his ability to deal with such a devastating dose of poison. The speed with which he had collapsed didn't bode well.

Teferi considered himself fortunate in that he hadn't seen any guardian patrols. Apparently, most of the guardians were at the ceremony.

Fortunate for them it is only me and not a gang of bandits seeking gold.

Actually, at this point, bandits would have been a welcome distraction, but he couldn't be that lucky.

His entire plan was based on a supposition. He had many times seen people go into the small building behind the temple. Several times, he had seen more people enter or emerge than could have possibly fit inside. And on several occasions, he had seen people, including Anok, go into the small building and emerge from the front of the tomb.

Assuming there was no magical trickery at work, the two buildings had to be connected underground. He had seen his unconscious (hopefully not dead) friend dragged back into the tomb. Anok would either still be inside, or he would be coming out through the smaller building.

Either way, I will find him.

A low wall surrounded the rear of the site. He considered scaling it, but it would be difficult to do quietly. Instead, he looked to an arched gate to the north. It was dimly illuminated with a single torch, and the lone guard seemed to be sleeping on his feet.

A single, well-placed arrow would have taken him down, but it also would mark Teferi a murderous invader. Considering the overwhelming odds against him, that would accomplish little. There was still the chance Teferi could bluff his way inside.

If not, Teferi had brought other traditional weapons of his people, weapons of stealth. He also had a new weapon that he had recently picked up in Kheshatta. He wasn't as practiced with it as he would have liked, but it might serve him.

But after he reached into his bag, it was the traditional weapon he casually held behind his back. He walked boldly up to the gate, pretending to be out of breath and on the verge of collapse.

The startled guardian, a round-faced man, jumped to alert and raised his sword. "Halt, in the name of Set! Halt or die!"

Teferi pretended to ignore the sword, leaning over as though too tired to stand. "I come— I come for an important message— For my master— Anok Wati— An acolyte of Set— Aide to the mighty Priest of Needs— Ramsa Aál— I am his— servant—"

The guardian seemed to relax, convinced Teferi was more annoyance than threat. "No outlander may enter this sacred place—"

"But lord! My skin is Kush, but I am born of Stygia!"

He laughed. "Birth is nothing! Blood is everything! The noble blood of Stygia runs in all who enter here!"

Teferi could not resist glancing up at the man for a moment. His pointed, hooked nose was the only sign that a drop of Stygian blood ran in him. He rapidly hung his head and kept his contempt to himself. "But lord guardian! I have come far. I bring word from the temple in Kheshatta— Directly from the High Priest—"

"You have done well enough then. Give me your message and be gone!"

Teferi frowned. This wasn't going to work. "As you wish, my lord!"

He stepped forward, and from behind his back his arm flashed forward, his reach extended by a polished black knobkerrie, a knob-ended club. The ball of it smashed into the guard's jaw, and Teferi heard bone crack. The man's eyes rolled back in his head as he fell backward, bounced off the inside of the gate's arch, and thudded into the dirt.

Teferi quickly dragged him inside the gate, where he found a small gate shack a few feet to one side. He pulled the man inside and removed a pair of snares from his bag. The slip-knotted leather cords were used to bind the legs of killed and live game, and they worked just as well for men. He pulled the man's wrists behind his back, slipped the snare over, and pulled the knotted cord tight, then repeated the process on his ankles. He gagged the guardian with his own robe tie, flinching sympathetically as he felt the grinding of bone in the broken jaw. Certainly this unfortunate was not going to chew through his gag.

There was one more thing. He reached into the bag and removed a small box made of hollowed bamboo. He opened the lid and removed his new weapon, a steel dart with a tuft of fur on the back, careful not to get near the poisoned point. He jabbed the point into the man's neck, then drew it out and tossed it away into the darkness. According to the Kheshattan poisoner he had bought it from (and were they not the finest in Hyboria?), it would be at least a day before the man awakened.

Teferi slipped out of the shack, closing the door behind him. Keeping to the shadows, he moved toward the little outbuilding. As he peered around a corner at his destination, he spotted two laborers loading a cart with camel dung, probably from the heavily laden pack caravan he'd seen taken out just after sundown.

Ducking back into concealment, he removed two pieces of carved bamboo tube from his bag, put them together end to end, and twisted the connection to lock them together. Then he took out the little bamboo case and removed two of the tiny darts. He slid one inside the mouthpiece, careful not to let the poison touch the sides, took a deep breath, placed the blowgun to his lips, carefully aimed, then *blew*.

There was a rushing whistle, like a small bird flying quickly over. The nearer man slapped his hand to the back of his neck, then quietly slumped to the ground.

Teferi ducked back, reloading. The second shot would be harder. Speed was of the essence, and the target might be moving. He inhaled, popped out, aimed, and let fly.

The dark struck the second man in the cheek. He yelped slightly, swatted at the side of his face, and fell on top of his companion. Not an elegant shot, but it would serve.

Teferi put the blowgun into his quiver and ran to the men, dragging them inside the little building. As he had expected, there was a stairway inside.

Less welcome was the sight of a guardian at the bottom, facing away from him, armored so that a blowgun shot from the rear would be difficult to impossible.

Instead, Teferi extinguished the lone torch inside the structure and withdrew to the shadows. In a loud whisper, with as much authority as he could muster, he said, "Up here! Quickly!"

The guardian turned, walked slowly up the stair, weapon at the ready.

Teferi crouched just above the tunnel opening, another dart in his hand. He waited until the man was in front of him, then jumped down to land behind him.

He slapped his hand over the man's mouth and jabbed him in the throat with the dart, leaving his hand free to grab the man's sword hand. The guardian struggled briefly before going limp.

Teferi struggled to lower his armored form as quietly as possible. It would be nearly impossible to drag or carry him up the stairs without making too much noise, so Teferi left the guardian where he lay, moving cautiously down the stair past the fallen man.

He found a chamber below, illuminated by many lamps, divided by curtained partitions. He saw ceremonial clothing and various temple artifacts lying around and surmised he was in some kind of staging area for the ceremony in front of the tomb. Though he saw no one, there were people nearby. He heard voices, footsteps, saw moving shadows cast on the chamber's ceiling, but heard no indications of alarm.

PEERING AROUND A corner, Teferi spotted two acolytes removing ceremonial garb. He extracted the blowgun and carefully readied two darts. With such powerful poison, he had learned from experience that it was dangerous to get in too much of a hurry.

One of the acolytes, an ivory-skinned Stygian, stripped down to his loincloth, becoming an easy target. An easy puff, and a dart appeared between his shoulder blades. The man yelped and flailed his arms, trying in vain to reach the dart.

As he did, he spun, revealing the dart to his companion, who had only gotten as far as removing his headdress. The man's eyes went wide, and he opened his mouth to sound an alarm.

Teferi had already reloaded and hastily raised the blowgun to his lips.

The poorly aimed dart stabbed into the acolyte's tongue. The man stuck his tongue out grotesquely trying to grab the dart, but striking so close to the brain, the poison was almost instantly effective, sending the man first to his knees, eyes rolled back, then thudding to his side on the floor.

Teferi looked at the man, his dart-pierced tongue still hanging from his mouth like a sleeping dog's. He realized that, in his haste, he'd almost forgotten to take a breath before putting the blowgun to his lips. With this weapon, breath control was everything. *Lucky the dart ended up in his tongue, not mine!*

Teferi resolved that he'd taken enough chances with the unfamiliar weapon and stuffed it back into his quiver. He

quickly dragged the two men into a curtained dressing area
and drew the canvas over the front of it.

He crouched by the bodies for a moment, listening for
signs of detection, then slipped under the back curtain to a
similar, empty, cubicle on the other side. A servant's table,
with large carrying handles, stood in the center of the space,
loaded with jars of ceremonial herbs and oils. Alongside
them was a nasty-looking dagger, with a blade that twisted
from side to side like the body of a snake, its hilt in the shape
of a golden snake's head.

He shuddered when he thought of the countless inno-
cents whose blood it had likely spilled.

Curse this cult! Curse them that killed my brother!

He surprised and angered himself with the latter thought.
He should not yet give up his brother for dead, yet he knew
what the black cobra's poison could do to a man and how
quickly it could do it, even when the bite was on an ex-
tremity. Anok had been bitten on the throat.

No! My brother must live, or that damned priest must pay!

Teferi was startled as the far curtain was thrown back,
and he found himself looking into the eyes of a startled
priest.

Teferi grabbed the knobkerrie and swung it at the
man's head.

But the priest was fast, ducking and stepping back in
one motion, so that the club only succeeded in ripping off
the man's serpent headdress.

Teferi swung again for the man's midsection, hoping to
at least break a rib, but the man vaulted over the club, catching himself on one hand, somersaulting to land smoothly
on his feet several paces away.

He has skills.

Teferi was planning his next attack when the man raised
his hands and gestured—

Not magic!

"Bands of Crytos, this barbarian bind!"

There was a flash of light, and Teferi felt a tingling. Then
nothing. He moved experimentally, and felt no hindrance.

The priest looked confused, stumbling back to keep his distance from his attacker.

Teferi didn't understand, but he grinned.

As Teferi stepped closer, club pulled back over his head, the man gestured wildly. "Sands of Stygia, winds of home, strip man's flesh and show me bone!"

A bit of wind plucked momentarily at Teferi's clothes, then faded. The priest's eyes were wide with fear and confusion.

He slammed the club down in the middle of the man's skull, dropping him like a bag of rice.

You should have kept fighting. You would have had a chance.

"Well fought, Kush."

The voice came from behind him, and Teferi knew it well. Ramsa Aál! He spun.

The priest stood behind two other priests, who stood, hands raised, ready to make magic. A pair of guardians stood behind Ramsa Aál, Anok's limp body held between them.

"Don't kill him," said Ramsa Aál, with a cruel smile, "but you can break him a little."

One of the priests brandished his ceremonial staff as the second began muttering the beginnings of some slower spell.

The priest with the staff held it over his head. "By Set's power, bring forth his serpents!"

The staff seemed to transform in his hand into a veritable bouquet of poisonous vipers, which were immediately flung at Teferi, a hissing mass, fangs dripping poison.

He swung his knobkerrie. There was the sound of wood striking wood, and the spell was broken. The staff clattered to the floor, harmless.

Ramsa Aál's lips parted, and a look of surprise and wonder appeared on his face. He watched as the second priest completed his incantations.

"By Set's power, I draw forth your immortal soul!" He priest gestured.

Teferi felt a tingling that moved up his body like crawling ants, and danced around his head and neck, making him shudder. Then he threw the feeling off.

The priest fell back, a look of surprise on his face. He glanced at Ramsa Aál, who only smiled knowingly.

Teferi heard shouts and armored footsteps running down the stairs and in from the front of the Tomb. Suddenly, guardians seemed to appear from every direction.

Teferi tossed aside the knobkerrie and drew his sword, grimly prepared to fight, to make them pay for Anok's life, and his own, with as much blood as he could spill.

Ramsa Aál shouted. "Wait! I will talk with this inferior, if he can speak."

A captain of the guardians appeared from behind the massed soldiers, a look of confusion and rage on his face. "This outlander left one of my man with a busted head and a cracked jaw! Let us make him pay for it!"

Ramsa Aál waved him away. "Your fool was likely sleeping at his post. That he lives is probably more than he deserves." He look to Teferi. "I know you, Kush, from past times we have met. Anok painted you as a muscular fool to be his bodyguard, and I was all too willing to believe that. But my acolyte is far cleverer than that, is he not?"

Teferi glared at him. "He is now more dead than clever, as you shall be soon enough!"

"I see. You come to rescue your master?"

"I come to rescue my *brother*!"

Ramsa Aál laughed. "A barbaric Kush, even one so unusual as you, is no brother to any man of Stygian blood, even a poor half-breed such as this one. But have no fear. The snake that bit him had been fed mystic herbs and milked until its venom was weak. He will recover in time. But you—!"

"Pray you speak the truth, as it is worth your life!"

Ramsa Aál looked around at the circle of angry guardians, all aching to fight. "I think that is not an issue. I won't be foolish enough to waste magic on you again." He chuckled. "Clever, clever, Anok is.

"Just when I think I have his measure, he surprises me. To take a Zimwi-msaka as his bodyguard! Ingenious! And I had heard your kind were all dead! Had I but known earlier, your blood might have served in my counterspell against the protectors of the tomb. But it is too late for that now."

Teferi frowned. The name sounded something like the native language of his people. It might mean something like "spirit hunter" or "demon hunter," he couldn't be sure. But he had never heard the exact word before. How did a Stygian priest know it?

Ramsa Aál studied the look of confusion on his face and laughed. "Even better, a Zimwi-msaka who does not know he is a Zimwi-msaka!"

"What do you mean?"

"Anok must know. Ask him when he returns from his communion with Set. Or ask your friend Sabé! The blind scholar can tell you—if he will."

At that moment, Anok coughed, a bit of pink foam on his lips. But although he stirred, he remained unconscious.

Ramsa Aál made a gesture, and the two guardians carrying Anok lowered him facedown onto the floor and stepped back.

"If you want your master, take him. We are done here." He snapped his finger at a servant, who watched, cowering, from behind a curtain. "You! Find two fresh camels for my acolyte and his servant, with extra water and provisions to return to Kheshatta."

Teferi thought of saying he had no need of these things, but to do so would hint that Fallon still waited for them in the desert. Better to keep some things to himself. Forcing a calm on himself he did not feel, he again pretended to be the good servant. "My master would thank you, if he could."

Ramsa Aál nodded. "That's more like it, Kush. Your loyalty is admirable, but remember your station, and that each breath you take from here on out you owe to *my* mercy."

Teferi swallowed his anger, and the taste was bitter indeed. *I do this for my brother's life.* He put away his sword and moved carefully to attend Anok, kneeling at his side.

Trickles of blood ran from the fang marks on his neck. His skin was cool and damp, his pulse fast and weak, his breathing slow. His eyes were opened a slit, showing only their whites. He looked up at Ramsa Aál accusingly.

"He communes with his god. If he is judged worthy, he will return. If he is weak, then none can help him."

"My brother is not weak!"

Ramsa Aál nodded. "No. I do not think he is."

5

TEFERI LEANED AGAINST a heavy wooden case stacked with ancient tablets of slate and stone, part of the greatest library of ancient knowledge in all of Kheshatta. The man who owned the library paced angrily back and forth across the room of the little house.

Though the man, Sabé, whose eyes were bound with a ragged cloth blindfold, could not see, he moved with vigor and confidence. He knew every crack and corner of his home, and there was little danger he would bump into anything save a misplaced visitor.

Teferi was careful to keep out of his way. He liked Sabé, the two having become friends since Teferi had come to Kheshatta as Anok's bodyguard. But he kept some distance from him now.

Sabé was infamous as the "blind scholar of Kheshatta," but they had recently learned the old man was not blind at all. In his youth he had been a follower of Set, and magical corruption had turned Sabé's eyes into the eyes of a serpent: evil eyes that twisted Sabé's vision of the world.

He chose to live as a blind man rather than allow the terrible vision of evil guide him.

Learning that had only increased Teferi's respect for the old scholar, but still he shuddered when he thought of those eyes, and he shied away whenever the old man came a little *too* close.

Sabé stopped his pacing and turned toward Teferi. "I have heard of this thing, though it was not done in my time. The priest candidates are infused with repeated and increasing doses of snake venom. The snakes themselves are fed rodents, who in turn eat only magical herbs, giving the venom special properties. Those so treated have powerful visions. Some say they commune with Set himself."

"Wait," said Teferi, "did you say 'repeated'? You mean, they will do this to him again?"

"As I have heard it, the cobra is but the beginning, to build his immunity to the venom, and to train his body to resist the poison with magic. Later will come the venom of the sons of Set, the most sacred serpents of the cult."

"Madness! What purpose can that serve?"

Sabé frowned. "To break his resolve. To destroy his resistance to corruption, so that he will fall totally under the influence of Set's cult."

"But he has the Band of Neska. Won't that help him?"

Sabé hung his head. "You have said it yourself. Anok places too much faith in that ancient object. It is an anchor to sanity and reason, nothing more. It gives him something to hold on to in the dark times, a reference point to guide him through evil places, but he must find his own way, he must pull himself back from evil. These treatments are intended to weaken just that kind of resolve. He is in terrible danger."

"Then," said Teferi, "let us go to him! Even now, Fallon sits in vigil at his bedside. He did not waken during the journey from the Tomb of the Lost King, nor has he wakened since."

Sabé's mouth hung open in surprise. "Go? What can I do?"

"You can be there to guide him when he awakes. If he has visions, you must be there to tell him what they mean."

Sabé looked unhappy and confused. "Go? I can't leave all my ancient texts—"

"Your house is guarded by a thousand magical traps and snares. They will be safe for a time."

Sabé sighed, and suddenly looked like an old and frail man. Teferi wondered how long it had been since the old recluse had left his house.

Never mind that Sabé was even older than old, preserved by dark magic long past his natural lifetime, and never mind that he was more than a little frail; his power of personality had always made him seem younger and stronger than he was.

This momentary glimpse at fragile reality was somehow as disturbing to Teferi as seeing Sabé's dread serpent eyes.

Teferi tried to make his voice reassuring. "Anok needs you, and he cannot be moved. You must be strong, and go to him. We will not be gone long."

Sabé licked his dry lips. "Yes, you are right. Of course." He pointed to a stool on which assorted clutter was piled. "Get my satchel, cloak, and walking staff. We will go."

Teferi handed him the cloak and staff. He carried the heavy satchel himself. "I could summon a cart."

"It is but a few streets away. I am old, not dead!"

They stepped out of the house. The door clicked shut, and Sabé fiddled briefly with the strange and complex brass lock mechanism. Teferi had a feeling that it, like so much of their surroundings, was fraught with hidden sorcerous danger for anyone who would trespass upon this place.

Sabé allowed Teferi to lead him down the flagstone walk, through the fence gate, and out into the busy streets of Kheshatta. He pulled the old man aside as an oxcart, laden with large casks of poison and guarded by fierce-looking Shemites armed with axes, rolled by noisily on the cobblestone street.

Kheshatta was famed as a city of sorcerers, but it was also the city of poisoners, Stygia's famed masters of potions and powders, both terrible and, occasionally, beneficial.

The poisoners, in their palaces in the green, forested hills west of the city, guarded their secrets, and their powers, as jealously as the sorcerers did.

The two main power factions of the city maintained an uneasy truce, each trading with the other, each making use of the other with not a grain of trust between them. It was an interesting and colorful city, but Teferi could not say he would be sad to leave.

They walked in silence for a while, until he felt Sabé hesitate, and they stopped on a street corner in front of one of the city's many museums of mystical relics.

"I'm sorry," said Teferi, "I walk too fast."

"Not a bit, young friend. It's just that I sense something troubles you, something beyond your concern for Anok."

Teferi hesitated to answer. His concerns didn't seem very important right now. Still, he did not know when he might next find himself alone with Sabé.

"I had a troubling encounter with the priests of Set at the shrine. Several of them tried to use magic to harm me, and their spells all failed. At the time, I thought perhaps it was fear that had caused them to misspeak their incantations. But the priest Ramsa Aál said it was something else. He said I was a—" He paused, trying to remember the term exactly. "A Zimwi-msaka."

They began to walk toward Anok's villa again, slower this time. "I have seen this term in some of the old texts."

"You once told me that some souls are drawn to magic, and some are anathema to it, and that I was the latter. You told me I could read aloud from the dark texts forever and 'not raise enough magic to turn a grain of sand.' Is that all it is?"

"So I thought at the time, but perhaps there is more to you than this. You say your family fled Kush to escape the magical corruption of the dark lands to the south?"

"So I have been told. Dark forces of sorcery and be-witchment came south out of Stygia into Kush and the lands beyond, and corrupted the souls of our people. My forefathers fled north, but were captured, and kept as slaves in Stygia until most of the slaves there were eventually set free. Then they lived in exile and poverty, scratching out their lives in this evil land."

"Did you ever question this? If the evil that corrupted your people came from the north, why flee north? And if it corrupted all your people, how were your forefathers spared?"

He felt a flash of anger. "Are you saying my father lied to me?"

"I am saying the story may have become twisted after countless retellings through the generations. I am saying that certain facts may have been left out to protect their daughters and sons—you—from the secrets of your own origins."

"You talk in riddles. What is a Zimwi-msaka? You know, don't you?"

"I know what I have read in the texts, and know that it could be as twisted and suspect as what you have told me. It is said that in the ancient times, the Zimwi-msaka were a clan of warriors that appeared in Kush. They were great fighters, and great hunters, but they were more. It was said that no magic could be used to harm them, that magic rolled off them like raindrops off a goose. Even their blood was resistant to magic. Some of the old texts list blood from a Zimwi-msaka as an ingredient in the most powerful counterspells, and it was said that it could be used to poison demons and supernatural monsters."

Teferi shook his head in confusion. "You think I am one of these warriors? How could I be? I was born in a Stygian slum, eldest son of a poor family. I am nothing."

"I have always known you were far more than nothing, my young friend, though I could not have dreamed how much more. It is said the power of the Zimwi-msaka is passed down the line, to all of pure Kush blood.

"But most of the texts say that the Zimwi-msaka are no more. All agree that they could not be corrupted by the dark forces that took Kush, Darfar, and the Black Kingdoms beyond. Some say they were killed to the last woman and child during the dark times. Others say they remained in secret, fighting against the dark forces for generations, until they were all killed.

"Perhaps, instead, the last survivors of that noble line came to Stygia, to live in secret and rebuild their numbers. Perhaps, in time, they even forgot who they were."

They approached the gate in front of Anok's rented villa. Teferi paused. "You are saying then, that it is my destiny to return and liberate Kush from the evil forces that ensnare it?"

Sabé shrugged. "Who can speak to the destiny of one man? But of your bloodline, perhaps yes. Perhaps one day your children, or your children's children, shall reclaim your lost homeland."

Teferi shook his head. It was too incredible. And yet, in his heart, he somehow knew it was true. In some confused way, perhaps he had always known. "Ramsa Aál thought that Anok knew of my heritage. Could it be so?"

"I don't see how. Yet great men, be they sorcerers, or warriors, or leaders, sometimes have an almost supernatural way of drawing to them in life the very people that they need. Perhaps your friend has ever needed a champion who can stand against the very magic that corrupts him." He held out his hand at Teferi. "And there you are."

He nodded and turned to go through the gate. "Then perhaps I do have a destiny. If I cannot save my homeland, perhaps I can at least save my greatest friend."

THEY TOOK TURNS watching over Anok. Late in the evening, Fallon called to them.

"He awakens!"

Sabé and Teferi hurried into Anok's sleeping chamber, where Fallon sat on the edge of the bed. She wiped his fevered brow with a cloth damp from a basin on the side table, and he moaned and stirred, his eyelids fluttering.

He flailed his arms weakly, as though fending off some imaginary menace. Teferi caught a glimpse of the Mark of Set on his left wrist. The mark of power, burned into his skin, took the form of a snake curling around his wrist, the tail pointed back up his arm toward the heart, the head running down the back of his hand.

The mark was the source of much of Anok's mystical power, and also of his troubles, for use of the Mark of Set inevitably led to corruption. Only recently had they learned that Sabé also bore the Mark of Set, and that it had led directly to the old scholar's self-imposed blindness.

Now, Anok struggled to avoid meeting a similar fate, or perhaps one even worse. With Sabé's guidance, and the aid of his friends, Anok had obtained the lost Band of Neska, now locked around the bones of his right wrist, to help him resist the influence of the dark magic. Watching his friend suffer, Teferi wondered if it had all been for nothing.

Anok's eyes opened wide, staring up at nothing. He sat up with a start. "Father!" He stared off into space, panting for breath. Then, slowly, his eyes seemed to focus. He looked over at Fallon, blinked, then blinked again. "How long?"

"Nearly three days."

He looked around the room. "Kheshatta. We are back in Kheshatta."

"Teferi brought you out of the shrine, and we brought you back here, seemingly on the verge of death."

"I'm not dead." He almost seemed surprised.

Teferi smiled. "You look well, for a dead man, brother."

Fallon reached out and touched his face gently. "His fever is broken."

Sabé nodded. "His body has thrown off the venom through instinctive use of magic. Were there visions?"

Anok noticed the basin of water, reached into it, and tossed a handful of water into his own face. He wiped his eyes with his fingers, then drew them back through his dark hair. "There were visions, but that is not what concerns me. Before the trial, more of Ramsa Aál's plan was revealed to me. We must act quickly. I feel he is close to something. Something very dangerous."

"I fear," said Sabé, "that you may be right. But I am concerned for you as well. You should rest."

Anok pushed himself up and swung his legs over the side of the bed. "I have slept for three days. What more rest can a man stand?"

He sat there for a time, collecting himself, then looked at Fallon.

Teferi glanced at her expression and realized she was hoping for something tender from him. It was not to be. "Ramsa Aál loaded a pack caravan with mystic armor that he took from the temple. Did you see it?"

She looked disappointed but quickly hid the emotion. "I saw it at sunset that day, headed out on the camel road back to Kheshatta."

"Then go, try to find out what happened to it when it arrived, and especially what happened to its cargo."

She nodded grimly and stood. "I'll go to the taverns where the caravan drivers congregate. Perhaps someone there will know something." She headed for the door. "And perhaps while there, I can find a drink."

Teferi watched her go with some concern. He and Fallon had their differences, yet he also found he had a growing affection and sympathy for the Cimmerian. She was right when she said they had many things in common, not the least of which was their shared concern for Anok. He knew also that she was a flawed—and, in her way, fragile person.

Whatever potential she had to aid Anok could easily be washed away by strong drink. Anok had just sent her away to the source of her greatest weakness, with ample reason to surrender to its embrace.

"Perhaps," said Teferi, "I should go with her. Two might learn more than one."

Anok considered for a moment, then nodded. "I would like to speak with Sabé in private, anyway. Go, but come back for him later. He should have an escort home, and I don't know that I'm yet equal to the task."

Teferi quickly headed for the door, his mind and emotions a tangle. He was still reeling from Sabé's revelations about his heritage. His concern was torn between Anok and Fallon, and he wasn't sure how best to help either of them, much less both.

But one more thing bothered him as he left Anok and Sabé alone. He was disappointed that, after all they had been through, his adopted brother still felt it necessary to keep secrets from him.

ANOK TOOK A few minutes to wash the bed sweat off, using water from the basin. Then, feeling refreshed, he pushed himself off the bed to search for proper clothing.

He wobbled as he stood, his legs weak and uncertain. His stomach twinged with nausea, and his head pounded. He tried to ignore it all, taking a clean set of robes from a cabinet against the wall. As he did, he noticed his father's medallion, which someone had removed and hung on a hook just inside the cabinet.

He started to put the medallion's chain over his neck, then thought better of it. He pulled on the robe, tied it at the waist, and shuffled back over to sit on the edge of the bed. Sabé perched on a stool a few paces away, waiting patiently.

Anok looked at the plain, iron medallion in his hand. "It's time," he said to Sabé, "that we talked about this." He held the medallion between his hands and, with practiced form, gave it a precise series of twists and turns, until it finally clicked open in the middle, like the shell of a clam. Inside, an ornate, golden object glittered.

Though he could not see, Sabé immediately reacted to the now-revealed Scale of Set. "What is that? What did you just do?"

As a former practitioner of sorcery, Sabé had senses keenly attuned to the supernatural. Though the cold iron of the medallion had kept it well hidden, Sabé could still detect the Scale.

Anok held out the Scale, and Sabé reached for it, taking the object in his hands, carefully examining it with his fingers. "You have not talked of the Scale of Set since just before you went to look for the Tomb of Neska, when you first revealed it to me." He turned his face toward Anok and thrust the Scale back into Anok's hands. "I should not even touch this. The temptation of power for one such as I is too great. You should not have it either. You should entrust it to Teferi."

"It is my responsibility, not his. My father entrusted it to me moments before he died. It has something to do with my past. Something to do with my destiny. Yet I don't really know what it is." He looked at Sabé. "Help me."

"It is good that you asked. I feared you had already been seduced by its power and jealously hoarded it for yourself. If so, you might have been beyond my help."

"I, too, sense its power, yet it seems useful for little. It is not a weapon, in any sense that I can reason. Perhaps it could be used to drive serpents against one's enemies. I think Ramsa Aál used his to command the cobra that bit me. But there are many magical ways to summon and command beasts, some far more effective and useful."

Sabé leaned on his walking staff and nodded. "Indeed. That the Scales can be used to command cold-blooded creatures seems to be but an accident of their true power. Many objects of great power have secondary abilities that are incidental to their intended purpose. One does not fill a cup so full without spilling a little."

"Then what is their intended purpose?"

"That is a mystery. There are many tales written, of how the Scales were made and what they can do, but who can say if any are true? For their true power to manifest, all three Scales would need to be brought together, linked by metal forged in a sacred fire, and that has not happened since before they were first separated. All the legends agree on that. At times, two have been brought together, but never three. Only with all three together will their true power and purpose be apparent. Some say it would be a portent of the end of the world."

Anok thought back to the moment before the black cobra had struck him, and shuddered. "As I said, I think Ramsa Aál used the power of the Scale to command the cobra. Sensing that, I tried to repel it with the power of this Scale. I know I risked revealing it, but I was desperate. Ramsa Aál overwhelmed its power somehow. I fear he has two of the Scales already."

Sabé frowned. "Perhaps this cold-iron shell you carry it in muted its power. Or perhaps the corruption in Ramsa Aál's soul makes him better able to command the Scale's power."

"Perhaps, but I think not. And if so, in that moment, the three Scales were within an arm's reach of each other. Ramsa Aál could have simply reached out and taken it, and that ancient power would have been his."

"Perhaps it would have been just as well if he had. For the true power of the Golden Scales, the so-called Scales of Set, was never meant to be wielded by man. He could no more hold that power in his hands and live than ride the lightning. No, though men have sought the Scales through history in a misguided quest for power, they are the tools of gods, demigods, demons, and monsters."

The old scholar leaned back, considering for a moment. "There are many tales of how the world came to be. Each land and people has its own, though many common themes show up again and again. There is one version that concerns the Golden Scales.

"In this story, it is said that a great, golden serpent circled the world, holding his tail in his mouth, guarding it so that nothing could grow there. It was a lifeless and empty place."

"Set?"

"It is said this was long before Set or any of the other gods. An eternity passed, then a hero came."

"If nothing lived, where did the hero come from?"

Sabé scowled at him. "You think like a rational man, and such tales are never rational. They are full of such contradictions. Simply accept that it is so."

He paused for a moment, trying to remember his place. "So the hero came and challenged the snake for possession of the world. The serpent would not yield, and there was a great battle that filled the heavens with fire. Finally, the hero was mortally wounded by the snake, but with his last breath he struck a mighty blow. The snake was crushed, and the world was free to grow and become fertile."

"What about the Golden Scales?"

"Patience! You are like a child sometimes! That is the next part.

"From the hero's blood came the first creatures that would eventually become men. They were brave and strong, but forever tainted by the serpent's venom, forever doomed by their own flaws.

"The snake's shattered bones became the snakes and crawling things of the world, the small bones into natural snakes and lizards, his large bones into supernatural serpents, dragons, and other such monsters. The golden snake's scales fell and became the gods, demons, and other supernatural monsters that torment men, all but three scales from where the hero's blow struck."

"The Golden Scales."

Sabé smiled slightly. "Now you see! The Scales are the missing parts that bind man, gods, and the crawling things together. Some say that is why most gods require their followers to bow before them, to crawl on their belly like a cold-blooded creature."

"You believe that this story is true?"

Sabé shrugged. "There is a touch of truth to many such stories even if much is also fancy. All are only things men tell to explain things that are truly beyond their understanding. Who can say what really happened? But we know the Scales are real, and their legendary power as well. They were not meant for men."

"Is Ramsa Aál a fool, then, that I should sit back and allow him to destroy himself?"

Sabé grunted, sneered, and seemed to think for a while. "This is not all his doing. Kaman Awi, High Priest of Set in Kheshatta, guides his hand. For all his arrogance, Kaman Awi is a dangerously brilliant sorcerer in his own way."

Anok knew Kaman Awi well by now. He was unlike any priest of Set that Anok had ever encountered, and yet in his own way, he was even more corrupt than most. "He is obsessed with the study of what he called 'natural law,' the study of things in the natural world, and how they may be applied by men. I am not sure it is truly sorcery at all."

"Nor am I, though he makes use of sorcery, alchemy, and the arts of the poisoners in his schemes. He seeks to blend the most powerful forces that man has dared to tamper with, and I fear that nothing but evil can come from it. And if he is involved, then they have a plan, though I cannot fathom it."

Anok looked grimly at the golden trinket in his hand. It looked so harmless. How could such a small thing be so ancient, so evil, so full of potential dread?

At length, Sabé spoke. "Any plan that includes the power of the three Scales of Set could remake the world."

6

TEFERI HAD TRIED to follow Fallon out into the street, but in such a large and busy city as Kheshatta, even a head start of a few minutes had been too much. She was nowhere to be seen when he left the villa, and he was forced to make the rounds of the various taverns and roadhouses where he thought she might be.

He started at those places frequented by camel drivers. They were easily identified simply by sniffing the front door. A camel's odor was pungent and unmistakable, though few in Stygia considered it objectionable.

On his third stop, a tavern located under a brothel on the west side of the city, he found a drunken Shemite who remembered seeing her. "Big woman," he said, "dark hair. Large"—he giggled—"humps! Owns the white camel that is kept boarded at the western station. Is that right?"

Teferi rolled his eyes but only nodded.

"She asked about a caravan the snake worshipers brought in, full of some kind of armor, all tied up in tight bundles, like they were afraid it would get away."

"What did you tell her?"

The Shemite looked up at him and grinned, displaying gaps from half a dozen missing teeth. "A drink for a thirsty traveler, just in from the desert?"

Teferi briefly considered removing a few more teeth, then put a few coppers on the table. A blond bar wench brought over a fresh mug of beer, and smiled at Teferi in hopes of a better tip.

The Shemite took a deep swig, then looked up at Teferi in surprise, as though he had just materialized out of thin air.

"What did you tell the woman?"

"I told her they took the stuff somewhere along the road leading east along the lakeshore." He took another swig.

"Is that all?"

The man didn't answer and started to lift the mug again.

Teferi put his hand flat across the top and slammed it back to the table. "Is that all?"

"She asked about strangers coming to Kheshatta. I told her I just came in with a caravan full of tinkers and smiths, and that word is they've been coming in from all over Stygia for weeks." He laughed. "Tinkers and smiths? What need has a city of wizards and poisoners for so many tinkers and smiths?"

Teferi left the man to his drink and departed the tavern. Kheshatta was not famed for tinkers and smiths; but like any large city, it had its share, and they had their districts. He thought about going to the jewelers' district, but the armor, though golden in color, had not truly looked like gold, and it *was* armor. Instead, he went to the district frequented by blacksmiths, bladesmiths, and armorers.

Smiths, as a rule, were not generally talkative people, and in fact, quite suspicious of strangers asking questions. Many jealously guarded family metalworking secrets handed down through dozens of generations, and assumed anyone nosing around was either a potential competitor playing ignorant, or a hired spy.

Teferi spent several frustrating hours wandering from forge to tavern, tavern to smithy, smithy to forge, learning nothing. He even went so far as to put a down payment on a very expensive dagger with a seemingly knowledgeable bladesmith, but he refused to pass along any gossip or even discuss Fallon.

His search might have ended there, had he not stumbled onto a broken-down old blacksmith in a bar near the lakeshore who admitted having spoken with Fallon.

The old man wore a patch over one eye, and his hands and arms bore the scars of countless burns. His eyebrows were entirely missing. Yet there were still ropes of muscle under his thin, leathery skin, and his good eye twinkled as he looked at the hearthfire in the back of the tavern.

"Oh, I seen your Cimmerian lady, but she's a friend of mine. Walked arm and arm with me over to my smithy, where my worthless sons are running the business into the ground, then made a big fuss over me and even gave me a kiss on the head while they was looking! That'll put those little rat bastards in their place for a while, think their old sire is used up and worthless!" He chuckled. "Friend of mine, so I will not tell you nothing."

It took Teferi at least an hour of talking and the buying of many drinks to convince the old smith he really was a friend of Fallon's and just wanted to find her.

"I do not know where she went, for sure, but she was asking about all these smiths coming to town. I told her that the Cult of Set built themselves a fancy new forge out near their guardians' east garrison and been bringing in folks from all over. Outlanders. Pay them big money, too. They will not have nothing to do with us local folk. Figure we would talk too much I guess." He spat on the floor. "Cursed snake-lovers!" He lowered his gruff voice to a whisper and looked around suspiciously. "You did not hear that from me, of course."

Teferi pressed some silver into the pretty tavern wench's soft palm and left the tavern, walking northeast around the end of the lake. He could see the garrison there, far around the lakeshore beyond the edge of the city sprawl, a utilitarian square-cornered fortress of moderate size surrounded by a walled stockade.

Though Kheshatta was historically a city besieged by border raiders and bandits, it was well protected by private armies financed by the poisoners and sorcerers. Their hired troops manned the formidable southern wall, which protected the city against raiders from Kush, and the various approaches by trail and caravan road. There was even a small freshwater navy of fast, shallow-draft fighting ships, equipped with both sails and oars, that plied the lake and patrolled its extensive shoreline.

Though they were mercenaries, the ones Teferi had met were a proud and disciplined lot. Resignations were rare, and there were never many openings in the ranks unless a raid resulted in casualties. Most of the officers had served steadfastly for years, and some families had been in service of the city's forces for generations.

The guardians of Set were more tolerated than welcomed within the city's boundaries, and massed troops could never appear without provoking a confrontation with this private army. It had to be galling to the guardians, as their authority was near absolute throughout most of the rest of Stygia.

Still, if the cult had something of importance to guard, this was the one place, besides the Temple of Set itself, where they would logically keep it.

That he could see the garrison did not mean it was close. It was a considerable walk, and he was considering what to do when he spotted an old, and in this case useful, acquaintance. He stepped into the street in front of a mule-drawn carriage and waved.

The brown-skinned, bald-headed driver waved back, and Teferi stepped to the side as the colorfully painted wagon rolled up next to him and stopped. The driver, moving spryly for a man of his age, jumped down from his seat. "Teferi! A pleasure as always! I have not see you for a while." He looked around. "Where is your friend, Anok Wati?"

Teferi found himself frowning slightly at the mention of the name. "He is otherwise engaged today, but I am in need of transport and perhaps the latest gossip."

"Well then"—the man gestured at the bench seats in the back of the open carriage—"get in." He climbed back up onto his driving bench and picked up the reins. But before moving on, he looked back, an apologetic look on his face. "I am afraid I was not sad that you were alone today. Master Anok, I must admit, I find his presence sometimes— unsettling." He snapped the reins, and the two mules started moving at a stately pace.

"I've known him since we were boys, Barid, but I do understand. My old friend has changed much this last year or so, and I fear it is not for the better. My quest is to end his troubles and restore the friend I once knew. It is in this cause that I today seek information."

"Of information, perhaps I can help. I talk to many and hear much. As for the rest, where do you wish to go?"

"Back the other way. I wish to go near the guardians' fortress off around the lake."

Barid glanced back, a look of puzzlement on his face. "What business can you have there?"

Teferi grinned. "Nosy business that the guardians would not approve of, which is why I only wish to go near. To get closer and see what I wish to see will require care and stealth."

"You are interested in the forge?"

Teferi raised an eyebrow in surprise, but Barid was, through his passengers, his friends, and his seemingly never-ending supply of brothers, well connected in the city. "What do you know of a forge?"

"My third brother, Mesha, is one of the finest brickmasons in all of Kheshatta." He seemed to consider this for a moment. "Well, he is at least one of the fastest masons in all of Kheshatta, which seems to be why the priests of Set hired him. They have been building a new compound next to their stockade, and at its center, a great forge for the smelting of metals. The forge is finished, but he still is working on the sheds and walls that surround it. He says they value speed over all things, and they seem to care little that the brickworks might collapse after a few monsoon seasons."

"That is indeed useful information. I would like to get a look at this compound."

Barid glanced back over his shoulder and grinned. "Well then, how would you like to go inside?"

ANOK RETURNED TO his sleeping chamber and drew the curtains, trying to rest, but that didn't last long. He lay awake, staring at the painted and plastered arch of the ceiling and snatching flies out of the air, crushing them dead and flicking them carelessly into the corner of the room.

He tossed restlessly, thinking about all that had happened to him since leaving Khemi. Despite his recent vision of Parath, his mission seemed less clear than ever.

He had set out to join the Cult of Set, to learn its secrets, and use those to strike at it from within. In the former he had been successful, in some ways beyond his wildest expectations. He was now on the path to become a priest of Set, to have some real power and autonomy. As he had learned, acolytes were often little more than servants and sorcerous foot soldiers who danced at the whims of the priests.

As for secrets, there seemed to be no end of them, and if he seemed no closer to finding his father's killer and unraveling the mysteries of his death, he found himself truly enjoying the acquisition of sorcerous secrets, the study of arcane objects and tomes, and he even hungered to delve into Kaman Awi's "study of natural law."

Now, with the might of the Mark of Set, balanced against the control of the Band of Neska, he finally felt ready to apply some of the sorcerous knowledge he possessed.

But with all this power and knowledge, he had little idea how to use it in service of his goals. With all his power, he could not last an hour, perhaps not even a handful of minutes, against the sorcerers and armies of Set. Ramsa Aál and Kaman Awi seemed to be planning something that would put all that power to shame, something that Sabé said could remake the world.

But wasn't that exactly what Anok wanted to do? Didn't he want to wipe the foul Cult of Set out of existence, bring vengeance on those who had wronged him and those he cared for, free the people of Stygia from tyranny and wickedness?

He sat up suddenly in his bed.

That was it! It had been there all along. That was his mission! He was not to hinder Ramsa Aál in his plot to re-make the world. He was to embrace his role as a new priest of Set and Ramsa Aál's strong right hand. He was to aid the priest in every way possible.

Then when the day came, he was to steal the dark priest's plot *and make it his own!*

7

INSTEAD OF PROCEEDING directly to the garrison, Teferi and Barid turned west, into a neighborhood where many of Barid's Vendhyan countrymen resided. It was a colorful place, every building, wall, and pillar elaborately decorated with brightly hued paint, turned wood, and carved stone. Arches and rounded forms predominated, and many buildings were topped with ornate columns and slender, needlelike towers.

Everywhere there were carvings, paintings, and statues of strange beings who might have been Vendhyan gods or deities: women and men with many arms, a man with three heads, a hairy man who seemed part-ape, and a strange creature with the body of a man and the head of an elephant. Pungent and exotic cooking odors came from many shops and buildings, some so strong that they nearly made Teferi's eyes water.

He knew little about Vendhya, beyond that it was a large country far east across the arm of the Southern Sea. What he had heard of it sounded attractive—fertile, warm, a beautiful, ancient, and civilized land. Yet Barid and his clan seemed quite happy to have left it.

Apparently, one's lot in life there was largely decided by which caste one was born into, and Barid and his kin were at the very bottom of that society.

Here in Kheshatta, Barid claimed, a man's station was limited only by his boldness, intelligence, and enterprise. He made this corrupt and dangerous border city seem like a paradise.

Perhaps, to Barid, it was.

Barid drove them onto a side street, where they came on a large brickworks. Teferi saw storage sheds, piles of clay and sand, stacks of fuel, wooden troughs where mortar was mixed, wooden forms for the molding of bricks, and beehive-shaped kilns, all tended by industrious Vendhyans, mostly women and children. The few men either did the heaviest work, or seemed to be there just long enough only to load bricks onto stout cargo wagons or mules with baskets lashed across their back.

A woman stepped away from poking at a kiln fire to greet Barid with a warm smile. Her face was almost as dark as a Kushite woman's, but her features were narrow and delicate, and her eyes large and dark. She wore a red jewel somehow attached in the middle of her forehead. Though it was difficult to judge her age, something of her face spoke of wisdom and experience. "Barid, honored brother-of-my-husband, what brings you here today?"

"Lovely Hema, I come to ask a favor. My brother still works for the priests of Set?"

"He will finish within the week. But yes, he is there today, finishing a wall."

Barid looked slyly about. "I would wish to deliver a small quantity of materials to him, perhaps some brick, in my carriage. I would wish also to borrow clothing so that my friend and I could appear as masons in my brother's company."

"You would be doing us a service. Mesha ran short of some special brick this morning, and I have not had workers free to deliver it. As for the clothing, that is nothing for our rich brother. We are ever in your debt."

Barid laughed. "Mesha finished repaying my loans years ago."

She bowed her head respectfully. "In spirit, we are in debt to you, dear brother. Always."

She turned and started yelling at the men working in the yard, instructing them to load a small pile of yellowish brick onto the back of Barid's wagon. Barid in turn led Teferi to a shed where the workers' clothing hung on wooden pegs along one wall.

The clothing was uniform, and very drab by Vendhyan standards, loose pants, vests with pockets, a loose overshirt that could easily be removed in the heat, and a turbanlike headdress that Barid had to help Teferi put on.

Barid looked disapprovingly at the pant legs, which ended at Teferi's calf, and the sleeves, which didn't reach nearly to his wrists. "These are the biggest here, but I'm afraid the Vendhyans are not such a large people."

Teferi looked down at himself. "If I am not too conspicuous, these will do."

Barid smiled sadly. "Trust me that I know matters of class. The guardians look down upon the non-Stygian laborers and craftsmen they hire as little better than draft animals. As with the lower classes in my country, such people are practically invisible to them. They will not notice you in their ranks. You will be beneath their notice."

Teferi nodded. "Normally, I would not consider that a good thing, but today, it suits me fine."

ANOK FINISHED DRESSING and placed the yoke of Set around his neck. He felt a curious sense of pride as he did so. For the first time, it seemed to mean something, to stand for the trials that he had survived and would yet survive.

Not that he was proud to be a follower of Set. Of course not! But there was some satisfaction in his growing rank in the cult and the power and authority that would soon be his.

He pushed back the curtain over his door, and was surprised to see Sabé sitting at a table in the parlor, playing a solitary game of spirit tiles, his fingers reading the carved inlays in the tiles arranged on the table. As Anok watched, he selected two tiles from the pattern and removed them to the "Realm Eternal" pile.

"What are you still doing here? I thought you would have gone home."

Sabé turned in his direction, one gray eyebrow peeking up over the top of his blindfold. "Am I no longer welcome in your home?"

Anok suddenly felt on the defensive. "No. I didn't mean that. I just didn't hear anyone out here. I thought everyone had left."

"Obviously not. I thought someone should stay to watch over you during your recovery."

You're poorly qualified to watch over anyone! But he held his tongue. "I can care for myself. I am feeling much better."

"Clearly, since you are dressed to go out."

Anok looked again, to be sure the cloth over Sabé's eyes was still firmly in place. "How did you know that?"

"I could hear your sandals on the floor, and the sound of metal plates in your yoke rubbing together when you move. The hem of your temple robes also make a slight sound as you walk."

"Well then, yes, I'm dressed to go out."

"You are not well. You are recovering from an ordeal."

"I feel fine. Actually, I feel better than fine. I feel invigorated, as though I've taken a tonic."

"In a manner of speaking, you have. But it is not the sort of tonic that will bring you benefit."

Anok found himself becoming annoyed, and suddenly realized that he was hungry. He spotted a bowl of fruit, selected an orange-skinned custard-apple, and bit into it. Beneath the papery skin, the flesh was soft and sweet, a trickle of juice running down his chin.

"And how do you know? As a boy, I was stung by scorpions so many times that I developed an immunity to the poison. Now, to be stung by a scorpion is little more than a call to alertness. When I went on my Usafiri into the desert, I had collapsed when a scorpion sting revived me. Without it, I might not have survived."

"This is different."

"This is different, how?"

"The snake that bit you had been milked to thin its venom and dosed with herbs having mystic properties. What entered your veins was more potion than tonic, a potion concocted in the service of Set. This tradition started after my time with the cult, so I can say little about what it might do to you, but I doubt it can be good."

Anok laughed harshly. "You doubt? But you do not know. Perhaps these infusions of venom will offer me immunity not only to the serpent's poison but also to the serpent's influence."

He considered for a moment what that might mean. "Perhaps it will prevent the horrible transformation that has caused you to blind yourself. Perhaps what happened to you caused the tradition to begin. Had you considered that possibility?"

He expected Sabé to argue the point, but instead, the old scholar seemed taken aback. "I cannot say that is not so. I have never heard of another priest transformed by corruption as my eyes were. Yet until you, I have never heard of another who is cursed with the Mark of Set. Even if the treatments do offer some protection from the physical transformation, they will do nothing to ease the spiritual corruption. That would not be in the interest of Set."

"Then it will still be better than nothing. I will take care of the rest myself."

"So you say. So tell me, where are you going in such a hurry?"

"To the temple. Ramsa Aál may be back from the shrine, but if not, perhaps I can extract some information about his plans from Kaman Awi. I suspect he may know more about this part of it anyway. It concerns metal, and that is within the realm of his study of natural law."

"And if Ramsa Aál is back?"

"Then it is well that I make an appearance as soon as possible so as not to show weakness."

Sabé turned back toward him, frowning. Though the old scholar could not see, Anok had the feeling of being stared at, of intense scrutiny.

Finally, Sabé spoke. "To show him you have recovered from the venom ritual?"

"Yes, I suppose."

"So that he can decide you are ready for another?"

"If that is what must be done, I am prepared. I have endured it once. I have no doubt I will do better, now that I am properly prepared."

"You sound almost *eager* to repeat the ritual."

Anok started to deny it, then stopped and reconsidered. There was some truth to that. In surviving the ritual he felt a sense of accomplishment, of having proven himself. It was a challenge, and Anok had always enjoyed challenges. "I do what must be done. I have come so far; now I feel I am close to my goals. Is it unexpected that I should be anxious to speed the process along?"

Sabé turned his head slightly and smiled, a rare, and, somehow frightening, thing. "You think you have mastered it, don't you?"

Anok frowned. "Mastered what?"

"Sorcery and all that comes with it: corruption, madness. You think you have mastered it, and that you can act as you will without consequences. Well let me tell you, you have not!"

"You don't know what you're talking about."

"But I do! I was just like you once."

Anok felt his face redden with anger. "How so? Did you have the Band of Neska to counter your Mark of Set? Did you take the rituals of venom to protect you from the influence of serpents? I tire of hearing how our paths are the same. They are *far* different. I travel a different road than you. I will not end up as you have!"

He stomped past Sabé, picking up his satchel on the way out.

As he walked out the door, he heard Sabé say, in a voice so low that perhaps he wasn't intended to hear, "You travel a different road, and I'm afraid it ends in a place far worse than mine."

8

BARID'S WAGON WAS made for city streets. Near the
edge of the city, the road turned from cobblestone to hard-
packed dirt, full of potholes and deep ruts. Teferi swore he
could feel each of those potholes in his kidneys as they ran
through them with bone-jarring regularity. A chilled wind
blew in from the lakeshore to their right, bringing with it a
stink of marsh-muck, rotting vegetation, and dead fish.

Barid seemed to take it all in stride. "With the building
of the forge, many heavy wagons have traveled this way of
late, and the road is ill suited for such traffic. Fortunately, it
is not much farther."

Teferi looked up the hillside to their right. The slope
was steep, and outcroppings of crumbling yellow rock fre-
quently showed through the dark tangle of brush and trees.
Piles of stones, and even boulders, made of the same rock
lay at the base of the hill and along both sides of the road,
suggesting that falling rocks and small avalanches were
common.

Unlike the hills west of the city, these were ill suited
for building, and therefore almost uninhabited. It was no

wonder the powers that controlled the city had been willing
to cede this place for the guardians' garrison.

They rounded a gentle turn that hugged the edge of the
lake, and Teferi could see that the hillsides ahead fell back
from the lake, creating a flat apron of land on which the
stockade was built.

The place looked even more austere close up. The
square-topped towers and ramparts were almost totally
lacking in decoration or ornament. It could have been a
prison as easily as a fortress.

This was not a place to be celebrated, or to draw attention to itself. It was a tangible sign that the Cult of Set's
rule over Kheshatta was tenuous at best.

The towering fortifications were built right up to the
lake's edge, doubtless to defend against attack by water,
but likely also to reduce the danger from falling rocks and
boulders. The road curved sharply left, passing inland of
the fortification. But as they rounded that bend, Teferi
could see that it had been recently rerouted even closer to
the slope, to allow for a small, walled compound to be
built nestled against the much taller stone walls of the
stockade.

The smell of woodsmoke was strong. Beyond the wall
he could see several small buildings, thatch-topped huts
that might be living quarters for workers, fuel sheds, a
small barn or warehouse. The tall tapering chimney of a
forge belched clouds of gray smoke.

They drove past the main gate of the stockade, and
Barid waved at the gate guards as they passed. The men
barely glanced at them.

As they drove along the wall of the new compound,
Teferi could see several places where it was incomplete,
workers still placing bricks along the top. They pulled up
to a smaller gate with a wooden arch, leading into the
compound.

A bored-looking guardian leaned against one side of the
arch. He glanced up as they approached, stepped out in
front of them, and held up his hand. He walked up to them,

a suspicious look on his pockmarked face, scrutinizing the wagon. "This doesn't look like a work wagon."

Barid smiled. "It is not—usually. My brother, Mesha tells me this job is behind schedule, and asks my help. My servant"—he gestured at Teferi—"and I have brought brick for him, and will unload it for him as well, saving time for his more skilled men. I would not do it"—he looked around cautiously before continuing—"but I owe him money, and I dare not anger him. As you know, masons have strong arms, and hands hard as stone. He could snap me like a dry reed!"

The guard walked around to the back of the wagon, peered under the leather tarp at the stack of bricks, and, after a moment's thought, waved them through.

Barid waved at one of the masons as they passed, and he waved back with a smile, apparently recognizing the carriage driver. Though the masons were all Vendhyan, the men working the forge were of other races, Shemites, and dark-skinned men who might have been from metal-rich Punt.

As they rolled past, Teferi got a better look at the forge. The base of it was an arch of brick as tall as a man, half-buried in a tall mound of earth to keep in the heat. Even from this distance, Teferi could feel the heat of the burning coals inside, as a chain of men passed a stream of charcoal from an adjacent fuel shed.

On the other side of the forge, but just as close, stood a locked shed. The walls were conspicuously sturdier than those of the other buildings, with a roof made of wood shingles rather than thatch. There could be little doubt that it protected something of value.

It was, Teferi observed, more than large enough to hold the armor he had seen removed from the Tomb of the Lost King. They drove on, to a nearby gap in the wall, where three men busily placed mortar and brick.

The oldest of the three men looked up as they approached, stopped his work, and came to meet them.

He was younger than Barid, with more hair. Corded muscles rippled under the coppery-brown skin of his arms.

In that, at least, Barid had not lied to the guard. Despite the differences, his close relation to Barid was obvious to anyone who looked at their faces. It had to be Barid's brother.

Mesha greeted Barid as he stepped down and began to speak to him in Vendhyan. He glanced suspiciously at Teferi and asked a question, likely wondering who this stranger was.

Seeing Teferi's discomfort, Barid answered in Stygian so that he could understand. "This is Teferi, a friend and regular customer. He wished to see the cult's mysterious forge with his own eyes, for reasons of his own, and I offered to oblige him. I hope I have not caused you trouble."

"Of course not, brother. In a day, we will be done and free of this foul place. Though I cannot say what there is to see, other than shoddy workmanship. The priests of Set assure me this forge will only be used for the span of a month or so, then left to crumble."

Teferi observed the curious mechanism used to operate a large bellows. It was driven through a series of peg-gears, which were turned by a pair of mules lashed to a pole that rotated on a fixed post. As the mules marched endlessly around their circular path, the leather bellows pumped up and down.

With each blast of air, the fire grew brighter, and sparks shot from the top of the chimney. He looked at the thatched roofs, and wondered how long it would be before one of them caught fire.

In the center of the fire sat a tall crucible, a glowing red mass of liquid metal visible in the top. There was a curious quality to the metal. It did not boil, and the crucible itself was quite steadily placed. Yet the metal seemed to be in constant motion, little waves and ripples appearing in the surface, moving upward with curious slowness, then falling back.

"They seem," said Teferi, "to have been anxious to begin their work."

"They have been at it for a day now," said Mesha. "Now and then, two of them will go into that shed with hammers and chisels. They will pound for a time, then come out with a bit of gold-colored metal that they add to their pot."

Teferi nodded. "Gold-colored, but not gold, yes?"

Mesha looked at him with some surprise, and nodded.

Barid threw back the tarp and picked up a brick. "We had best unload these before our friend at the gate becomes suspicious."

Mesha pointed out a spot near the wall to stack them, and the three men made quick work of the load. When they were finished, Barid threw the tarp over the back of the wagon, then led the two of them on a contrived errand that took them nearer to the forge.

Teferi noticed a strange, slack-faced expression on the men who tended the fire. They moved slowly, as though sleepwalking. There were other, more-alert men as well, but they kept back from the forge and worked with long-handled tools that allowed them to work from a distance.

Once they were out of earshot and headed back toward the carriage, Teferi asked about this curious arrangement.

"I do not understand it," said Mesha, "but we have strict orders that no man is to come within twenty paces of the forge in any direction. A priest comes here once each day, and I believe he places a hypnotic spell on the fire-tenders to dull their minds. It is a very curious thing."

They walked past a smaller building, a smithy, from which a smaller chimney emerged, also belching smoke. From inside, they could hear constant hammering, but the windows were too high to see in, and the door was kept shut.

Having seen all they were likely to see, Teferi and Barid climbed back into the front seat of the carriage. After giving thanks to Mesha, they headed for the gate.

The same guard awaited them, watching as they approached. Once again, he stepped out and put up his hand. He walked around the carriage, looking inside, and stopped at the rear, looking at the tarp.

Barid frowned at him. "You searched us going in. What is the point of this? My brother needs more brick, and I must hurry about my business."

The guardian ignored him and lifted the edge of the tarp. His eyes widened, and he looked up at them, and quickly drew his sword. "You'll be going nowhere," he tossed back the tarp and jumped back as he did, "until you explain how this barbarian woman got in your carriage!"

Teferi looked down, and saw Fallon crouched behind the carriage's rear seat, one hand uncertainly on the hilt of her sword, a look of supreme annoyance on her face.

ANOK LEANED IMPATIENTLY on the wall surrounding his villa. A gray cloud passed in front of the sun, threatening rain and casting a chill across the busy street.

Twenty minutes before, he had sent a boy to fetch Barid and his carriage. There had been plenty of time for the boy to find Barid at his livery and return, and he was becoming annoyed.

An empty carriage rolled by. He considered flagging it down. But he did not recognize the driver, a disreputable-looking Shemite with a jagged scar that ran from forehead to jawbone down the right side of his face. Riding alone with an unknown driver could be just as dangerous to the likes of Anok as walking unguarded to the temple by himself.

He watched the carriage disappearing as it traveled west down the street, when a flash of motion caught his eye. Someone was running toward him. He recognized the ragged orange kilt, the tanned skin, and the unruly mop of black hair. It was the boy he had send for Barid.

The boy ran up and slid to a stop, his threadbare sandals offering little purchase on the slick paving stones. He bent over, leaning hands on knees, gasping for breath. "Master Anok Wati! I did not find Barid. He was not home. His carriage was gone. I beg pardon!"

Anok snorted in disgust. The cursed Vendhyan was never around when needed. "Go then. I've no more time to wait."

The boy stood, hesitating, his eyes nervously on Anok. "What do you want?"

The boy bowed his head apologetically. "When Master Teferi sends me on such an errand and Barid is not to be found, he usually gives me a few coppers for my trouble."

Anok sneered. "Do I look like a Kushite? I am not Teferi, boy! You'll get my coppers when you bring me what I sent you for. Better luck next time." He swung the back of his hand toward the boy as though swatting at an invisible fly. "Now away with you!"

The boy frowned and took a few hesitant steps.

Anok drew his dagger, and as he did, whispered the simplest of spells.

The boy's eyes went wide with fear, as the blade seemed to transform into an angry serpent that hissed and struck at him. He shrieked and ran away down the street as fast as he could.

Anok laughed, shaking the dagger so as to break the spell of illusion. The curved blade of the dagger returned to its original appearance, and Anok slid it into its scabbard on his belt.

The cloud moved past, and the sun again shown on Anok's face. Perhaps it would not rain after all. That decided it for him. With Teferi and Fallon both out spying for him, he would simply have to walk, no matter the risk.

He headed down the street at a brisk pace, dodging street vendors, scholars on errands, and assorted street rabble, low-level followers of one cult or another.

Some of these latter gave him contemptuous looks as he passed, but they were not the kind to trifle with even the middling sort of wizardry most acolytes of Set could easily wield.

He was many blocks from the villa before he realized that he'd forgotten to put on his swords. That caused him to break his pace briefly, more out of confusion than concern.

How had he forgotten his swords? For half his life they had been his constant companions, almost as much a part of him as his fingers and toes. Those early weeks as an acolyte, when he'd been unable to wear them, had been torture.

How could he simply walk out without them and not even notice?

He smiled. *Because I do not need them. I fear nothing!*

His sorcerous abilities more than compensated for the lack of weapons. He had his dagger, if blood needed to be spilled in the old way, but he could barely imagine how that could possibly be necessary.

He turned south, headed toward the Temple of Set, becoming bolder by the step. Now, as people spotted his acolyte robes and sneered at him, he sneered back. If they brushed against him, or even bumped him, he did not hesitate to bump back.

If there was to be trouble, let there be trouble. He welcomed it!

No, he wanted it. He remembered his first encounter with the followers of the Jade Spider Cult. Now, they had been worthy adversaries!

He fantasized about a new encounter. When last they had met, he had gained the respect of Dao-Shuang, a local master of the cult, by saving the life of his student, Bailing. But the circumstances had been humiliating for Bailing, and he might blame Anok. Perhaps he would seek Anok, hoping for revenge.

There would be a battle. *Oh, yes, my victory would be sweet!*

But there was no sign of the Jade Spider followers, or any other adversary worth mentioning. Nothing but street scum, who quickly looked away when they caught the anger and determination in his eyes.

He could see the Temple of Set over the tops of nearer buildings, and was losing hope that this journey would offer any excitement, any challenge, at all.

Then he stopped in front of the entrance to a dark and narrow alley.

The passage was cluttered, dirty, and anything but straight. He could see no more than a dozen yards before an offset in the alley hid the rest of its considerable length from sight. He could see no one along this length, but

echoing in the distance he could hear voices in some unknown language, the barking of dogs, and the ominous
beat of large drums he felt as much as heard.

There was a stench, not just of rotted garbage, but of
death, from the alley's mouth. Human death.

This, Barid had cautioned him once while passing, was
home to the Zamboulan Cult of Hanuman. Hanuman was a
beast god with a reputation for bloodlust and corruption
that equaled that of Set, seemingly without the theatrics
and fakery sometimes employed by the followers of Set to
frighten the masses.

It was a small but feared cult, and they had no love at all
for Set and his worshipers.

Anok took a step toward the alley. For him, in his acolyte
robes, to enter would almost guarantee he would be attacked, and the followers were known for their savagery
and mastery of dark spells.

He hesitated only a moment more before marching into
the narrow confines of the alley.

"Have at me," he said quietly, "if you dare!"

9

TEFERI LOOKED FIRST at Fallon, then at the guardian. He was only a lone soldier, but just over the stockade wall was the largest concentration of guardian troops that side of Khemi, and they could be upon them in a minute.

He blinked. Then he looked at the guardian, and smiled reassuringly. "The woman? Oh! The woman! Well!" He looked again at Fallon, who seemed to be as interested in what he had to say as anyone. Still, her hand remained wrapped around the hilt of her sword, and he knew it would take but a moment for the situation to turn bloody and doom them all.

"Oh," he said, "you mean the *whore*!"

Fallon glared at him but said nothing.

"Yes, well," Teferi continued, "you haven't lived until you've felt the powerful thighs of a barbarian woman wrapped around your middle!"

Fallon tilted her head, looking at Teferi in a most threatening fashion, but again she remained silent.

The guardian's manner relaxed only a little. "Then explain to me what this *whore* is doing in the back of your wagon?"

Teferi looked desperately at Barid, who shrugged.

"She was—a present! Yes, a present, for the anniversary of Barid's brother's birth! That was it!"

Now the guardian looked confused. "But I searched your carriage going in. There was no woman hidden here!"

"She was—" Again he looked at Barid, who again just shrugged. He continued. "She was enchanted! Yes! Enchanted into the form of a brick! You looked right at her and did not know!"

The guardian looked at him, eyes narrow with suspicion. "A barbarian brick woman?"

"Yes! Why, it's the latest thing for smuggling slaves, all the rage in Black Kingdoms! Turn them into a brick, take them where you will, say the magic incantation and return them to living human form!"

"A brick?"

"Ingenious, is it not?"

He looked at her again. "If you brought him a whore, why was she only here but only a few minutes?"

Teferi chuckled nervously. "Mesha, he is not as young as he used to be. That's why we brought him a whore. We knew it would be a cheap present!"

The guardian opened his mouth to say something, when a shriek of terror from behind him made him turn.

They all looked back toward the forge, where workmen with long poles jabbed at the crucible, which had become unbalanced and was threatening to fall over. The ends of the wooden poles flared into flame where they touched the red-hot crucible.

A quantity of molten metal splashed out of the container and began to flow in a burning red rivulet along the ground.

Men ran back and forth frantically, fetching more poles, babbling and yelling in languages Teferi could not understand. Then the tiny river of molten metal seemed to shudder, and rose from the ground like a snake.

The nearest man cried out at the sight of it, then screamed as it struck forward. It wrapped a flaming tentacle around his middle, quickly budding off a dozen smaller tendrils that whipped around the man's neck, body, and limbs. His clothing sizzled and burst into flame. The stink of charred flesh filled the air.

A number of men appeared carrying buckets of water that they tossed on the screaming man. There was a loud hiss. The water flashed into a cloud of steam that rolled into the gray sky.

When it dispersed, the screaming had stopped.

The charred and blackened corpse hung limply, suspended in a framework of cooled metal twisted around his disfigured body like some ghastly sculpture.

The guardian turned away. "That is the second time this week," he said. Then he blinked in surprise as he looked at the back of the carriage. It was empty.

He looked at Teferi and shook his sword in the air. "Where is the woman?"

Teferi looked at him innocently. "What woman?"

"The barbarian whore!"

"Well," he said, "she was definitely a barbarian, but I am not certain about the whore part."

"You *hired* her!"

"I made that up. Actually, I have never seen her before in my life. But you didn't seem willing to take that for an answer, so I tried to think of something."

He pointed his sword at Teferi's face. "You are in serious trouble! I'm taking you to my commanding officer!"

Teferi looked toward the stockade. "Well, if we must. Certainly, he will want to know how the woman slipped past you and got into the compound. We'll tell him everything we know." He looked at the guard. "Of course, he may have questions for you as well. She was trying to get out of the stockade, not in, meaning she already slipped past someone. Perhaps you."

The guardian scowled, chewing his lip, considering.

Teferi had been dealing with guardians all his life. He knew that common soldiers such as this one often had limits to their loyalty, especially when no one of authority was watching, and preferred to avoid the scrutiny of their superiors whenever possible. Doubtless, he had other minor misdeeds he wished to keep hidden.

The guardian grunted, then sheathed his sword. "Speak of this to no one. You never saw the woman. She was never here. Now leave!" he said. "And don't come back!"

They rolled quickly out of the gate, around the back of the stockade, and back along the lakeshore. Teferi kept looking back for pursuit, but none came.

They had just moved out of sight of the stockade when they passed under the low-hanging branches of a tree. Fallon dropped out of the foliage into the rear passenger area of the carriage, crouched, looking carefully over the back of the rear seat until she was satisfied that no one was coming after them.

Then, still keeping low, she duck-walked forward and sat on the floor of the carriage, keeping her head down. She looked up at Teferi, her lips in a tight frown, her eyes narrowed with annoyance. "Whore? I'll give you a taste of my barbarian thighs when I use them to snap your *neck*!"

THE ALLEY STANK of death. Human death. He rounded the projecting end of a building, stepped around a stack of empty baskets, and looked into a row of faces.

Dead faces.

The heads hung from a window overhang, twisting in the cold wind, like one might see chickens hung in a marketplace. They were bodiless, but not severed. From each hung an artfully extracted spine, each glistening with bits of gore, grotesque tadpoles hung by the neck.

He studied them, anger rising in his chest. On each face an expression of horror, mouths wide as though in a scream, gagged by a swollen, black tongue. Several were women, one, smaller, a child. Girl or boy he could no longer tell.

Butchers!

At least most victims of Set died quickly, watching with fading eyes as their lifeblood spurted out, or their hearts were cut out. Death by torture was a fate reserved for special victims, and special ceremonies.

Even the priests of Set would never visit it on a mere child.

He heard them moving in the shadows, stirring from their hiding places, the cursed followers of Hanuman. Some were Zamboulan, others Shemite Kush, and even a few Hyborians, yet they all looked the same—dirty, clothing ragged, eyes sunken and bestial.

They had sold their souls in the name of power, and their humanity was all but gone.

They were two dozen strong. They faced Anok with no fear. Some drew swords. Some crouched and growled, baring sharp teeth filed to point.

Anok flexed his fingers, cracking his knuckles as he turned them and balled them into fists. His left sleeve fell back, revealing the Mark of Set. He looked at it, letting his anger flow into it.

They do not know fear.
Then I will show them fear!

ON THE WAY back into the city, Teferi and Fallon sat in the back of Barid's carriage. Teferi sprawled in the rearward-facing front seat, Fallon facing him, arms crossed over her chest.

For a time, they did not speak, simply staring at each other. The carriage bounced roughly along the lake road, but the sun had broken through the clouds, making the trip back more pleasant than the trip out. Still, there was a chill in the air, the kind that had more to do with personal discord than the weather.

Teferi finally broke the silence. "What were you doing back there? You could have gotten us killed!"

She laughed harshly. "What was I doing there? What were you doing there?"

"Investigating the caravan of enchanted armor sent from the Tomb of the Lost King."

"And how did you manage to find where it went? By following my trail perhaps?"

Teferi grimaced and looked away. Finally, he said, "Yes, but I didn't expect to find you there. Your path led through so many taverns—"

Her eyes narrowed. "So you assumed I would have drunk myself into a stupor before ever reaching the forge?"

Teferi frowned and averted his eyes. "Perhaps," he finally said.

"Then you have judged me wrongly, and badly. I was doing fine, until you came along and stirred up the smiths so I had no choice but to hide in this carriage. I would be fully justified taking my revenge out of your hide!"

"Perhaps you would."

The silence returned, and again they stared at each other.

Fallon parted the gloomy cloud with a sly smile. "I cannot claim I was not tempted by drink. Sooner I would face the guardians' entire garrison armed with but a pointed stick, than to pay good silver for watered beer. And yet I did."

"Why?"

"Because I knew, if I came home drunk, you would be there to judge me, and your harsh assessment would not have been wrong. Too long I have mourned the great Cimmerian warrior I may never be and drowned my sorrows in drink. Yet if I continue, I will never be any kind of warrior—any kind of Cimmerian, at all."

She bit her lip, and looked out at a needlelike galleon rowing swiftly across the lake. "I have faced pirates, bandits, and monsters from beyond the veil without yielding, but this monster frightens me most of all."

"Then I will stand with you. Despite our differences, I always have."

She smiled sadly. "You are a good friend, Teferi. What would wretched creatures like Anok and I do without you?"

He frowned and sighed at the mention of Anok's name. "I fear I have not been a good enough friend to my brother. I have been thinking, of late, that he might have been better without knowing me at all."

Her eyes widened in disbelief, and she laughed. "How can you possibly say that?"

"It was I who convinced Anok to go on the Usafiri, the journey into the wilderness. It was there he had the visions that put him on this mad quest."

"Who are you to say this was not his fate all along? Who is to say the Usafiri did not save him from an even darker path? I hope you have not given up hope for our friend. These are difficult days, but his fate is far from sealed, and his spirit is yet strong."

She shook her head in puzzlement. "This is strange to me, you people of the south, always looking to gods for answers and guidance, assuming they know better how to guide your life than you do yourselves."

"Cimmerians don't pray to—Crom is it?"

She nodded. "Crom. He is called by some the Lord of the Mound, for he lives in a great mountain that bears his name. By our birth, he gives us strength, bravery, will, and passion. That is all Cimmerians need. He does not hear our prayers. He does not want our worship. He does not care for our sacrifices. He will not live in our temples. He is a stern and distant god, but he troubles us not, and I have heard it said, that whenever a Cimmerian emerges bloody and victorious in a battle, that Crom may smile—just a little."

Teferi chuckled. "Perhaps that is not so bad."

He watched as they passed beyond the edge of the city, where the houses grew taller and closer together. A group of squealing Kushite children ran through the street, chasing a young goat that had slipped its rope. "I wonder now even about my own Usafiri, when my visions told me to leave my family behind, so they would have one less mouth to feed, and seek my own way. It told me nothing of my true destiny, my true birthright, or whether it was shared by my brothers and sisters. Perhaps I should be with them still."

"Did you not say yourself that your god, Jani, only gives the traveler what he needs? That is different than Crom, but not as different as the more meddlesome gods of so-called *civilized* men. Why should Jani tell you what you will discover for yourself? Perhaps he sent you to Anok, and perhaps even to me, because he knew you were what *we* needed."

He laughed. "Jani sent me to a Cimmerian whose own god will not care for her?"

She shrugged. "It is a theory."

He laughed again, but his frown soon returned as he thought of Anok. "Still, my brother grows more distant from me by the day. He keeps secrets from me." He sighed. "He has *always* kept secrets from me, but in the past, I always felt that he was trying to protect me. Now I feel he no longer trusts me. He believes the Band of Neska has relieved the dark influence of his sorcery, but I fear it has only blinded him to his downfall. I do not know how to help him."

"Nor do I. I have heard it said, no man can be helped who will not ask for help. But I vow I will stay close to him."

Teferi smiled slightly. "You care for him, do you not? You make a great show of being a wanton tart—"

She laughed. "And well I was!" He expression turned serious, and she looked away. "Yet I fear this warrior's heart softens. This, too, I fear, for if it is broken, Crom will offer me no solace, nor even pity."

Teferi nodded in sympathy, then looked south, up above the city's skyline. A dark cloud twisted angrily amid the broken overcast, casting a dark shaft of shadow down into the streets below. There was a rumble, and he could see a shaft of lightning dance across its dark surface.

Fallon looked at him. "What is wrong?"

He shook his head, uncertain. "I do not know, but I have a dire feeling." He turned around. "Barid, please hurry us back to the villa. We must learn what has happened to Anok."

AS ANOK STOOD in the center of the alley, rain suddenly began to fall, washing the blood from his face and robes. He stepped over the body of a fallen worshiper of Hanuman, feeling ribs crack under his feet, toward the snarling Hyborian who watched him with wary, yellow eyes, like those of a feral dog.

The man muttered some incantation. As Anok watched, he began to transform: hair growing from his exposed limbs, his nose and jaws thrusting out into a snout filled with deadly fangs, his ears becoming large and pointed, his fingers shortening, and growing long, curved claws.

He was becoming the very image of his beast god.

The beast creature moved forward, growling, foam dripping from his black lips, then pounced with sudden fury.

Anok dodged to once side, not quickly enough to avoid the claws that shredded through his robe and raked his side just above his left hip.

He spun, laughing, licking the mixture of rainwater and enemy blood that ran down his lip.

The beast crouched, a rumbling growl coming from deep in its throat.

Anok smiled. "Come," he said quietly.

The beast's body launched itself like a thrown spear, arcing toward Anok, claws out, fangs bared.

He did not dodge. He held up his hands, feeling the power coursing through him, through the Mark of Set.

"Stop!"

The creature's eyes went wide with surprise. It floated in the air above Anok's head.

He reached up, putting his hands, one above the other, around the beast's neck, feeling meat and bone beneath the wiry gray fur. One last time he summoned the power, even as he pulled his two hands apart. "Rend!"

There was a sound of tearing flesh, ripping tendon, and cracking bone, followed by a syncopated plopping sound, like someone pulling a large string of beads out of the mud.

Anok laughed as hot blood splashed down on his face, and he drew forth the creature's head and spine, holding them high as he let the headless, hollowed corpse splash to the rain-soaked cobbles at his feet.

Anok held his prize overhead and shook it at the black sky, cackling with joy, though there was no one there left living to see it.

10

THE GATE GUARDS stared wide-eyed at Anok as he approached the temple gate, his robes ripped, wet, and bloody. He ignored them and marched across the forecourt into the temple entrance.

Acolytes and servants stopped to look as he walked by. He could see them whispering when he was out of earshot, and he could easily imagine their words.

It was becoming annoying. He reached down and touched his wounded side through a ragged slit in his robe. Though he was still sticky with blood, the Mark of Set had already healed the wound. He sighed. He did not have a spell to fix his damaged clothing (perhaps he would have to work on that), but at least he need not look half-drowned.

He stopped in the center of the temple's central dome, a busy crossroads of traffic through the temple, and casually spread his arms.

"Desert wind!"

A warm breeze whipped around him, faster and faster, until it began to howl. A group of young acolytes watched from a doorway, both admiration and fear visible in their eyes.

Around him, everyone stopped. They watched, mesmerized as a visible column of wind, like a dust devil, snaked up from his feet to the skylight in the center of the dome.

Anok ignored them, casually pulling off his head-cloth and shaking his dark hair free, letting the dry wind lift it up and greedily leach out every trace of moisture. He looked down at himself, and his bone-dry clothing. So total was his mastery over the elemental magic that it took an act of will to end the wind. *Enough!*

The wind faded, even more quickly than it had come. Many eyes watched him as he replaced his headcloth and straightened his robes, then marched on through the central chamber and out into the temple's courtyard.

People still looked at him, but he no longer drew the kind of attention he had upon entering the temple. He checked the chambers assigned to Ramsa Aál and was told that although the Priest of Needs had returned to Kheshatta, he had left the temple on an errand and would not be back until later.

At loose ends, Anok realized that he was hungry.

From across the courtyard he could smell fresh bread, and some kind of stew or soup cooking in the temple's dining hall. Sorcery, he realized, exacted a physical as well as a spiritual toll.

He loaded a platter with flatbread, fresh fruit, sweet cakes, and a large bowl of meat and vegetable stew. He found an empty table, sat down, and started using the flatbread to scoop large mouthfuls of stew. He had cleaned the bowl, was finishing his last grapes, and giving thought to going back for more when he spotted a red-faced Kaman Awi marching directly toward him.

Anok looked up at him as he approached. "Greetings, master. Would you care to join me? The stew is very good today."

The High Priest just stood at the end of the table, his hands clenched into fists. Finally he managed to speak, almost spitting the words. "What did you do?"

Anok tilted his head innocently. "What *did* I do?"

"Just ask anyone in Kheshatta. The rumors are traveling across the city faster than a man can walk. By nightfall, everyone will know that a follower of Set killed the entire Cult of Hanuman!"

"Not the entire cult, just the entire cult here in the city. They were a small cult. Not many at all."

Kaman Awi snorted. "Twenty-seven, by the reports. *Twenty-seven!*"

Anok picked up a last corner of bread and wiped the inside of his bowl to pick up any gravy that might be left there. "I only counted twenty-five. Perhaps I missed a few."

"You missed no one! You simply can't be bothered to count all the men you've killed! Not just killed, ripped their heads and spines from their bodies."

Anok looked up at him, suddenly aware they had a large audience. He played to that.

Anok chuckled harshly. "Their manner of killing was in accordance with their own customs! I spilled their blood in the name of our god Set. How can that be bad? Have you not claimed countless victims by your own hand in the name of our glorious lord Set?"

Kaman Awi's hands shook. "That's *different!*"

"Is not their cult an enemy of Set?"

"Yes, but—"

"Please," Ramsa Aál's deep voice seemed to come out of nowhere, and the crowd of watchers suddenly parted to let him walk through, "Tell us, Kaman, how it is different? Young Anok has done us a service. I only regret that I did not do it myself."

Kaman Awi turned, a look of pure exasperation on his wide face. "You do not understand, Ramsa."

Ramsa Aál's eyes narrowed at the mention of his name. "You do not understand, *master.*"

Kaman Awi blinked in surprise, then bobbed his head in submission. "As you wish, *master.* But this is Kheshatta, not Khemi, not Luxur. Set does not rule all here. The city exists in a state of equilibrium, of balance between many powers. Your"—he gestured at Anok—"*student* has upset that balance! The Cult of Hanuman is a small one here, but there is an unspoken truce between the cults. There are disputes, even murderous ones, among the followers of various sects. But there is not open war, no wholesale slaughter, no desecration of temples."

Ramsa Aál looked down at Anok in mock surprise. "Acolyte, did you desecrate their temple as well?"

"If," said Kaman Awi, "there is truth to what is said on the street, the bodies of the slain are spread across its interior walls, reduced to little more than paste."

Ramsa Aál turned back to Anok. "Is this true?"

Anok pointed at a half-full bowl on an adjacent table. "There were chunks," he said, "more like the stew."

Ramsa Aál couldn't help himself. He chuckled, then broke into laughter, as Kaman Awi looked on with distress. At length, the Priest of Needs calmed himself and wiped a tear from his pale cheek.

Finally, he looked back to Kaman Awi, addressing the High Priest. "If the peace in Kheshatta is ultimately shattered, it will not be today. What will happen today is that the other cults and sorcerers, even the poisoners, will fear us—*as they should!*" He raised his voice, turning to play to all those watching.

"*Rejoice!* For today, of all days, the Cult of Set will be treated, in this foul city of heretics, with the respect that it *deserves*! Know that you may walk the streets, look into the eyes of all you pass, and see *fear*! Know that this is only the beginning, that our cult's rule over Stygia will be absolute, and this will only be the beginning!"

There was an agreeable murmur through the assembled.

Ramsa Aál reached down, put his hand on Anok's shoulder, and directed him to his feet. "Witness here the champion of the day, the ideal to which you should all aspire. Raise your voices for Anok Wati!"

Around them, people began sounding a rhythm, pounding the platters, mugs, even·discarded bones, on the tables. "Anok, Anok, Anok, Anok!"

Anok could not help but smile. *Yes, celebrate the heretic of Set, fools!*

But still he smiled and could not help but enjoy their adulation.

"Anok, Anok, Anok!"

TEFERI AND FALLON arrived back at the villa to find Anok missing and Sabé pacing the parlor. He stopped as they walked in the door. "He is gone." There was exasperation in his tone. "To the temple he said, but I heard no carriage come, and I found his swords hanging on a chair in the corner."

Teferi looked at the swords in amazement. How could Anok forget his swords? "He is in danger. I must go look for him!"

Sabé held up his hand. "There is little point. He left long ago. He is either safely there, or danger has already found him.

"But in truth, I fear he is more a source of danger to others, than in danger himself. He is now more drunk with power than ever, and he cannot see it. I cannot say what he will do next."

Teferi sighed. "Then what are we to do? Sit here and wait for our friend to go completely mad?"

"No, of course not. But he is more tangled than ever in the dark affairs of Ramsa Aál and Kaman Awi. Have you learned anything?"

"We have." Teferi described the forge, and the melting of the metal from the mystic armor of the Tomb of the Lost King. He went on to recount how the spilled metal had come alive and killed the worker.

Sabé rubbed his chin and frowned. "This armor was made by the Stygian wizard Mocioun. It is written he had discovered the magic to give metal objects the power of motion when directed by an external will. By Anok's account of the battle at the tomb, the armor was so sensitive that even the weak will of the undead spirits trapped within was enough to give it life."

"Then what happened at the forge?"

"In its melted form, the metal may be even more sensitive, more volatile. You say the men tending the fires seem as though they are sleepwalking? Then they have had their wills suppressed through some means, hypnotism, poisons, sorcery, or some combination of the three, so that they cannot influence the metal when they are near. When the spilled metal came too near the conscious will of a worker, it responded."

Fallon shook her head unbelievingly. "It *killed* him!"

But in some way, Teferi understood. "This is sorcery. There is always a cost."

Sabé nodded. "It may be most sensitive to those thoughts of self-destruction and self-hatred that eat at the edges of all men's minds. *That* is the power of sorcery to consume the unwary. That is why a powerful sorcerer needs no enemies to destroy him. Not when he has his own human weakness of spirit," he said sadly. "That is the universal flaw of man that brings all good plans to ruin."

Teferi found himself angered. "You speak as though we are doomed from birth. I will concede that you are wise in some things, scholar, but this I will not accept! Not while there are still a few men"—he glanced at Fallon—"and women, of good heart and bravery in this world. Though the sand may shift beneath our feet, still may we climb the dunes and cross the deserts wide. *No* path is closed to one with the will to walk it. That is what I believe!"

Fallon nodded in agreement. "Aye!"

Sabé could not help his lopsided grin. "You are young, my friends, and that gives you power, not just of body, but of spirit, that I no longer possess. Who am I to say what you can or cannot do? The fates have only so much power over optimists and fools."

Fallon raised an eyebrow. "Fools?"

Teferi chuckled. "It is better we do not ask."

Sabé sat wearily in the chair where Anok's swords still hung. "If I am not wise in all matters, believe me in this one thing that I tell you. You three are stronger together than alone. Accept that in some things, Anok is stronger than you can ever be, and that right now, he needs *your* strength more than ever. Alone, none of you can succeed in your quests. Together? Who am I to say?"

Teferi looked at the door. "There may be little sense in it, but I am going to look for my brother."

Fallen nodded. "I, too, will go."

Just then they heard the rumble of chariot wheels and the sounds of large horses pulling to a stop on the street just outside.

Teferi and Fallon looked at each other, and Fallon jumped on a table so that she could look out one of the high front windows.

"It is a chariot from the Temple of Set," she reported. "Someone is getting out, but I cannot see who for the trees." She jumped down and moved to another window. "I see two guardians, but they are leaving."

The door opened, and Anok walked in. His robes were slashed in many places and covered with dark, rusty streaks and splotches that might have been bloodstains. He stopped at the door, looked at them, and blinked in surprise.

Teferi rushed toward him. "Brother! Are you well?"

Anok wobbled on his feet, then threatened to fall over, just as Teferi rushed to his side, steadying him. The Kush giant helped his friend to a couch, where he collapsed in among the pillows limply, staring at the ceiling.

As his head went back, Teferi saw the fresh fang marks on his neck.

Anok blinked. "Is it time for supper yet?" His voice was weak. "It has been a very long day."

11

ANOK'S RECOVERY FROM the venom ritual was rapid. For this, Teferi was unsure if he should be pleased or alarmed. By the midday meal, Anok had his color back and was eating ravenously.

Teferi watched as he deftly sliced a melon into wedges with a knife, separated the green, sweet-smelling meat from the rind, and diced the meat into chunks that he could easily eat from his knifepoint. He chewed eagerly, wiping a bit of juice on his sleeve as it ran down his chin.

"If you keep eating like that," said Teferi, "you will need to ask the temple for an increase in your expense payments."

Anok chuckled. "I expect there will be one due me when I am inducted into the priesthood."

Teferi frowned. "Do you not mean *if* you are inducted into the priesthood? Ramsa Aál's plans seem to be progressing rapidly. Perhaps this will all be over before things go that far."

Anok took a chunk of melon away from his mouth and looked down at the blade, turning it so that the reflected sunlight from the window played across his face. "You speak as though we can simply thwart his plan and go home?"

"Is that not your intent?"

Anok bit off the rest of the melon, then stabbed the point of the blade into the tabletop, so that it stood there, quivering. "If Ramsa Aál can be thwarted without revealing myself as a heretic, why should I leave? I can continue to work within the cult to bring about its downfall, and I can do that most effectively with the mantle of priesthood. The higher my rank, the more power I will have, and the more harm I can do."

"You speak as though that is your true avocation, Anok. You must decide, are you a heretic or a true follower of Set?"

Anok laughed humorlessly and leaned back in his chair, putting his hands behind his head. "You know the answer to that."

"Do I?"

He leaned forward, his lips pressed together into a thin line. "What do you mean by that? Do you doubt me?"

"I worry about you, brother, that is all. If I remind you of your mission, it is only because I feel I must. Do not lose sight of your true goals. You may be closer than you think, but not if you become entrapped in Set's snare." He pointed at the marks on Anok's neck, already healing. "How could you let them do that to you again so soon?"

Anok chewed the corner of his lip and did not meet Teferi's eye. "I did not let them. I asked for the ritual."

"What? Why?"

"You don't understand, Teferi. My status in the cult is growing by bounds. I am celebrated. Ramsa Aál's trust in me grows. Whatever his plans, I am now confident I shall be at his side when they are executed. I must continue to convince him of my loyalty to the cult."

"By subjecting yourself to poison?"

"It isn't so bad. The Mark of Set offers me some protection, and the venom is weak. In some respects, it is exhilarating."

"You speak of it like a bath in a hot spring. This is poison, Anok. Poison further tainted by Set's evil magic!"

"I am equal to the challenge. I will not yield."

Teferi sighed and paced the length of the room. "Fallon was here earlier while you were in the garden."

"I haven't seen her this morning. Where has she been?"

"On the streets, trying to pick up more information about Ramsa Aál's plans. She heard some interesting gossip this morning, and in fact, says she has heard very little but. A follower of Set entered the alley of the Hanuman cult and single-handedly slaughtered them all."

He looked at Anok, who said nothing, his face emotionless. Finally, he said, "The Hanuman Cult is a foul one, even by the standards of Set. Unclean, animal-fornicating baby-killers. It is for the best."

Teferi looked at him, his eyes narrowed. "So say you." He waited for Anok to say something else. When he did not, Teferi continued. "Why did you do it, Anok? Another creative act to impress your new master, Ramsa Aál?"

"That was the result, but it was not my intent."

Teferi frowned. It struck him as significant that Anok had not denied the part about Ramsa Aál being his master. There was a time when he never would have let a thing like that go by. Now he merely quibbled about details of intent.

"Then why did you do it?"

Anok frowned. He pushed back the chair and stood, yanking the knife from the table, wiping it on a cloth, then pushing it back into its scabbard on his belt. "Since I have returned from the Tomb of Neska, I have sought a *true* test of my power and control. No such opportunity has presented itself, so I was forced to contrive one."

He spread his hands and looked down at himself. "As you see, even after that and the ritual of venom, I am whole. I am not mad. When I face my battle with Set, I will know what weapons are at my command and how to wield them. I did not know that before."

"And this slaughter brought you favor at the temple?"

"In truth, many were outraged, including Kaman Awi." He smiled as he remembered. "But Ramsa Aál jumped to my defense, in front of half the temple!"

Teferi sniffed. "Listen to yourself, Anok. You speak of this with pride! Ramsa Aál is not your father!" The words were out before he had thought them through, and they landed in the middle of the room like a boulder from a catapult.

Anok just stared at him, his expression unreadable. Finally, he shook his head and turned away.

"Anok! I should not have said that! It was unfair of me."

Anok took a deep breath and slowly released it. "No. No, it needed to be said. Perhaps there is some truth to what you say. My father's death at such a tender age, it has left a great void in my life. Perhaps I have always had a secret need to fill that void, and in my foolish way, I have let Ramsa Aál step into that role."

He just stood there for a moment, then turned his head and spat angrily on the floor. "What was I thinking?" He stomped to the open garden doors, leaning on the doorframe, looking out at the greenery, still lush from the previous days' showers.

Teferi wondered if he was being too harsh, or not harsh enough. Still, Anok seemed genuinely repentant. He stepped up behind his friend and put a hand on his shoulder. "You have lost your way, brother. Let us help."

Anok laughed. "I can't believe I left my swords behind." He turned, and looked at them, still hanging on the chair in the corner of the parlor. "Do me a favor, old friend. Let us spar as we did in the old time. Let us take up arms and make the simple music of steel."

Teferi frowned. "Do you think you're up to it?"

Anok chuckled and walked over to pick up the sword harness. "I told you, I feel fine. Better than fine, now that I have rested some."

That did not make Teferi feel any better, but he said nothing. The villa's garden was small, but lush, surrounded by a high wall. It had been neat and well tended when they had moved in, but it had become somewhat overgrown since their arrival.

Of the three of them, only Fallon showed any interest in, or knowledge of, tending plants. Teferi gathered that her knowledge was gained during her time as a youthful slave. She did not speak of it much, but it was clear that her interest in such work was tainted by troubling memories; and she tended to work in the garden only occasionally and only for a short time. On occasion, they would hire someone to come in to clean the villa and tend the grounds, but this was not Khemi, and such labor was not cheap.

They stepped out into the garden, following the flagstone path to the brick-paved center court. It was a sunny day, and bees buzzed around them seeking honeysuckle and the flowering shrubs that grew along the wall.

Teferi turned to face Anok and drew his sword. "You recall," he said, "our last attempt at sparring did not go so well."

Anok tilted his head. "Has it really been that long? I suppose it has. When I first saw this garden, I always assumed we would use it to practice our swordsmanship."

"As Fallon and I have."

Anok strapped on his own sword harness and drew one of his swords. He extended it forward and tapped the blade against Teferi's larger weapon. Then he drew his second sword, moved into a relaxed stance, blades high, feet apart.

There had been a time, on the streets of Odji, the slums of Khemi, when the swords of Anok Wati had been a source of terror and awe. He had been called the "two-bladed devil," for his two-handed fighting style. He could fight as well as any man with left hand or right, and fight just as well with two swords as one. He could fight a man to a standstill with a sword in his right hand, then toss it to his left just to create confusion. He had been fast, agile, cunning, winning battles through speed, skill, and misdirection.

That seemed an eternity ago. Mastery of the sword only stayed with those who lived by the blade every day, or by those who practiced it daily without fail. These days, it seemed like Anok wore his swords more out of habit than anything, and the previous day's adventure seemed to show that even this habit was fading. "I will go easy on you," he said.

Anok just grinned, shifting his weight from one foot to another, crouching slightly in anticipation of an attack.

He waits for me to move first? So be it.

Teferi put his left arm back for balance, waving the point of his sword to confuse his intent, then lunged at Anok's right side.

Anok dodged left, using his right sword to deflect the point of Teferi's weapon up and out, even as the left sword swung at Teferi's exposed flank.

Teferi spun and dodged, freeing his blade in time to swat Anok's right sword away. His heavier weapon knocked Anok's sword and arm wide, giving him an opening.

Teferi lunged forward, stabbing at Anok's midsection, prepared to stop the sword before it could do real damage.

He need not have bothered. Anok was not there to meet the point when it passed.

He dived to one side, used his sword to guide Teferi's blade into the soft earth, then jumped onto a boulder while Teferi struggled to extricate his weapon.

Anok laughed down from his perch. "First blood! I believe you have skewered a worm!"

Teferi grunted, swung his blade at Anok's ankles. Anok jumped at the last moment, so that the blade sliced only the air under his feet, then stabbed at Teferi's face.

Teferi dodged the blade, only to dodge immediately the other way to avoid its twin.

The first blade slashed.

He stepped back and deflected it.

The second.

Again he stepped back, steel clanging against steel.

The blades moved faster and faster, so that all Teferi could do was fall back and defend himself.

Out of the corner of his eye, he saw the shadow of a palm tree behind him. He angled toward it, saw the slight smile on Anok's face that indicated that he thought he was going to corner Teferi.

He felt the solid trunk against his back, saw the point of Anok's blade coming at his face.

He ducked and dodged right, using his sword for defense as he stepped around the tree, and the point of Anok's blade stabbed deep into the wood and stuck there.

Before he could remove it, Teferi lunged forward, using the tree as cover, forcing Anok to abandon one of his blades.

Teferi grinned. "Now," he said, "things are more even."

Anok grinned back and shook his head. He reached for his dagger with his right hand and drew it. "I am *still* the two-bladed devil!"

If the different reach and balance of his two weapons bothered him, Anok did not show it. He was quickly on the offensive again, using his sword to keep Teferi's blade busy while he stabbed and slashed with the knife. Always, Teferi was able to keep just out of his reach, but it was a distraction, and Anok was very fast with the dagger.

Teferi feigned a thrust, then stepped back, swung the sword overhand, and brought it down in a powerful two-handed slash.

Anok crossed his blades, catching Teferi's sword between them, then suddenly fell back, using the power of his larger opponent's blow against him.

Teferi tumbled forward, off-balance, as Anok fell onto his back into a cushioning flower bed.

Suddenly Teferi found Anok's feet against his belly, carrying him over, tossing him head over heels onto the flagstone walk.

There was a thud as he hit the rough stone, and he felt a hunk of skin scraped off his back. He grunted, rolled over, and came up crouched on all fours, sword still clutched in his hand, braced for Anok's attack.

Instead, Anok had run back and was recovering his second blade from the tree trunk. As he yanked it free he turned and smiled. "So, things are again not so even!"

Teferi looked over and spotted a section of fallen branch next to his left hand. It was nearly as thick as his wrist, and roughly three feet long. He grabbed it and scrambled to his feet. "Then," he said, "let us find another way to even things!"

Near one corner of the garden, a trio of upright boulders were artfully arranged in a triangle. Anok turned and ran toward them, leaping nimbly onto the farthest one, then spun back to face Teferi, his twin swords at the ready.

Not willing to give him a moment's rest, Teferi roared a battle cry and charged across the center court at him, sword held high over his head, his makeshift wooden weapon held diagonally in front of his face in a defensive pose.

He charged between the other two boulders, stabbing at Anok's stomach.

The smaller man danced aside, just as Teferi swung the branch at his ankles.

He jumped, stepping across the blow and landing on the boulder to Teferi's right.

Teferi instinctively dived back just as the point of Anok's blade struck the stone behind where his neck had been.

Anok jumped again, landing even as he made a slashing blow that Teferi deflected with the branch.

Anok had the high ground now, and took full advantage of it, stepping from rock to rock, his twin blades darting down from every angle. Teferi felt like he was trying to dodge lightning bolts, yet there seemed to be a rhythm, a pattern, that he could anticipate—

Suddenly one of the swords reversed, the other slashing unexpectedly. He caught it with his sword as an awkward angle, the branch in his other hand poorly positioned and useless.

The heavy pommel of Anok's sword came down on the top of his head. There was thunder with the lightning, and he saw stars.

Before he could see, one of Anok's swords was tangled in the guard of Teferi's blade. The blade was ripped from his hand, flying away to spin across bricks of the center court.

Teferi managed to block a blow with the wooden branch, but he was instantly at a huge disadvantage.

Anok toyed with him, herding him away from recovering his blade, keeping him busy responding to one attack, one feint after another, pushing him ever back.

Then the blades swung in from two directions at once. He ducked back and held up the branch to defend himself, instantly realizing that he had been fooled again.

The swords were not for him. They cut into the branch from either side, allowing Anok to use the strength of both arms to pull it from his hand and toss it aside.

One of Anok's blades was stuck in the branch, but he let it fly away as well, and instantly the dagger was in his hand.

He shoved Teferi back, jumping onto his chest as he fell.

Teferi landed with a painful thud, Anok's knees driving him into the ground, his sword across Teferi's throat, the point driving his chin back.

He lay there, grunting, knowing that in a true battle he could be dead. "I yield!" he managed to gasp.

The sword still lay sharp against his jugular, the point driving ever deeper into the soft flesh of his chin, until he felt a tiny trickle of blood.

He realized something was wrong, and though his head was forced back, he managed to catch Anok's eyes.

His friend, his brother, panted, his face red and covered with sweat, and his eyes wide with rage and bloodlust.

"I yield!"

Anok just looked down at him like an animal, the hand holding the dagger trembling.

"Anok!"

Anok jumped back, dropping his sword, and casting aside the dagger. He staggered back, turning his face away, slumping as though he barely retained the strength to stand.

He stood there for a moment, then laughed. "I— I had you fooled, did I not!" He laughed again, and it rang hollow in Teferi's ears.

"You thought me weak and out of practice. I surprised you, didn't I?"

He turned back, a half smile on his face, but it was a mask, hiding the receding bloodlust, and something else.

Fear.

Some part of him knows, even if he will not admit it to himself.

Anok turned and walked hurriedly back into the house. "We must do this again soon. But not today."

Then he passed into the house and vanished around the corner.

ANOK LAY ON his bed, staring at the ceiling, trying to make sense of what had happened in the garden earlier. What madness had possessed him?

He tried to remember the last time he had been in such a fight, one with swords, not with magic. He supposed it was during their trip by caravan, when they had been attacked by bandits and forced to fight for their lives against and overwhelming force of mounted Kushites.

But even then, when all had been lost, he had ended the battle with sorcery, and that was different.

To fight with arms was a fight of passion and emotion. One felt anger, fear, the fever of battle in one's blood. But fighting with magic was different, less of emotion, more of intellect and will. In a way, even at its most desperate, its most violent, it was—cold.

In that, fighting with arms was different than what he had become so used to. He realized now that it was more than the sum of swordsmanship, speed, and skill. It was emotion. And in this case, rather than too little lust for battle, he had succumbed to too much.

That was all. He was simply not used to such primal, animal combat anymore. His emotions had gotten the best of him. That was all.

It would be better next time.

He would remember.

He lay there, quietly, watching the shadows through the window grow long, the light orange, and still he could not entirely convince himself.

This was getting nowhere.

He had to stop brooding, to find some distraction to lift his spirit. Perhaps just this once he could leave behind his robes of Set, dress as any common man, and slip out into the streets, find a tavern, and get happily drunk.

When was the last time he had done that?

Just then, he heard Teferi's voice in the room outside. It had been quiet for so long, Anok had assumed he was long gone. Evidently, he had been mistaken.

"Fallon, you have returned."

Anok quietly stood and moved closer to his door in order to listen.

"I have been prowling the bars for gossip, and I overheard a camel driver saying a caravan of fifty fresh troops arrived at the east garrison this morning by the Pteion road." Her voice was just the tiniest bit slurred.

"You've been drinking again."

She chuckled, a throaty sound that Anok found appealing.

"Just a little. I had to keep up appearances, and even watered drinks have a cumulative effect."

He heard Teferi grunt. He sounded only barely satisfied.

"About the troops then. Replacements?"

"Reinforcements. When we were there yesterday, you saw only the forge compound. I thought little of it at the time, and you gave me no chance to mention it later, but I got a look inside the stockade itself. Already it is crowded with guardian troops, busy drilling as though practicing for some coming battle."

"Why would they be massing troops? It would take far more than that to take Kheshatta, yet it is far more than they need to defend the temple and their garrison. That many guardian troops would never be tolerated in the city. In fact, there will be grumbling when word gets around that they are even *close* to the city."

Anok had heard enough. He swung open the door and stepped out. "Perhaps they are going in search of the third Scale of Set."

Teferi frowned at him. "I thought you said Ramsa Aál already had two?"

"I was wrong about that."

"But the power of his Scale was able to overcome yours at the first venom ceremony. Is his more powerful than yours?"

Anok looked down. "I do not think so. I think they are all equal. But I assumed he used the power of two against one. Since that is not the case, there must be other reasons. Perhaps the Scales are more readily commanded for evil than for good."

Teferi just stared at him, as though he wanted to say something but was holding back.

"You have something to say, Teferi?"

"You have found yourself drawn back to the ritual of venom. Perhaps that day, some part of you wanted it, wanted to surrender yourself to Ramsa Aál's evil."

"That is absurd!"

"Is it? I can no longer be sure."

They stared icily at one another. Finally, Teferi looked away and turned toward the door. "I must go speak with Sabé. He will want to know of this."

And you will tell him of my doings as well, will you not?

But he said nothing, just watched Teferi walk out the door. "I may be late," he said to Fallon. "I may be very late."

Fallon, confused, turned back and looked at him, her eyes wide. "What devil has possessed him this day?"

"We were sparring in the garden earlier. He lost. Badly. I think it angered him."

She grinned and laughed in surprise. "You beat Teferi? In a fair fight?"

"In a fair fight."

"No magic? No sorcerous trickery?"

He casually took a step toward her, noticing how beautiful she looked in the light of the setting sun. "Nothing but muscle and blade. Oh, and he picked up a stick at one point, but I quickly relieved him of it."

She giggled. "A stick! Tell me it is not so!"

He pointed out into the garden. "It is still there, with my sword marks upon the wood. Go see for yourself."

She giggled again. "I will take your word. It is just so funny, to imagine Teferi fighting you with a stick."

Anok smiled, slid a step closer. The sunlight glistened off her hair like a halo of fire. She smelled like flowers and honey.

She caught the look in his eyes and seemed surprised. Without thinking, she let the tip of her tongue slide along her upper lip. Her smile faded, laughter gone. She looked at him, and her eyes fluttered in surprise. "Anok, what is in your heart this late day?"

"Us," he said.

"Us? As in, you and me?"

Anok looked around mockingly. "I see no one else here. Yes, you and me. It is well past time that we talked."

She looked nervous, averting her eyes, but she did not step away. "Long there have been things I wished to say to you, but I have held back. Though we have lain together several times since leaving Khemi, always it has seemed a matter of lust and convenience, and little has been said afterward."

He smiled slightly. "And you did not share that lust?"

"I did, I admit. But I was not always so sure of *you*. Always it seems I was the one coming after you. There was some reserve, something held back. And I did not question it, did not challenge it."

"Perhaps," he said, "there is some truth to that."

"I know that your heart belonged, perhaps still belongs, to another, now gone. And though time has passed, I know those wounds are still fresh."

He stepped closer. "Sheriti is dead and gone, I know that now. Once, perhaps, that stood between us. No longer."

She looked up and met his gaze, her eyes wide with wonder. She looked open. Vulnerable.

He reached out and took her hand. "If I have held back from you, my heart, my passion, then you may find that things have changed. That they have changed very much."

He jerked her toward him. She gasped, too surprised even to feign resistance, finding their bodies pressed together.

He put his arm around her waist, yanked her hard against him, hungrily found her lips.

She made a muffled cry of protest that turned into a moan, her lips yielding to his tongue.

He spun her around, pushed her back, slamming her against the wall next to the bedroom door. She gasped as he instantly was on her, his hands roaming over her body, his teeth biting her lips, their hips grinding together.

He felt a powerful lust wash over him, and growled, low and deep in his throat. He unbuckled her sword belt and threw it aside. "You are defenseless now," he whispered.

His open hand slid up her chest, between her breasts, until his fingers curled around the yoke of her tunic. His hand clenched tight around the cloth.

He yanked, hard. There was a hesitation, a ripping, and then the garment came away in his hand, leaving her half-naked before him. He threw the tattered rag aside, drinking her with his eyes as she shrank against the wall.

He pushed himself against her again.

She pushed weakly at him with her hands, but he subdued her with the power of his kisses. His hands gently slid down past her heaving breasts, his fingers counted her ribs, gently caressed her soft flanks, until they found the waistband of her skirt.

He grabbed it with both hands, pulled until something ripped, until he could pull the skirt down over her hips, so that it fell, useless, around her feet. She gasped.

He took her shoulders roughly, pulling her away from the wall, guiding her backward through the door into his bedchamber.

"You say I held back from you? Well, you have all of me now. All of my passion, all of my heart, all of my lust, nothing held back. No quarter asked—" He shoved her back onto the bed. She landed on her elbows, her legs akimbo, her mouth parted, from lust or surprise he could not tell, and really did not care.

He eagerly pulled off his own clothes, feeling the cool evening air against the heat of his body. He climbed on top of her, pushing her back, his hands holding her wrists, pushing her legs apart with his own.

He pushed his weight down upon her, entering her roughly.

She cried out, struggling weakly against his arms, her body twisting under his.

He silenced her with his mouth, and at last, there was nothing between them.

Nothing at all.

12

TEFERI SAT IN the little walled courtyard behind Sabé's house. It was small, even by comparison to their villa's garden, and nothing grew here. There were a few pots and planters, but they contained nothing but dirt, a few brown sticks, and dead leaves. Until recently, even the doors connecting to the house had been boarded over by Sabé.

Fallon had convinced him to open them again. "You live like a hermit in a cave of your own making," she had chided him. "You are not too blind to feel the rain on your face or the wind in your hair!"

Sabé had relented, and now, on clear nights, he spent much of his time here, often with Teferi for company. The old scholar sat reading at a heavy table set up for that purpose, his fingers sliding along the writing in gloom so deep that Teferi could barely see the tablet at all.

Teferi leaned back, watching the sky as the clouds parted like a curtain, revealing a sparkling carpet of stars. "You have nothing to say, Sabé?"

"What would you have me say? I am reading here."

"I've told you what happened today. I fear we are losing him, despite all our efforts. I came to you for counsel."

Sabé growled with disgust and pushed his chair noisily back from the table. "And I am reading! I am a scholar! That is what I do! That is what you came to me for, and that is how best I can help you!" He rose out of his chair, shaking his finger in the air. "I have forgotten more mystical lore than most men will ever hope to know!"

Then he sighed and slumped back into his seat. "The problem, my young friend, it that I have *forgotten* it. Lo, these many years, the evil Mark of Set has kept me whole and of reasonably good health. But it has limits, by flaw or design I do not know.

"My mind is aging faster than my body now. I struggle even to remember all the volumes and tablets I have here, much less what is in them. So, to aid you, I must constantly review the relevant works. Surely you have noticed that I have asked you to bring me the same tablets again and again."

Teferi frowned. "I had, but I assumed you searched them for subtleties that you had missed previously."

"Once that was true, and perhaps still, a little. But now I read them so as not to forget. When you told me you were Zimwi-msaka, I dimly remembered that some of my texts referenced that lost clan. I could not find them until now.

"Fifty years or more ago, I purchased a small store of materials that belonged to a wizard who had studied ancient Kushite magic."

"I did not believe that the Kush had magic, that it had all come from Stygia and beyond."

"Then you were wrong. There were good sorcerers—so-called witch doctors who aided the Zimwi-msaka—and evil sorcerers or witches who were outlaws and feared by the people. Sorcery was not a part of everyday life, as it is in Stygia, but it was a part of life nonetheless."

"Then what do these texts tell you, and what does it have to do with Anok?"

Sabé lifted the tablet in front of him and put it on the stack with the others that he had read, then put his elbows on the table, far apart, his chin resting on his knitted fingers. "I have learned this of your history. There were many ways that the Zimwi-msaka protected the people from evil, and many tools they used to do so. Among those items I obtained long ago is what I believe is one of those tools."

He stood. "Come with me."

Teferi followed Sabé into his house, through the large central room, cluttered with tablets and scrolls, and down the narrow corridor into the west wing of the house, where Sabé's personal quarters were located.

Teferi had only rarely ventured there during his visits. Sabé was still intensely private, and this part of the house was still windowless and constantly dark. On the way in, Teferi took an oil lamp from a wall sconce, knowing full well there would be no lighting within.

The air was stale and full of strange smells, incense, exotic herbs, burned things, decaying things, dead things. They entered a small storeroom full of trunks, boxes, and odd objects. What seemed to be a full-size mummy case leaned in one corner, a demonic mask on the lid suggesting the occupant was not entirely human.

Sabé ignored all of it, instead pointing to a large chest in the center of the floor. "Push that aside."

Teferi placed his lamp on a nearby shelf, put both hands on the edge of the lid, and leaned into it. To his surprise, the chest moved easily on hidden rollers of some kind, revealing a trapdoor in the floor. "Should I open this?"

Sabé nodded.

Teferi took the iron ring and pulled. The counterweighted door opened easily, with a rusty creak and a cascade of choking dust. Teferi put his hand over his nose and mouth to keep out the dust, and recovered the lamp.

By the time he had turned back, Sabé was already halfway down a staircase hidden under the door. Teferi rushed after him.

They descended into the darkness, entering a cave running under the house. In places, the stone had been carved away to create flat floors and sizable rooms, but the essential form of the original cave could still be seen.

Teferi held the light out, trying to determine how big the cave was, but passages vanished into the darkness in at least three directions.

Around them were stacked countless tablets and scrolls, boxes of artifacts, statues, strange weapons. What seemed to be a complete stone sacrificial altar, still streaked dark with blood, leaned in pieces against one wall.

He looked around in wonder. "How much is down here, Sabé?"

"More than you can know. You should know that, when I am dead, you must not return here. The first to enter after my death will trigger a spell that will collapse these caves, returning all these secrets to the earth."

"All this will be lost?"

He laughed. "Most of what is here is so dangerous, it should never have been found. But perhaps, there are a few exceptions. Now, where did I put that box?"

Teferi heard a dry scuttling noise behind him. He turned to find himself looking into the hairy gray face of a spider the size of a barn cat, its eight eyes glowing like emeralds in the light of his lamp.

He cried out, jumping back as he drew his sword.

The spider clung to the wall at eye level, and as he watched, it scuttled along the wall toward Sabé. It stopped, turned briefly back toward Teferi, and hissed a warning, then headed on toward the old scholar.

"Sabé! Look out!" He dashed forward, stabbing the nasty creature through its torso, pinning it to the wall.

Eight hairy, gray legs flailed at the air, a spray of webbing spewed from the thing's rear, piling up harmlessly on the floor, and a steam of greenish-black ichor flowed down Teferi's sword to drip onto the floor by his feet. Then the thing shuddered and fell still.

Sabé casually turned, reached up, feeling the dead thing

to identify it. "I should have warned you," he said casually. "Those are a problem down here. Be careful."

You choose now to tell me!

Sabé turned, and as he did, his fingers brushed an oblong wooden box with an inscribed lid. He hefted the box and held it out for Teferi. "Can you read it?"

It was old Stygian. He struggled with the words. "Beware, to he who uses magic. To use these things within, means—dinner."

"Not dinner. Death. Which is why I will let you open the box."

Inside were a number of objects. Carved stones, like marbles, necklaces and other jewelry, totems made of gold, and a large, heavy wooden object that ran the length of a box. It was a stick, perhaps intended as a scepter or ceremonial club, wrapped with leather and drawn metal wire, decorated with rock crystal and beads carved from bone and shell.

Teferi looked at Sabé. "This is all Kush."

He smiled. "More specifically, they are all Zimwi-msaka. The significance of most of them, I cannot say. Perhaps they are trinkets or trash. Perhaps they are of great importance. I cannot say, but they are yours now. But it is the stick for which the box was made, and it is the stick of which the warning inscription speaks. Pick it up."

Teferi hesitated.

"Go on! It cannot harm you. You are Zimwi-msaka. You are the only one who *can* use it!"

Teferi lifted the stick from the box.

It was almost as long as his arm, the knots and shape of the original limb still visible, though it had been stripped of bark, polished, and intricately carved with tiny pictograms. It was heavy enough, and solid enough, it could have been used as a club, but somehow that did not seem to be its function.

"Yesterday, when I was sparring with Anok, I picked up a piece of wood, about this size and shape, to use as a weapon. Do you think that means something?"

Sabé pursed his lips, thinking. "It is possible. Now that

you know your true nature, I think your instincts are guiding you in ways you do not yet understand."

He looked the stick, shaking it. Some part of it had been hollowed out, and it made a soft, rattling sound as he moved it. The beads and decorations clattered together musically. It was a pleasing sound. "But this is not a weapon, is it?"

"Not in the sense that you mean. The texts say it is called a Kotabanzi. It is a 'dream stick.' If a person's mind is troubled by evil, he can invite a Zimwi-msaka into his dreams, and the Kotabanzi will supposedly let him travel there to deal with it."

He looked up in surprise. "You expect me to go into Anok's dreams? In his present state, why do you think he would even consider inviting me into his dreams?"

Sabé smiled. "He already invited you into his dreams when first he met me. Do you remember that?"

Teferi blinked in surprise. "The day we first came to your house. Anok came to see you, and I was dozing in Barid's carriage outside."

"I believed Anok to be an enemy, and we had a battle of minds. He called on many allies in that battle, including you."

"That strange dream! It was real?"

"As real as dreams are"—he turned and started back toward the stairs—"and as dangerous as they can be. There are real dangers in dreams. People die in their sleep every day."

Teferi followed him, watchful for more of the big spiders. "But will this even work on me? You said I was immune to magic."

"You cannot be harmed by spells intended to harm you directly; nor can you initiate magic yourself. But although the Kotabanzi can be dangerous, its purpose is not to do you harm, and thus you can use it. The magic is already within the stick, a fact of its creation, so you are not precluded from using it in that way, either. This was made by an ancient witch doctor of your people to be used by your kind, and your kind alone."

They climbed the stair, where Teferi closed the trapdoor and replaced the chest that hid it. They returned to the courtyard. Teferi put the box on the table and stood with the Kotabanzi in his hand.

"I wonder," he said, shaking it, and listening to the soothing sounds, "if Anok is asleep. Can you tell me how to make this thing work?"

Sabé smiled, seemingly from far away. "I think it is working already." His voice seemed to echo away into nothing, and Teferi turned. Behind him a flight of stairs climbed up into the sky, over the wall, and up into the stars. The stairs consisted only of the treads, perfectly black, which hung in the air with no apparent means of support.

He began to climb, higher and higher. Though the black stairs were difficult to see, his footing was sure, and he did not hesitate in his ascent. He was amazed to look down upon the city far below, the many yellow lamps, torches, and fires flicking in warm echo to the blue diamonds that sparkled in the sky above.

Still he climbed, until the world was small, mountain ranges like anthills, oceans like puddles of quicksilver, and surprisingly, he could see the last pink light of a setting sun far to the west, over a horizon strangely curved, as though the world were like one of Anok's crystal balls.

Still he climbed, until the sky was black all around him, and he could not see the stairs at all. It should have come as no surprise when his foot sought the next step, and it was not there.

13

TEFERI STUMBLED SLIGHTLY as his feet landed on hard-packed clay. He held up his hand and squinted against the light of the midday sun. The sky around him was deep blue, fading to hazy red near the horizon. The air was cool, dry and thin, and Teferi immediately knew he was on a mountaintop, or somewhere very high.

He turned, and saw before him a stunning sight. The rim of a canyon, a hundred times larger and steeper than Teferi had ever seen in his travels. He was only a handful of paces from the near lip. The far wall faded with the haze of distant, as though he were looking at a distant mountain range. Colorful stripes of different rocks wrapped around every cliff and tower, like layers in a sweet pastry. Far out over the canyon, a large dark bird, a falcon, or perhaps an eagle, circled lazily.

Unable to see the bottom of the canyon, he stepped closer, looking cautiously over the edge. He gasped. Far, far below, a narrow blue ribbon of water snaked along the canyon bottom, reflecting both sunlight and sky. He felt

that, if he slipped, it might take an hour for him to reach the
bottom. It was not, however, something he wished to test.

Just then somebody ran past him, close enough to brush
against his back, and he tottered on the edge, struggling to
keep his balance. As he waved his arms, trying to keep
from falling, he remembered what Sabé had told him.

People die in their sleep every day.

A cascade of pebbles tumbled away down the canyon
wall before he was able to step safely back from the edge.
He looked over to see who or what had brushed him, and
spotted a man running along the lip of the canyon.

It took him a moment to recognize the man. "Anok!"

Teferi ran after him. He was taller than Anok, with longer
legs, so there was little trouble in closing the distance between them. It was just that Anok had such a head start.

There was also the matter of caution. Some places, a
large, flat plain butted up against the canyon edge, but at
other places the path narrowed until it was a shelf little
wider than a man's foot. In those places, Teferi slowed considerably, even then fearing for his life with every step.

But Anok did not slow. He ran at a steady pace, tireless,
his eyes fixed on the far wall of the canyon, even as his feet
seemed ever on the verge of slipping and plunging him to
his doom.

As he ran after his friend, Teferi caught a glimpse of the
bird in the corner of his eye, and realized it was no longer
circling. It was growing larger against the sky.

Teferi redoubled his pace, keeping his distance from
the treacherous edge whenever he could. But ahead, always Anok ran right along the edge, rock crumbling under
his feet.

There was a monstrous screech, and Teferi looked up to
see the bird diving toward Anok, black wings wide, and its
strange white head now more clearly visible. This was no
falcon, no eagle. He could see that it was much bigger,
wings spanning at least half a dozen paces, talons large
enough to lift a calf—or a man.

It dived toward Anok, and still he did not see.

If only I had my bow!

As if by magic, it was there in his hand, the familiar weight of the quiver on his back. He drew his heaviest iron-tipped arrow, nocked it on the string, pulled back, and took aim. The monster-bird moved very quickly, and he would have only one shot.

He tracked the thing, letting the string slip from his fingers. The bow snapped, the arrow arched away from him and struck the monster at the base of its neck.

It screeched, flapped its wings frantically, and flew past Anok.

As it did, Teferi got a clear look at the monster's head, and saw that it was not a bird's head at all. It was the head of Ramsa Aál.

Even as he ran after Anok, Teferi watched the man-bird warily. It climbed higher, and higher, black wings pumping against the sky. At some point, the arrow fell free, as though it had not truly penetrated at all, but only caught in the monster's feathers. He saw no wound, no blood.

Again, it circled, gaining height in preparation for another attack. He had to warn his friend. "Anok!" He yelled, but Anok did not seem to hear.

The bird circled higher, then turned for another pass.

Teferi found another arrow, and already had it nocked in the bow before he realized this attack was not to be against Anok. The monster had turned its attentions on him.

Worse, the trail was very narrow here. There was no place to stop, no place to stand. He kept moving, kept walking, bow at the ready, as the monster grew larger and larger, heading straight for him.

Still walking, he drew back his bow, having to trust that his feet would find purchase.

Closer it came. He could see Ramsa Aál's face, screaming in fury. He aimed for the mouth. If he could kill the beast, even if he was swept into the canyon, his friend would be saved.

Closer.

He drew back the bow. Prepared to shoot. Prepared to die.

Then an arrow flew in from the side, penetrating the thing's right wing. It shrieked and veered to one side, missing Teferi, who released his shot.

He stumbled, the rock giving way beneath his feet. He scrambled for footing, but found none.

A strong hand grabbed his arm, lifting him back onto the path. He looked at his rescuer. "Anok!"

Anok looked at him, surprised, his bow still in his hand. "Teferi! What are you doing here?"

"I came to find you, brother."

Anok turned, distracted, looking on up the canyon. "I must go." The bow was gone, and again, he was running along the canyon rim, this time with Teferi dogging his heels.

Teferi glanced into the sky. Again the man-bird was climbing. The arrows that seemed to have wounded it were already gone. "It will come again."

"It always comes," said Anok, not looking back. "Again and again. I grow tired of it, but there is little I can do."

"Brother, why must you run so close to the edge?"

"So I can see. You can see so far from the edge, yet not far enough. The answers I seek are over there"—he pointed out across the canyon—"somewhere. I must find a way to get closer, so I keep running."

Teferi looked up at the monster-bird. "Brother, it comes again. Step back from the edge. It is a long way to fall."

Anok kept to his path. "I will not fall."

Teferi looked down over the edge. On a shelf of rock, far below, he could see seen the broken shape of a fallen man lying in a splatter of his own blood, which ran down the side of the rock, dripping into the abyss below. "Brother," he said, "you have already fallen."

ANOK AWOKE WITH a start, sitting up in bed. He was panting, sweating. He looked frantically out the open window into a blue sky: but there was no black shape of a bird there, only few wisps of cloud, and a buzzing bee.

It was morning. The air was warm, and scented with flowers. The smell made him remember—

His hand went to the bed next to him, and it was empty, only a rumpled spot where Fallon had been. He threw back the sheets, using a corner of them to wipe the sweat from his naked body, then found a simple tunic and kilt to wear.

He stepped out into the parlor. The doors into the garden were open. He could hear birds singing. It was a beautiful day, which did nothing to ease his growing sense of dread.

He found Fallon sitting in a chair at the edge of the garden. She sat as though she had been waiting for him, her face tense, but unreadable. And she was dressed. No, not just dressed. She was dressed for *war*.

Garbed in leather and mail, heavy shin guards strapped to her legs, iron bands around her wrists, she leaned forward on the hilt of her sword. She was relaxed in her pose, but something about it suggested she was instantly ready for battle.

"We need to talk," she said, "about last night."

Her manner made him chuckle nervously. "I thought that was what you wanted."

"I wanted to be closer to the man who had won my heart. I am not so sure he was there last night."

"What do you mean?"

"You were quite forceful."

"It was what you wanted, was it not?"

"You were forceful, and you would not stop."

"You did not want me to stop."

"That is not the issue."

"You did not want me to stop."

"If I had wanted you to stop, I *would* have stopped you if I had to cut off your manhood and feed it to you. Make no mistake. But that is not the issue either."

"Then what is the matter?"

"If I had told you to stop, would you have stopped yourself?"

He blinked in surprise. "You didn't want me to stop!"

Her voice became louder, more forceful, and she quietly

rose to her feet. "Look into your heart! Would you have stopped?"

He laughed. This had to be a joke!

But her expression remained deadly serious.

"Would you have stopped?"

He licked his lips, thinking. *What could she mean? What happened was—*

She took her sword in two hands and lifted it over her shoulder. *"Would you have stopped?"*

His breath caught in his throat as the horror of it struck him. His shoulders sagged. She could strike him down now, and he would hardly care. "No," he said weakly, shocked at his own conclusion. "No."

She slowly lowered the sword. "That was the correct answer," she said. "That was the answer that the Anok I know would have given. If you had lied to me, if you had failed to see your own heart, I do not know what I would have done."

He shook his head sadly.

"I put down a rabid dog once," she said. "I loved that dog, too." She smiled slightly but did not relax her grip on the sword.

"I came to tell you," he said, "about a dream. Now it makes more sense to me."

Just then, Teferi appeared at the garden door. He looked at Anok, then Fallon. "What is going on here?"

"My brother, I have been shown the error of my ways. I have come to the edge of a great abyss, and even now, I may be falling into its depths." He looked them in the eyes, first Teferi, then Fallon. "My friends, please help me, for I cannot help myself."

14

IT WAS NEARLY dawn as Fallon quietly emerged from Anok's sleeping chamber. She wore a silk tunic and a leather skirt. Her only weapon, a dagger, was strapped at her waist, but her sword leaned against the wall, never far from her sight.

Though he could not see her, Sabé reflexively looked up as she emerged.

She came and sat down heavily in the chair across the table from him.

"How fares he?"

"He sleeps soundly. The fever is past. His body fights the venom off faster each time. It is his mind I fear for. This is the third venom ritual in the span of a week. Though he fights, I fear it will not be enough."

She looked out through the doors into the villa's garden, where a bonfire burned, sparks dancing into the predawn sky, and Teferi knelt, the Kotabanzi, the "dream stick" held in his raised hands. "I fear for him, too. Each time he holds vigil over Anok's nightmares, and each time he emerges more troubled."

"He is strong," said Sabé, "as are you."

"I do not feel strong. This is no enemy I can fight with muscle or steel." She leaned closer to Sabé, across the table. "You must help us to fight for him! You must show me some mystic weapon, some talisman, some magic sword, like the Kotabanzi, so that I can help Anok."

Sabé smiled sadly. "There is nothing for you, my beautiful warrior. You have no hidden secret of blood, no foretold destiny, no hidden talents beyond those you already know you possess by birth and training."

She slammed her fists angrily on the table. "Then what good am I! What worth has a Cimmerian woman if she cannot battle for the man she—" The words hung in her throat.

Sabé reached out, felt for her hand, and gently put his wrinkled fingers over hers. "I know well how you feel. For all my study, all my learning, I can be of only little use in this affair. I know a thousand magics, none of which I can use. I am worse than useless"—he touched the cloth tied over his eyes—"I am a *burden*. I am blind, and a cripple in the one way that counts in this matter."

"You are too hard on yourself, Sabé."

"As are you. Nonetheless, in Anok, I see the culmination of everything I have struggled for all these many years. I never had a son, but if I did, I could not have asked for one better. Yet I cannot seem to help him to triumph where I have failed." He patted her hand. "But perhaps *you* can!"

"You just said—"

"A statement of fact which does not minimize your abilities. You are, like most Cimmerians I have met, what you are. There is no subterfuge, nothing hidden, nothing veiled. You may hide your feelings, even from yourself, but you cannot hide what you are. It goes against your nature."

"Then what am I?"

He smiled slightly. "If what I have heard you speak of your god, Crom, is true, you are what he has made you, and he has made you everything you need to be. Do not seek to be what you are not, for it is the Cimmerian sense of purpose and identity that makes you stronger than any civilized woman or man can ever be. We seek endlessly what you were born with." He leaned back in his chair, putting his hands on his knees. "Be who you are, Fallon, and know it will be enough."

She rose from her chair, stepped around the table, leaned down, and gave him a gentle kiss on the forehead. "You would have made a good Cimmerian, old man."

He grinned. "It is a lie, but it is good that you said so."

BARID'S CARRIAGE PULLED up at the gate of the Temple of Set. Anok looked at the portal without enthusiasm. One of the guardians raised his spear in salute. Anok turned away from him. "I have no wish to go here today," he said.

Fallon leaned over and put her arm around him. She leaned close to his ear. "Then do not go. What could be easier than that?"

"I have been summoned by Ramsa Aál. I must go."

She frowned at him, met his eyes with her own and looked deep into his soul. "You *must* do nothing! The only chains that bind you are of spirit and mind."

"Those are the chains broken with the most difficulty."

"Come with me! Barid can take us to the camel station. We can be on Fenola, riding far into the desert by nightfall. Barid could take word to Teferi and Sabé, tell them where we have gone."

"Where would we go, Fallon?"

"Back to Khemi. We could find a ship. Across the border to Kush. Or east, past the Mountains of Fire, into Shem and the lands beyond. We could take a ship across the Southern Sea, around the horn of Vendhya, to Kambuja, or Khitai. It matters not where we go! Just that we go!"

"But that I could. I have come too far, seen too much. I

sense today is important, though I know not why. I cannot leave when the answers I seek may be so close."

She took his face in her hands. "You are being a fool, Anok!"

He glanced nervously at the gate guards. "We are being watched," he said.

"Then let them watch this!" She kissed him hard and deep upon the lips, arms around his neck like tender serpents, whose coils he might never wish to escape.

But I must.

Gently, he pushed her away, the perfume in her hair still lingering. "I must go. I must."

He stepped out of the carriage, nearly stumbling as he did so. He walked with grim determination, not looking back, lest it destroy him.

The guards grinned at him. One slid closer, leering. "The Cimmerian whore—is she good? I could go for a taste of wild game if the price is right!"

Anger flared in Anok. He glared at the guard, and made the slightest gesture with his left hand.

The guard's eyes went wide. He grabbed his throat, opened his mouth so that his tongue was visible, as it blackened and crumbled into dry dust that cascaded down his anguished lips. He made a strangled cry and fell to his knees as Anok walked away.

He clenched his fists, all his accumulated rage welling up in his heart. He could turn the man to fire, fill his living skin with carnivorous ants, make his blood boil in his veins. But only if he turned back.

Keep walking. Keep walking.

He reached down and twisted the little silver ring on his right hand, the one Sheriti had bought him in the Great Market at Khemi, so long ago. He looked at the engraving, the little two-faced demon, Jani. The merchant who had sold it to her had told him that Jani was good luck for those in peril because he could see in any direction, but because of that ability he traveled only in circles.

"He can never leave the wilderness," Anok said to himself, "nor can I." He rubbed the ring. "Oh, Sheriti, what would you think of me now?"

He walked into the temple, knowing all the while that all he need do was turn and walk the other way.

He wandered like a sleepwalker through the halls and chambers of the temple. Many turned to look as he passed. Many offered greetings that were not returned.

He was well-known at the temple now, respected, even feared (and doubtless would be more so, after word of his encounter with the guard got around). He saw the eagerness in the faces of the young acolytes. They wished to stay close to him, to be his friend, or his follower, so that some small portion of his power and reputation would rub off on them.

This is how it begins, how a priest gains followers to do his bidding. Without trying, I am already the perfect priest of Set, gathering toadies on whose stooped shoulders I may stand.

His self-loathing seemed to know no bounds. He hardly noticed as he wandered into Ramsa Aál's chambers, and the priest looked up from his desk, where he had been writing with a reed pen on papyrus. Next to him, a tattered and faded map lay unrolled.

"Acolyte. Are you unwell? Your face is ashen."

Anok blinked, as though awakening from a dream. "I am still not fully recovered from the last ritual of venom, master. It will pass, I am sure."

Ramsa Aál washed the tip of the pen in a bowl of water and wiped it on a rag before placing it in a cup at one end of the desk. "No candidate for priesthood has ever gone through the trials of venom as rapidly as you, Anok Wati."

Anok could not hide his surprise.

"Normally," continued the priest, "they might be spread over a year or more. Sometimes two in those more frail. But matters progress too rapidly. I cannot wait for you to stand at my right hand as a full priest."

Anok looked inward at his own heart. *What is that? Pride? Stop it! You are a heretic, not a priest!*

But it was hard. Part of him was proud of his own strength, his own perseverance. Never had he asked for quarter, never had he begged for mercy. Always he had taken what had come his way, and always he had returned ready for more.

Ramsa Aál gestured him over. "Today we ride east to meet an army of three hundred men. We will take with us enough acolytes to serve us in those matters where magic will better serve than force of arms. We ride to claim a second Scale of Set and to strike at Set's enemy, Ibis."

He tried not to show his concern at the mention of the ancient Moon god. "Ibis? Master, Ibis was driven from Stygia in the ancient times."

"So you have been told. But long has the priesthood known there were pockets of Ibis worshipers in Stygia. Always when we could find them, they have been captured and tortured to death in sacrifice to Set. But there are always more, and we have long believed Ibis somehow retained a stronghold in Stygia. But never could we find it—until now."

Ramsa Aál reached down and spread the map flat so that Anok could see it better. "This was taken from an Ibis spy many years ago. It purportedly shows the location of the stronghold in some secret form, but never were the priests in Khemi able to reveal its meaning."

Anok examined the map. Though it was obviously not the work of a professional mapmaker, it was carefully done, obviously by one with the skills of a fine scribe. He could make out the Western Sea, the River Styx, Khemi, Kheshatta, Luxur, and the other major cities. The writing was Aquilonian, and something about the hand was strangely familiar—

Anok's blood suddenly ran cold in his veins.

My father's hand!

This was his father's map! *A spy for Ibis?* Is that what Ramsa Aál believed? Anok tried to parse it out. He was beginning to suspect that Ramsa Aál was acting in some way as Parath's agent. Yet if both his father and Ramsa Aál served Parath, why would he believe him to be a spy?

It may well be that Ramsa Aál only pretends to serve Parath, even as he pretends to serve Set. If he could lie to one god, why not two? Yet he serves only himself, and his own lust for power!

The priest reached inside the neck of his robe, grasping the golden chain there, and lifted the Scale of Set over his head.

Just one, not two as Anok had believed. But if, as he claimed, he had found the key to finding the second one, then he needed only the hidden one that Anok carried to complete his plans.

Ramsa Aál laid the Scale casually on the map, then put the fingers of his left hand on top of it. "It was Kaman Awi who solved the riddle. His cleverness can be an annoyance at times, but he has his uses. The Scale of Set was the key."

He slid the golden scale across the map, then rotated it, until the rounded point at the bottom fit precisely into the northern border of Stygia, nestled in a crook in the banks of the great River Styx.

The engraving on the face of the Scale was identical to the one Anok possessed, a flaming sword, two curved serpents facing inward toward the blade. Ramsa Aál tapped the sword with his finger. "The sword points the way." He traced a line away from the point of the sword, angling south toward Kheshatta. "There is no town, no settlement, no habitation along this line, save one. A small desert oasis, Nafri, far from the main caravan routes, far from anything of value or interest." He looked up knowingly. "It is a wonder that anyone would live there at all."

Just then, a young acolyte entered, looked nervously at Anok, walked widely around him, and whispered something in Ramsa Aál's ear. The priest's eyebrows went up, and he glanced at Anok, his expression otherwise unreadable.

The acolyte hastily scuttled out of the room.

"Anok," said Ramsa Aál quietly, in the tone one might use for scolding an ill-behaved child, "you are about to set out into battle with three hundred heavily armed guardians at your back. Let us hope none of them are friends with the guard whose tongue you just turned to ashes."

15

THEY RODE OUT of Keshatta on horseback to meet a contingent of mounted guardian soldiers at the East Garrison. Anok learned the foot soldiers had been dispatched, in secret and under cover of darkness, days earlier to begin their march to Nafri.

Preparations had begun weeks earlier, with caches of food, water, and animal feed hidden along the way. With no need to carry, or wait for the delivery of, large quantities of supplies, the march would be a rapid one.

Anok did not consider himself an expert horseman. There had been little enough opportunity to practice the skill growing up in the city, and since coming to Kheshatta, there had been little cause to ride anything but camels, with which he now considered himself quite proficient.

So it was that he found the journey especially difficult.

For the sake of speed, they rode Kushite warhorses. Lean and nearly tireless, they were also skittish and ill-tempered. His mount, a black stallion whose ribs and hipbones poked out as though he were half-starved, seemed especially difficult, throwing him twice on the first day, to the great amusement of the guardians riding with them.

That night, he found himself aching and saddle-sore to an extent that he was forced to use the healing abilities of the Mark of Set. He did so reluctantly. He felt that his resistance against the magical corruption was very fragile, and the sudden trip had taken him far from the help of his friends.

He sat alone and bone tired in front of the fire, an uneaten ration of bread and dried meat in his hand. They had traveled east most of the day, along the lake, and into lands where some fraction of Kheshatta's rain occasionally reached. By midafternoon they had turned north, climbing though a low pass in the mountains and into the desert. They had brought no tents, and each man had little more than a blanket.

Anok wrapped his food in a cloth and stuffed it in his bag for later, then wrapped his blanket around his shoulders. He watched the sparks from the fire curling into the air through heavy eyelids, and wished that he were home.

"Brother," said Teferi, "I am with you still."

Anok looked over to see Teferi crouched by the fire, his Kotabanzi in his hands. "I must be dreaming," he said.

Teferi looked around. "You are in the desert. There are many soldiers around us, many horses. To where do you ride?"

"To an oasis, a secret enclave of Ibis, to find another Scale of Set."

"I will tell Sabé. Perhaps he will know something." He stood, and without moving his feet, drifted away from the fire. "I will find you in your dreams."

Anok jerked awake, finding that the fire had burned down to embers. He found a soft spot on the ground, wrapped the blanket around him, and went back to sleep.

.   .   .

TEFERI LOOKED UP from the fire, suddenly aware that Fallon was standing next to him. "How long have you been there?"

"Hours," she said. "Someone should watch over you when you go on your dream journeys."

"He is safe and well," said Teferi. "Ramsa Aál has taken him on another one of his quests, this time to an oasis in the north."

"We should be there to watch over him."

"He has an army with him, the guardians you saw training, and more still from other places. I expect he has little need of our swords." He looked at the Kotabanzi. "This is what he needs now."

"Then again," she said wistfully, "I am useless."

Teferi smiled at her. "As you said, I need someone to watch over me while I search the dreamworld. Even on the best of nights, Kheshatta is not safe. It would be foolish to die on the tip of some bandit's dagger in our own garden."

"Then I will be your faithful protector," she said.

"I can trust that you will not fall prey to drink and leave me defenseless?"

She frowned, but to Teferi's surprise, held her anger. "I have sworn off strong drink since—"

She did not complete the sentence, and the troubled look on her face told him not to question her further.

Finally, she said, "This is no time for weakness, for carelessness. We must ever be at our guard." Then she rubbed her eyes. "But I will be better at my guard after some rest." She looked at Teferi curiously as they walked together back to the villa. "Do you ever sleep?"

He grinned. "While I dream-walk, I *am* sleeping. Truly, it can be quite refreshing, when the dreams are not too fearful."

But she did not smile back. She seemed lost in her own troubled thoughts.

"Do the cravings for drink trouble you?"

She glanced up at him, surprised. Then she looked away. "At times, yes."

"Perhaps I could help," he said. "Perhaps you should invite me into your dreams."

Then, finally, she did laugh. "You only wish that it could be so!"

IT TOOK ANOK and Ramsa Aál two days by fast horse to reach the hills above Nafri. They found a vantage point, among a cluster of jagged boulders, where they could observe the place unseen.

To Anok's eyes, it did not appear to be a stronghold of Ibis, or anything else for that matter. Rather, it appeared to be the sort of place that was barely holding on to itself, a cluster of huts, barns, and small, simple buildings of mudbrick and stone. Even from here, he could smell the woodsmoke of cooking fires, the odor of roasting meat, and of penned animals.

Except for the smoke curling from the chimneys, the movement of palm trees in the wind, and the milling of goats, ducks, and other animals, the place was strangely quiet. There were a few men and fewer women visible, clothed like nomads, sitting in doorways, or in the town square near the well, but none of the morning activity one would expect in a small village.

"This does not seem right to me," he said to Ramsa Aál. "Where are the children? Where are the old people?"

The priest scowled as he looked down on the oasis. "Curse Ibis; somehow they have anticipated our coming."

"Are you sure we have not been misled? I see no temple of Ibis here. No temple of anything. Could we have been led to a trap?"

Ramsa Aál held up his hand as though feeling the air. "I sense no spells of cloaking or deception. Nothing is hidden here. What we see is what we see. And yet I am sure what we seek is here. The map is too old, its meaning too obliquely hidden, for it to be a deception. They may have moved the Scale of Set, but the temple is here. I know it!"

Ramsa turned and walked away from the ridge, back toward his horse. "If this is a trap, then they will find us well prepared for their treachery. Come."

They rode down to where perhaps a third of their forces were gathered, along with several dozen acolytes who would doubtless serve as Ramsa Aál's mystical soldiers. "The rest of our forces are gathered to the north and west of the oasis," he explained. "We will enter the town on three fronts."

He rode his horse in front of the assembled troops, finally approaching their commanding officer. He removed a crystal ball from a bag hung on his saddle.

Anok assumed it was a crystal of speech and vision, and that its companion crystals were in possession of the officers leading the rest of the forces.

"Move our forces into the city on my command," he said. "Be at the ready, but do not attack. We will let them show themselves first. At the first show of aggression, return it with all your fury. Kill anything that moves, man, woman, or child, but with one exception. Anyone who wears priestly robes is to be kept alive. Report anything that might be a temple, shrine, or of mystic importance. Is that understood?"

The commander nodded, and the others spoke their affirmation through their crystals.

"Into the town," he ordered. Keeping close ranks, they began their march down the hillside.

As they descended, Anok could see two other columns of troops approaching as well, one from the far side of town, one from their left. As they rode in among the simple buildings and through the narrow dirt streets, there was no resistance, little sign of notice at all.

Anok scanned the surrounding rooftops, acutely aware of the danger from archers.

Ramsa Aál leaned closer to him and whispered, "Worry not. The acolytes protect us with a spell of deflection. I would hardly offer myself as such a tempting target otherwise. It is a shame the spell is only powerful enough to protect us of the temple, but the guardians are expendable."

The locals, if that was what they were, watched them with unfriendly stares as they rode past. As he studied their sunbaked and unwashed faces, Anok noticed something else. "None of these people have a drop of Stygian blood in them," he whispered to Ramsa Aál. "I see Shemites, Kushites, Hyborians, but no Stygians. They are a rough-looking lot, and many carry scars."

Ramsa Aál nodded. "Foreign mercenaries, most likely, with no loyalty to Stygia and not enough fear of Set. Well, I wager we will teach them that fear."

The logic of the priest's plan escaped Anok. He placed their troops at great disadvantage, vulnerable to almost certain ambush. Then the truth of it dawned on him. Ramsa Aál cared not even a little for the lives of his men. His only concern was in finding the Scale of Set, and he hoped that if the defenders were overconfident, they might feel less urgency to spirit it away into hiding.

Ramsa Aál looked back over his shoulder at the column of troops following them. "All our men will be within the borders of the town by now." He looked around expectantly. "It will happen soon."

Then, as if he spoke from prophecy, Anok saw a dozen archers appear over the roofs of the surrounding buildings. Arrows rained in on them from every direction. There were cries of agony as soldiers began to fall, but true to the priest's word, the arrows were deflected away from their horses.

Around them shields were raised over heads to protect the column of soldiers, like scales on a snake, and swords were drawn. Anok instinctively reached for his blades as well, though it did not seem that they were in immediate danger.

There was a battle cry from some hidden voice, and all around them, doors were thrown open. From every hut and hovel, armored men poured out, armed with swords, axes, and warhammers.

They were surrounded!

16

INSTANTLY THEY FOUND themselves in the middle of fierce, hand-to-hand fighting against which the deflection spell offered no protection.

The savagery around him inflamed Anok's sensibilities. These were brutal mercenaries who sold their loyalties to the highest bidder. They would not offer mercy, nor did they deserve any. He was eager to enter the fray, but his horse could not move without trampling their own soldiers.

He watched a bowman moving along a nearby rooftop and decided not to wait.

He sheathed one sword to increase his mobility. Startling Ramsa Aál, he leapt from his horse, landing with his feet astride two of the upraised shields. Instantly they began to give way under his unexpected weight, but he was already moving, running rapidly from one shield to another, like a man crossing a pond by dancing over giant lily pads.

He jumped onto a stack of barrels leaning against the wall of a brick building. Using the tops of the barrels like a stair, he dashed up to roll over the top of the wall and landed in a crouch on the flat roof.

He kept low, seeing the bowman, who now was moving along the roof of the next building, loosing arrows on the guardian troops trapped in the narrow street below.

Anok instantly wished he had his own bow. *Well, if I want a bow, I will need to take one.* He reached for his dagger, and, crouching low, came as close to the man as he could before calling out to him.

The archer spun, just as Anok threw his dagger.

Guide me, Sheriti!

His dead lover's countless hours training him in the use of knives had not left him. The archer's eyes went wide, and he spat blood as the dagger buried itself up to the bolster in his throat. Anok was upon him, even as the man fell dying, sheathing his other sword and taking up the man's bow and quiver.

It was a lighter Shemite bow, not the more powerful Stygian bow that he was used to, but it would do. Almost as an afterthought, he reached down and yanked his dagger from the archer's gushing neck, wiping the blood on his robes and returning it to its sheath.

Then he scanned the rooftops for targets, and saw too many. Fortunately, they were all focused on the invaders in the streets below. He had not yet been noticed, but that would not last long unless he took action.

He sighed and called on the power of the Mark of Set, whispering a long-unused spell, the Walk of Shadows. It would not render him invisible, but it would help protect him from notice by the unwary. It was the sort of spell priests tried to avoid, one that used much magical power for a small result, but it would best serve him here.

He crept quietly across the rooftops, drawing closer to the next archer. He took out an arrow, drew back the bow, and let the string slip from his fingers.

It missed its intended mark but struck the man in the back of his left shoulder. He flailed madly, trying to reach the embedded arrow, and tripped, falling backward off the roof.

One of the other bowman turned at the sound of the man's cry, but did not see Anok, who was already prepared with another arrow. He pulled and shot. The man screamed as an arrow bloomed from his chest, plunging deep into his heart.

Several of the archers were suddenly aware they were under attack.

Anok moved swiftly. Though the spell might protect him from being noticed directly, his opponents would instinctively seek the source of the arrows that were felling their friends.

He jumped from rooftop to rooftop, firing as he moved. Another archer fell dead. Another was gravely wounded. One on a more distant rooftop suffered only an arrow through his draw arm before ducking out of sight, but it would take him from the battle.

The remaining archers were spooked, now more concerned with their own safety than the troops below, which was Anok's goal. He shot one more, then drew back on another, who suddenly began to move.

Anok tracked him with his aim as he ran, but held the bow too long, pulled too hard. It parted with a loud snap.

The archer instantly turned and fired at the sound.

Anok turned and leaned back, just in time to see an arrow fly by a thumb's length in front of his nose.

The man searched frantically for him, bow at the ready. Clearly the spell was not broken. The man fired wildly at every sound.

Anok drew his sword and ran at the man, dashing from side to side. An arrow jabbed through the hem of his robe, barely nicking his leg. He kept silent, despite the sting, and came on the man just as he was drawing another arrow.

Anok knocked the arrow aside, putting the archer off-balance, then jabbed his sword deep into his chest, yanking it back as the man fell with a groan off the edge of the roof, to land among a penful of terrified goats below.

He looked around. There had been more archers, but they had all gone into hiding or had dropped to street level in fear. He realized he had allowed himself to become separated from the guardian troops and had no idea what direction they had gone.

To the north, he could hear sounds of heavy fighting, and could see clouds of dust rolling up into the sky. That was as good a direction as any.

As he glanced down at his arm, he saw the Mark of Set, dripping with blood. He had awakened it from its slumber and drenched it in heart blood. Already he could hear its voice whispering in his ear, the bloodlust burning at him.

He growled in frustration as he made his way toward the battle. Teferi could help him in his dreams, but awake and in the heat of battle, when he needed help most, he was alone.

He steered his mind toward the calming anchor of the Band of Neska, about his right wrist. It alone was immune to the influence of the Mark of Set, the corruption of the magic.

In his imagination, he took that cool firmament, shaped it into a shield, and held it up against the evil influence of the Mark. It wasn't much, but it was something.

He came to the edge of a roof, looking down onto one of the wider streets, and found it littered with bodies, dead, dying, or badly wounded, a good two-thirds of them guardians. *Ramsa Aál has led them into a slaughter!*

Yet he felt a pang of guilt for himself, as well. If he had entered the battle with the full force of his magic, and not merely his swords, he might have saved many guardian lives. Though they served evil, it did not mean they were all evil themselves. Certainly, they deserved to die standing and fighting like men, not sacrificed in an ambush.

A confused, riderless horse staggered through the carnage below. It was not Anok's mount, but it would do. He jumped onto a canvas awning, slid down it, then jumped into the saddle.

The startled horse reared, and Anok held on for dear life as it first pawed madly at the air, bucked once, then sprinted headlong toward the battle.

He could see the fighting just ahead. He drew his second sword, holding both high, as the horse waded into the confusion. Anok began to swing his swords, jabbing and slashing as fast as he could sort mercenary from guardian.

Around him, the tide of the battle was turning. Though the guardian casualties had been grievous in the beginning, they had greatly outnumbered the defenders.

Now that the numbers were more even, the element of surprise was gone, and the terms of battle more balanced, the superior skill and training of the guardians were beginning to show.

Worse, for the defenders, some of their ranks had already judged the battle lost and were beginning to run for their lives.

Only so much loyalty can be bought.

Suddenly an arrow plunged into his horse's chest, and the animal fell forward, its front legs giving way. Anok jumped out of the saddle, sliding down the horse's neck to land on his feet, swords at the ready.

He ducked as an axe was swung at his head, then jabbed the attacker in the chest with his left sword.

He sidestepped as a spear jabbed at him, watched as that attacker was stabbed through from behind by a guardian, then turned, looking for other quarry.

They were all engaged, man to man, sometimes two on one. The battle was nearly won.

The Mark of Set urged him to end it with some great spell, but with the enemy mingled with their own troops, he had not the skill to do so without slaughtering both.

He saw a horse and rider approach from the other direction, and immediately recognized the priest's robe and yoke.

Ramsa Aál!

The horse stopped, reared. Anok saw Ramsa Aál's left hand over his head, gesturing, as his lips formed some spell.

For a moment, he thought the priest intended to sacrifice them all. Then the mercenaries began to stagger back and drop their weapons. Many were quickly felled by the guardians, but there was no need.

The defenders' faces began to draw in upon themselves, turning wrinkled and brown, like apples going rotten. They seemed to shrink in upon themselves, their bodies crumbling to dust and bone inside their clothing and armor. In the span of a minute, nothing was left that could be identified as ever having been human. Just brown dust that flowed away with the wind.

The surviving troops cheered, and the real purpose of Ramsa Aál's spell was apparent. Instantly, his questionable leadership bringing them into this place was forgotten. He had been at the heart of the battle, and he had ended it for them.

They would have followed him into the infernal pits if he had asked it of them.

"Spread out," he called to them. "Capture anyone left so they can be tortured for information." There was a roar of affirmation from the men at the word "tortured." "Look for any sign of Ibis, his priests, or his temple."

The soldiers began to fan out, a few staying to tend the wounded.

Anok looked up at Ramsa Aál. The priest's eyes were wide, with a strange, intoxicated look. He laughed, then glanced down at Anok. "I may not have your raw power, acolyte, but remember that skill, training, and experience still count for much!" He laughed again, joyfully, almost manically. "Too long I have left such magics to my followers. It is *good* to taste the great spells again!"

Anok felt a twisting in his gut, of envy, of frustration, of rage. The battle had ended too soon, the Mark of Set was still not satisfied.

Seeming to regain some of his calm and reserve, Ramsa Aál climbed from his mount and looked around. They were but a few houses away from the central square with its well, and he began to walk purposefully toward it.

Curious, Anok followed him.

The square was small, far smaller than the courtyard at the Temple of Set in Kheshatta. In the center, a low stone wall topped with a wooden cover marked the well. A heavy wooden archway over the well supported two wooden pulleys with matching ropes, one small, with a bucket attached, and one much heavier, ending in an iron hook. A small round opening in the center of the lid allowed for passage of the bucket.

Ramsa Aál walked around the well, examining the hoists and rigging. Then he picked up a stone from the ground and carefully dropped it through the opening. After what seemed like a long time, there was a splash far below.

Still, he did not seem satisfied. He dropped the bucket down into the darkness, letting out its rope till they heard it splash at the bottom. He pulled the bucket up, dipped his fingers in the water, tasted it.

Anok stepped up next to him and did the same. The water was cool and sweet. He dipped a double handful and drank, then splashed his face and hair, casually washing the blood from the Mark of Set as he did.

The maddening voices in his head grew a bit quieter.

He looked at Ramsa Aál, who was too distracted to notice. The priest ran his fingers along the edge of the lid, which Anok noticed, was not precisely round. At the four points of the compass, there were small projections, which rested just offset from four matching grooves in the wall of the well. He also noticed four stout iron rings attached to the wood around the center opening. The purpose of it all was not readily apparent to him.

Ramsa Aál walked around the well again, now paying notice to what seemed to be a water barrel, also with a wooden lid, set up against one side of it. He removed the lid, reached inside, and removed a pair of short, iron chains with hooks on each end. He smiled as though some secret had been revealed.

"Gather the men," he said, "as many as you can find. We will need both ready swords and strong backs, but"—he jumped onto the lid of the well and looked down into the hole—"I have found the temple of Ibis!"

17

RAMSA AÁL WATCHED with intent interest as the guardians followed his instructions. Anok watched as well, puzzled by the goings-on.

The two lengths of chain had been attached to the four rings around the center hole of the lid. These in turn had been attached to the hook on the larger hoist. Clearly the intent was to lift the large lid off the well, but the purpose of it escaped him.

A horse was harnessed to the end of the rope, and a dozen men took up the line. At Ramsa Aál's command, they pulled. The rope creaked and groaned, but the lid lifted a handbreadth above the stone lip of the well and swung free. Rather than allowing it to be lifted completely clear, the priest called a halt. Then, following his instruction, two men rotated the lid so the four tabs projecting from the sides lined up with the four grooves on the side of the well as the top was lowered back slightly below the rim.

Anok's eyes widened with understanding. "The lid can be lowered into the well!"

Ramsa Aál stepped up onto the lid, testing its stability first with one foot, then putting his entire weight on it. "When I was a young acolyte, I served at the Prison of Gems at the base of the Mountains of Fire. Lifts not unlike this one were used to lower slaves and prisoners into its hellish pits, to collect precious stones for Set's troves."

"Then you believe there are tunnels below?"

"Or caves, or catacombs. But the temple we seek is below." He inspected the rope. "I expect this will take the weight of ten men." He rounded up two of their best acolytes to maintain a protection spell, and six guardians with armor, much of it salvaged from fallen mercenaries, since the guardian force had traveled light and fast.

The acolytes, Anok, and Ramsa Aál positioned themselves closest to the center of the platform, with the guardians around the outside, swords drawn, shields raised. The rope creaked ominously under their weight, and though the platform was a tight fit in the well, it still shifted slightly with each movement.

Two more squads of ten men each stood ready to follow them in as reinforcements. The mood was tense, with only Ramsa Aál seeming comfortable, even gleeful, about the impending descent. He shouted the command, and men and horses began to lower them into the unknown depths.

Anok drew his swords and stood with his feet wide apart for balance. His heart was pounding harder than when the battle had begun. That enemy he could see, he could fight. He did not like the helplessness of the descent, or the confinement.

He could smell the guardians pressed tight around him, and he could smell their fear.

Down and down they went, so far that Anok had time to admire the masonry in the wall, so precise that the lid never caught on any projection, nor became so loose that it would be free to tip. The four grooves that guided them ran down the well with such precision, they might have been cut into the wall with a great knife.

The rope groaned and crackled. Occasionally, the edge of the platform would bump noisily against the wall, scraping along for a time until it bounced away, only to strike against the other side. Anok looked at Ramsa Aál. "This will not be a surprise," he said in a low voice.

"Again," said Ramsa Aál, "we will hope for their over-confidence."

It grew darker, the top of the well now a circle of light far above, bisected by the top bar of the hoist. Around them, four openings began to rise up the platform, the grooves now set into four columns. Beyond the opening, Anok could dimly see a much larger room, illuminated by a few hanging lamps.

They looked around, but there were no guards, nothing that suggested they were expected at all. Yet Anok knew that was impossible. "Perhaps they are hiding," he said.

Ramsa Aál knelt and put his hand through the hole in the center of the platform. There was a splash as his hand entered water. "Ingenious. We are on top of a cistern, or perhaps even an actual well. Anyone looking down the well, or dropping something in, as I did, would be fooled."

The highest ranking of the guardians looked nervously at the priest. "What shall we do, lord?"

He looked thoughtful for a moment. "Step off the platform. But slowly and carefully."

The officer nodded to his men, and they hesitantly began to move.

One, braver, or perhaps more foolish than the rest, stepped down first. The stone under his feet sank slightly, and there was a clanking sound, followed by the twang of a dozen or more bowstrings.

Anok had a flashing image of a large, steel-pointed arrow coming right for his face, when suddenly it was torn from its line of flight and vanished to the side.

Instantly, they were surrounded by a swarm of arrows, circling like angry bees until, one by one, their energy was spent, and they clattered harmlessly to the floor.

The man who had triggered the trap laughed nervously.

Ramsa Aál nodded. "Well done, acolytes."

Anok glanced over at the young acolyte next to him and noticed the mad look in his eyes, the trace of drool coming from the corner of his mouth, and the drop of blood just crawling down out of his nose. His companion looked little better. "I fear, master, they will not serve us again."

"It matters little. The next trap, if there is one, will be different. Now that my eyes are adjusting to the darkness; I see a passage that way." He pointed.

Anok's eyes strained into the darkness and could just make out a stone archway flanked by columns, painted with murals of god figures.

The officer looked unhappy, watching as the platform was lifted out of the chamber, blocking most of the light save a small circle on the water of the cistern. "Should we not wait for reinforcements, master?"

"No! There may be escape tunnels. At the very least, they may attempt to hide that which we came here to seek."

Several of the soldiers produced bags from which they removed smooth, fist-sized, white crystals, Jewels of the Moon. Each man with a bag made a small cut on his arm with his knife, and touched the jewels, one by one to the blood. As he did, each crystal flared into a cool, diffuse light, like the light of the moon, and he handed it to one of his companions.

The acolyte Anok had been studying earlier removed his own crystal from his pocket and casually rubbed it across the trickle of blood on his upper lip. As it began to glow, Anok could see the irises of his eyes, which were alarmingly turning yellow, the pupils narrowing into vertical slits.

Ramsa Aál glanced at the acolyte for a moment before turning away. He chuckled. "The Jewel of the Moon was discovered by Ibis worshipers. Now we use these to hunt them down and destroy them."

They made their way past the columns, ever watchful for traps. In the light of their jewels, Anok looked up at the columns as they passed. On one side was Ibis, pale, wearing the cusp of the moon as his crown, and on the other, Bastet, a lesser goddess of cats and of the new moon, who some believed was Ibis's wife. Her skin was as dark as Ibis's was light, and her features were those of a great cat with green eyes.

Through the portal, they encountered a wall and turned left, descending a stairway into a narrow, high-ceilinged hall.

Anok was immediately suspicious. It was curiously un-adorned for a place guarded by such a grand portal. It was also strangely warm, and they could smell wood or char-coal burning.

The floor was black and strangely slick. Anok scratched it with the tip of one of his swords, and the corroded patina came away, revealing a gleam of white metal beneath.

He shouted a warning, even as he tried to recall the spell of frozen death Sabé had once related to him from his an-cient tablets.

There was a rumble, and a huge clang of metal as something large fell. From a large slot above the door at the far end of the hall, a gushing wave of silver liquid rushed at them.

Anok was already reciting the spell, giving the Mark of Set full release to draw on its powers. The wave swept past the soldier at the front of the column. He screamed as the stuff came up around his waist, just as Anok whispered the last word of the ancient spell.

The air seemed to turn to ice, the walls of the tunnel covered with a glittering skin of frost. The wave of lead slowed like thick syrup, then stopped. The trapped soldier was, mercifully, frozen as well, a white statue, horror still visible on his rigid features.

Anok looked down. The molten metal had come within a single pace of his sandaled feet. He reeled from the power of the ancient spell, suddenly dizzy.

Ramsa Aál stepped up next to Anok, holding his arm so he did not fall.

Anok took a deep breath, composed himself, and shrugged off the priest's support. "I am fine."

"I did not know that prophecy was among your gifts, my student."

It was no such thing, but he found he rather enjoyed the pride in Ramsa Aál's voice and did not contradict him.

The priest led them back up the stairs. "This is a false passage. I understand the wrongness of it now."

They reached the top of the stairs in time to meet the next wave of soldiers, and waited for the third, who arrived soon after.

As they waited, Ramsa Aál studied the blank wall just inside the portal, running his hands over the stone. "This is a false wall," he announced. "Acolytes, a spell of disruption!"

The acolyte with the nosebleed gestured at the wall, then gasped as though a knife had been stuck between his ribs. He shuddered once and fell to the floor, spasming in agony. A red froth formed around his mouth, until he shuddered one last time and lay still, his open, unseeing eyes like those of a serpent.

Ramsa Aál sighed, watching as the second acolyte crawled into the corner, sobbing and babbling in fear. The priest looked at the closest soldier and ordered, "Kill him."

The guardian stepped up to the acolyte, pulled back his head, and in one, swift motion, snapped his neck.

Anok looked at the wall. "Allow me, master."

He drew back his hands, then threw them forward at the wall, feeling the power wash over him like a whirlwind. Masonry cracked, and blocks of stone began to fly through the air.

He had done this before, at the Tomb of the Lost King, but he was more practiced now. It was easier, almost joyful, as the stones ripped away under the force of his will, swooping through the air with the grace of playful birds, only to stack themselves neatly against the sidewalls of the passage ahead.

The found themselves looking into a great chamber of worship, with low, marble prayer benches before which the worshipers could kneel, and a great altar, flanked by flaming brass braziers and topped by a massive gold statue of Ibis, holding the moon overhead in his open hand.

Then Anok noticed one other thing: a golden-haired woman dressed in pale blue silk, who cowered against the base of the altar, caught by surprise. "There!" he shouted. "A priestess."

"Capture her! I need her unharmed!"

The soldiers fanned out, running up the middle and sides of the chamber. She tried to elude them, and was halfway into a hidden doorway behind the altar when one of guardians grabbed her and pulled her back. As he did, the door swung shut. Closing with a click, it vanished into the seemingly seamless wall.

Ramsa Aál ran up to the door, swept his hands over the smooth wall, then slammed his fist against it in frustration. He turned to the priestess. "How does this open?"

She struggled vainly against the two guards holding her arms. Her hair was ironically the color of sunlight, and fell in curls around her shoulders. Anok judged her to be older than he by a number of years, but still very beautiful. She wore a silver crest of the moon around her slender neck and a thin band of silver around her forehead. Though he had never seen her before, there was something strangely familiar about her face.

She glared at them, fire in her eyes. "I will never tell you!"

"Where are the others?"

"Long gone, escaping through caves that you will never find. Only the hired soldiers were left behind, and I, to protect the temple should you survive."

Ramsa Aál laughed. "One priestess to protect against an army? Are the worshipers of Ibis fools as well?"

She scowled. "I would have prevailed, if not for"—she glared at Anok—"his foul sorcery!"

Ramsa Aál laughed again. "But you did not prevail!" He leaned closer, taking her chin in his hand, forcing her face up so he could look into her eyes. "Now, where is the Scale of Set?"

She looked uneasy but did not shy from his gaze. "I know not of what you speak. Nothing with the taint of Set would ever be kept here!"

"Oh, you know. Some call them the Golden Scales." He reached under his robe, pulling out the chain to show her the medallion hanging there.

She gasped as she saw it.

"Oh." He laughed. "You know. Now tell me!"

"Never!"

Ramsa Aál licked his lips. "I has been too long since I enjoyed sacrificed a beautiful woman to Set—by slow torture."

He glanced up at the platform over their heads and the stairways to either side leading to the top. He looked back at her and smiled. "How would you like to be tortured to death on the altar of your own, false god?"

She growled and tried unsuccessfully to tear herself from the soldier's grasp.

"Take her," said Ramsa Aál, and they began to drag her up the stairs, as the priest drew up his ceremonial dagger and held it up, admiring how the flames reflected from its polished blade.

Anok felt his heart quicken in anticipation of the sacrifice.

Ramsa Aál walked past him and began to climb the stairs.

Follow! Observe the sacrifice! Taste the blood!

No!

The voices in his head were not his own. He had let the Mark of Set free of its cage, and now rather than his controlling it, it controlled him.

He heard the struggles above, as the priestess was drawn out on the altar.

Blood! Sweet blood!

No! Stop it! This is wrong!

In his mind, he flashed on the image of the priestess, as Ramsa Aál had lifted her face up and looked into her—

Eyes! His blood suddenly felt as cold as the spell of the frozen death.

He sought out the Band of Neska with his mind, sought its firm purchase, and with one, supreme, effort, shoved the Mark of Set out of his mind, screaming, back into its dark hiding place.

Eyes! Those eyes! His father's eyes! His *sister's* eyes!

He had found her, and any moment now, Ramsa Aál would begin flaying the skin from her flesh and the living flesh from her bones!

18

FRANTICALLY, ANOK TRIED to think of some way to save his sister. Certainly nothing he could say or do would dissuade Ramsa Aál. The only thing that would defer him would be to give him the thing he wanted most.

Briefly he flirted with the idea of presenting his own Scale of Set, announcing that he had "found it" somewhere. But it was possible Ramsa Aál's mystic senses could identify the three seemingly identical Scales individually. Or perhaps this was somehow simply a plan to get him to turn over his own hidden Scale. In any case, once Ramsa Aál had his Scale, Anok lost all leverage against the priest.

It was even possible Ramsa Aál would still torture her, looking for information on the location of the third scale. Or perhaps he would then feel free to kill her, and Anok would need to strike a deal.

As those thoughts rushed through his head, his eye fell on the front of the altar, where a decorative row of circular, silver medallions were set into the stone, representing the phases of the moon. At the center of the altar, below the rest, a lone circle of humble iron appeared, slightly larger than the rest.

He rushed over to examine it. It was identical to his father's medallion, where his own Scale of Set lay hidden. He pressed his palm against it, twisted, and felt it turn.

It had taken him years to discover accidentally the pattern of precise left and right twists that opened the medallion's hidden latch, but he had spent countless idle hours examining the medallion, opening and closing it.

Now he applied this pattern to the altar's seal, with practiced skill.

He heard his sister cry in pain.

There was a click, and a hidden panel cut into stone fell open. Inside, a cluttered assortment of religious objects, obviously hidden in haste, and among them, a *glitter of gold!*

Like Ramsa Aál's, this Scale hung from a chain of gold. He snatched it, held it over his head in triumph. "Master, I have found it!"

Ramsa Aál instantly appeared, looking down over the edge of the altar, his eyes wide, the tip of his dagger dripping blood. He smiled as he looked down. "Well done, acolyte! You have found a vital key to our greatest plan!"

He vanished, and Anok could hear him climbing to his feet, walking down the stair on the far side of the altar. As he did, Anok looked at the other objects in the compartment. There were small fertility idols, jewelry representing symbols of Ibis, and the phases of the moon, scrolls that were obviously holy texts, and—*a simple medallion of iron!* Anok snatched up the iron medallion and shoved it in his shoulder bag just a moment before Ramsa Aál appeared.

Anok glanced around. There were many guardians about, but most of them had their attention focused on the top of the altar. If any were watching him, they would have no context to understand the significance of the small theft. If it was not silver or gold or crusted in gems, it would appear to them to be worthless.

Ramsa Aál stepped up to him and took the Scale of Set. He seemed not to notice Anok's deception, his interest only in the Scale itself. He held it up to the light, then looked over at Anok, as though suddenly noticing that he was there, a strange, intoxicated look in his eyes.

"My pupil, we are very, very close to the dawn of a new age. You cannot imagine the power that will soon be ours." He looked up and shouted to the two guardians on top of the altar. "Bring down the priestess. I now have another purpose for her."

She was led down the stairs, her right hand bleeding slightly. *Thankfully, he had just only begun!*

Ramsa Aál stepped up to her and examined the moon amulet around her neck. "A High Priestess of Ibis will be very useful in our plans.

TRUE TO HIS sister's word, hours of searching by the guardians found none of the escape tunnels, only several more death traps. The latter were found in the most unpleasant way possible, and eventually Ramsa Aál was forced to call off the search.

"Doubtless," he said, "they are long gone, into the desert, or to caves in the hill. Still, we can ensure they never return to this place again."

After stripping the temple of any valuables and desecrating all its relics, statues, and shrines, Ramsa Aál had all the water bags and barrels filled. Then the corpses and dead animals were gathered and thrown down the well, fouling the waters.

Finally, every loose item that could be taken from the town, every box, barrel, awning, stick of furniture, and loose board was thrown down after them, doused with lamp oil, and set afire.

Only a few of the better buildings near the center of town were spared. These became the temporary quarters of the occupying force. As darkness fell, the surviving guardians gathered around the well to celebrate with plundered food and drink, and to sing grim songs of war for the dead.

Anok took advantage of the time to slip away from Ramsa Aál and the surviving acolytes and enter the house where his sister was being held. He found a pair of guards watching the windowless storage room where she was imprisoned, unhappy to be missing the festivities.

As he entered, he produced two jugs of wine he had pilfered from the gathering at the well. "I wish to speak with the prisoner alone. Enjoy your wine and wait outside. I will watch her, and in any case, she will not be able to get past you."

The guardians looked doubtful. "You doubt my authority? I am Kamanwati, the fist of Ramsa Aál!" He narrowed his eyes. "Would you rather have mouths full of wine, or your tongues turned to sand?"

Their eyes went wide, and their manner immediately became apologetic. "Of course, my lord! We appreciate the gift, and will wait outside until you summon us!"

He waited until they were outside to go to the door of the makeshift prison. He hesitated, feeling a strange tightness in his chest. That he was about to be reunited with his lost sister was only part of the reason. She was a symbol of his quest for answers and of his lost past. She might tell him even more, but for the moment she brought only questions.

Parath claimed that he had no sister, and at last he knew, with complete certainty, that the god's statement was false. Parath might have lied, but it seemed somehow that he simply did not know. How could that be? Had Anok's father hidden her existence from the god he served, and if so, why? Or was this only the beginning of the lost god's deception?

Steeling his resolve, he knocked before unlocking the door and looking cautiously inside. The prisoner had at least been provided with a lamp and cot, on which his sister—how strange that word suddenly seemed—sat.

She looked up at him, her eyes filled with piercing hatred.

He could hardly blame her for that. As for himself, he felt—*disappointed*. What had expected when he finally found his sister? That she could greet him lovingly, throwing her arms around her long-lost sibling?

No, it wasn't about how she was reacting. It was about him. He had expected—something. A sense of connection. A sense of fulfillment—*completion*.

But there was none of that.

She was just a stranger, with every reason to despise him. If he turned his back on her, she might kill him, never knowing the connection between them.

Yet he could not help but feel sympathy for her. Her blue silk robes were dirty and torn, spattered with blood in places. Her most holy place had been invaded, pillaged, defiled, and ruined. And the Scale of Set, the object she had stayed behind to protect, had been taken by her most bitter enemy.

How must she feel now, and what could he possibly say or do to ease that?

He reached into his bag and took out a cloth-wrapped bundle. "I brought you food. Perhaps they have given you something, but this is doubtless better." He reached into his bag again and took out a corked bottle. "I also have water, among the last from your well, I fear."

He noticed that she still clutched her injured hand. He put down the bottle, looked down at his own dirtied robes, and found a relatively clean spot near the hem, from which he tore a strip of cloth.

He uncorked the bottle, put one end over the opening, and briefly turned it over to wet the cloth. He stepped forward and pointed at her hand. "Let me see that."

She frowned, clearly confused and puzzled, but let him take the hand with only a little resistance. He dabbed away the blood, and examined the wound. It was a shallow cut across the palm, intended to cause pain rather than damage. "It is not serious," he said. "The priest was stopped in time. You have no idea what he would have done to you."

She frowned. "I have every idea." She held up the palm for him to see. "The first step of torture is to show the victim their own blood. The next is to cause pain. The next is to cause agony. The next is to destroy, as slowly as possible, their body, their mind, their dignity, and every shred of hope. I have seen what the worshipers of Set do to my people!"

He licked his dry lips and did not meet her eyes. Instead, he gently took her hand again and used the strip of cloth to bind her wound.

The instant he was through, she snatched her hand back. "Why are you doing this, snake-lover?"

He wondered if he should tell her. He wondered if she would even believe him. Ultimately, he took the coward's way out. "I have my reasons to attend your comfort." He glanced at the door reflexively, cautious that they might be overheard. "I want to help you."

She laughed harshly. "Help me? Likely this is just more clever torture. Build up my hopes, then dash them with violence and cruelty!"

He looked at those strangely familiar eyes, and knew what he had to do. "I'm going to help you escape."

She shook her head in confusion. "Why would you do that?"

He looked into her eyes. This chance might never come again. There were things he had to know. "What is your name?"

She hesitated, then seeing no harm in it, answered. "Paniwi."

He smiled slightly. "That is a good name. I am called Anok Wati, but once, I had another name. I was called Sekhemar. Does that name mean anything to you?"

She shook her head, and from the lack of recognition in her eyes, he was sure she was being truthful. There were many things he could tell her, but she might not believe.

There was one thing he could show her she could not help but believe. He removed the iron medallion he had found in the altar from his bag, pressed it between his palms, and with a few skillful twists snapped it open.

Her eyes went wide with shock as he showed her the empty inner compartment. "How did you know?"

He handed her the medallion, then removed its twin from under his robe. "This was given to me by your father." He hesitated, the words hanging in his throat. "*My* father."

Her eyes went wide with shock.

"He gave it to me, and with his dying breath told me to take it to my sister. A sister I never knew I had and, perhaps until this day, never really believed existed. Yet you are real."

She stared at the medallion, clearly wanting to ask the next question, and unsure if she could trust him enough even to ask.

He took the medallion between his palms and quickly opened it as he had the other. He turned it so that she could see the Golden Scale nestled within.

She glanced at it, in an instant pleased and alarmed. She snapped the medallion shut. She looked around furtively. "Do they know? Does the priest know?"

"I have hidden it from him. I do not serve him, though it appears that I do. I am no friend of Set or his cult. I seek only to do them harm."

Anger flashed in her eyes. "Then why did you use your magics to lead them into my temple? They why did you deliver to them my Golden Scale?"

He frowned at her. *Ungrateful!* "To save your life! It was the only way! I did not know you would be here, did not know you were my sister until I looked into your eyes and saw my father looking back!"

She frowned and sighed. "I would have died gladly to protect the Golden Scales from the Cult of Set. Yet I can see you meant well, and at least he only has one of the three."

Anok looked away nervously. "Truth be told, he has two."

"What!"

"It was sold to him by pirates some months back. I do not know where they got it."

"It is said the third Scale was thrown into the sea ages ago to keep it from a demon. Perhaps it washed up on some beach, or some creature of the depths found it and brought it back to the world of men. Set must not have the third Scale. You said our father told you to give me the Scale. Help me escape, and I will take it far from here, where Set's minions will never get it."

She tried to take the Scale, but he would not let it go. "No! I will help you escape, but you must leave the Scale with me. I have been able to mask the Scale from his mystic senses, but if you leave with it, he will know, and he will call forth every army of Stygia and every magic at his disposal to track you down. If you leave empty-handed, you will have a chance to escape, and perhaps I will be able to give it to you some other time."

"If you protect the Scale, then you must come with me!"

He shook his head. "Such treachery would not be allowed. I fear he would hunt me down, and you as well. Then he would have the third Scale anyway. But if I stay here, I will thwart his plans and scatter the three Scales so they cannot be used again."

She leaned back against the wall and drew up her knees to her chest. "If I cannot take the Scale, then I cannot go. It is my sacred duty to protect it with my life."

"You must go! I may not be able to protect you!"

"That changes nothing. I must take that risk to guard the Scale."

"I could guard it better without you."

"I doubt that. But we will see what we will see."

She is stubborn and willful! But he couldn't help but smile. *Perhaps she really is my sister.*

19

TEFERI LOOKED UP from his reading as Fallon entered the front door of the villa. From the rips in her clothing, the bruises on her arms, and scratches on her cheek and forehead, she'd been in another bar fight. From the smug grin on her face, she'd won.

He chose not to comment on the bruises. Since swearing off strong drink, she'd gotten much of her old confidence back, and he did not want to make her self-conscious of the fact. She had confided in him that when the urges became too strong, she would enter a tavern, order water, wait for the inevitable insult or comment, and promptly trounce the offender. It was, he had to admit, an interesting tactic, though word was getting around Kheshatta, and uninformed targets were getting harder to find.

So, instead, he greeted her casually. "Welcome home. There is fresh bread and fruit in the pantry."

"I ate at the Boar's Head not two hours ago. I heard gossip."

He pushed his scroll aside. "Then what news, sister?"

"Some of the metalworkers were eating there. It seems their task is done, and they have been released. They spoke Iranistani, and so did not fear being overheard." She grinned. "Fortunately, the tongue is not unknown to me."

Teferi leaned back in his chair. "Few are, it seems." He admired her Cimmerian gift for picking up language. He had heard a story that King Conan could curse in every language ever known to man, though as with most tales of the barbarian king, there was always some doubt.

She continued. "They talked much of 'the cursed metal.' It seems the man we saw killed was not the only one, and they were glad to be done with the job, despite the princely sum they were paid. None of them saw all of what they were building, nor did they know its purpose. But from the shape of the parts, they speculated that it was armor for a dragon or some great beast."

He frowned. "A beast? Not a man?"

"I am almost sure that is what they said. The words are not the same, but a beast, or an unnatural monster, or a great creature of some kind."

"Can the priests of Set intend to bring forth some great demon to do their bidding?" He noticed suddenly that she seemed not to be listening, but that she was smiling at him. "What?"

"You called me 'sister'?"

He was genuinely surprised. "I did?"

"You did."

He felt flushed, then chuckled. "Perhaps I am reminded of the old days on the dangerous streets of Odji, united with my companions in deed and purpose. Truly I thought those days were over."

"I am honored."

He chuckled again. "Well you should be." He stood, and as he did, noticed the blood-colored light of the setting sun streaming over the wall into the garden. "It will be time to begin the vigil soon." He picked up the Kotabanzi from the table where he had left it. "Let us go guard our friend's dreams."

THEY LEFT THE gutted remains of Nafri in flames. Paniwi
was led on a black mare captured in the town, her hands
tied. She kept her eyes directly ahead, not willing to look
back until the carnage was lost to the horizon.

Anok wanted to comfort her, but he could barely talk
to her without drawing attention to himself, and he supposed his words would bring her little peace. After all,
this was as much his fault as anyone's. Without his aid,
Ramsa Aál might have failed in his quest, and certainly
he would have had more difficulty penetrating the hidden
temple of Ibis.

They traveled with the full remaining complement of soldiers for a day before dividing ranks. While the mass of soldiers returned to Kheshatta with their plunder, a few of the
higher-ranking guardians, Anok, Ramsa Aál, and their prisoner, veered onto an even narrower, less-used road that
branched and branched again, finally leading deep into a
narrow desert canyon. To Anok's surprise, Ramsa Aál had
Paniwi blindfolded as they left the main trail. He wondered
what secret they meant to keep from her.

The canyon trail wound on and on, sometimes so narrow that the horses could barely pass. At last, after half a
day's ride, they came to an ancient temple, hewn from the
naked stone of the canyon wall.

Two great columns flanked the door, each entwined
with a huge stone serpent, their heads looking out from the
top. Over the door was a statue of Set, ten times as tall as a
man. In appearance, it was somewhat like the one on the
temple at Khemi, except the face was more snakelike, even
less human. Scales covered his exposed arms and legs, rep-
tilian claws on his hands and feet.

In the middle of the steps stood a great slab of stone,
which had clearly fallen from somewhere high in the
canyon. It was speared deep into the steps, and the exposed
part stood at an angle, leaning away from the temple, but
still higher than a man's head.

More guardians, priests, and others from the temple awaited them, and clearly they were preparing for some ceremony on the steps of the temple. A wooden platform had been placed on the steps flanking the slab of stone, and torches on tall brass poles had been erected to keep away the gloom that would doubtless come early in this deep, sunless place.

As they arrived, servants came to take the horses, and Paniwi's blindfold was removed. The first thing she looked upon was the great statue, and she looked at it with dread.

Ramsa Aál laughed. "Behold, Priestess of Ibis, the first temple of Set, where it is said our god first birthed forth from his serpent's den, far under the world. Behold the home of your god's most hated enemy, where today this one"—he clapped his hand on Anok's shoulder—"will become a priest of our mighty god!"

Anok did not know what disturbed him most, the news of the impending ceremony, Ramsa Aál's lies about his loyalty to Set, or the look of anger and disappointment in Paniwi's eyes.

They walked toward the temple. Anok was so distracted, he did not notice a huge snake coiled on a boulder until he was almost upon it. Disturbed, it rose, spreading a wide hood, its mouth opening to reveal dripping fangs.

Ramsa Aál showed no fear, walking up to the great snake, as long as two men were tall, and holding his open hand up before its face. Likely enthralled by the two Scales of Set he wore, the creature did not attack, but rather followed his hand in an eerie dance as Ramsa Aál waved it back and forth.

The snake was unlike anything Anok had ever seen, larger than any cobra, its scales iridescent in red, black, and yellow, like some of the greater Sons of Set, the holy constrictor snakes of the cult.

"Only here," explained Ramsa Aál, "in this holy place, do the native cobras of Stygia and the holy Sons of Set interbreed. These snakes are unique in all the world, able to kill by deadly poison or crushing coil. There are none more deadly or rare." He made a gesture, and the snake withdrew its hood and calmly slithered away. "Beautiful, are they not?"

Paniwi said nothing, but Anok was close enough to see her shudder. She was led away by a pair of guards, and Ramsa Aál led Anok away to a tent set up near the temple, to prepare for the ceremony.

He had expected robes, but although the other priests and acolytes were clothed in long robes of scarlet and gold, he was clad in only a red kilt and gold ceremonial jewelry, a wide belt, bands around his biceps and wrists, a band of gold around his head, and ornate sandals secured with golden serpents that curled around his ankles.

To his displeasure, he had no choice but to remove his father's medallion. The tent was a simple shelter with no floor, and left alone for a moment, he lifted a flat stone to find a hiding place. As he did, a squirming fistful of baby serpents, like the crossbreeds that he had seen earlier, hissed up at him.

With care, he placed the medallion in their little nest, even as he used a bit of its magic to calm them. "Care for this, little ones. I will be back for it."

As he waited he was able to examine the temple more closely. It became obvious why the ceremony was being held on the temple steps. Through the great front door, he could see that the interior of the temple had long ago collapsed. One look revealed only a jumble of boulders and broken stone columns that left a relatively small opening in the middle, like a cave.

As the participants waited, the guardians and servants gathered before the steps to watch. He saw Paniwi there, a look of disgust and disappointment on her face.

The ceremony began just after nightfall, as several guardians began to pound out a rhythm on large kettledrums. The priests assembled in rows flanking the platform and began to chant in old Stygian, keeping time with the drums:

> *Set, oh god of dark power*
> *We praise thee and thy works*
> *We praise thee and thy works*
> *We offer you this, our servant*
> *Enter him into your work!*

Two guardians in ceremonial armor and long crimson sashes stepped up and led Anok toward the stone slab. As they stepped around it, he saw for the first time the metal hooks that had been set into the stone, and that they matched grooves on the armbands he had been given. Before he could resist or protest, he was lifted and hung by the wrists on the slab. He struggled, but his own weight held the bands down on the hooks, and they were far enough apart that he could not use leverage against one to lift himself off the other.

Again, they chanted:

> *Set, oh god of dark power*
> *We offer you this, our servant*
> *May you shape his soul to do your work*
> *Give him the gift of corruption*
> *That he may wield dark power in your name!*

Far within the depths of the temple, something large stirred. He could hear large stones scraping against each other as it began to move.

He struggled again, looking for some way to free himself. Again they chanted:

> *Set, oh god of dark power*
> *We offer you this, our servant*
> *That he may become your servant*
> *Bring forth your sacred son*
> *That he may receive the gift of venom!*

Within the darkness of the temple, he could dimly see something move. Then two eyes appeared, big as soup bowls, the color of molten copper. A great, red tongue flicked out. The head appeared, wider than a man's shoulder, the scales glittering in firelight, three colors: the black of night, the yellow of gold, the red of blood.

A length of body, easily ten paces long, thrust itself out of the passage, barely wide enough for its passing. It reared up, the cold, flicking tongue tasted the air, metallic eyes scanned those assembled, as a man might study a banquet table.

Then its attention seemed to center on Anok. Hungry eyes focused on him, the slits of its pupils narrowing. Its wide slash of a mouth parted just a little.

It hissed, and Anok could not help but shudder. Desperate, he tried to call on the Mark of Set, but something about the ornate gold band around his wrist blocked it. Or perhaps it was simply that its power would not work against Set himself. It did not matter. He was helpless!

Then Ramsa Aál stepped away from the other priests and put himself between Anok and the great snake. He threw back his hood, and held his arms aloft. "Great Son of Set! Great son of Stygia! Hear me!"

The snake's head suddenly shot down, so quickly that Anok thought it would swallow Ramsa Aál in one gulp, and even the priests around him gasped.

Instead, it stopped, its scale-covered muzzle but a few feet from the priest's face.

Of course! With the two Scales of Set, his command of the great serpent would be almost absolute. "Oh, Son of Set, know this, our servant. Until this day he has been called Anok Wati, 'I am rebel.' Now, I give him a new name in your service, Anok Kamanwati, 'I am dark rebel.' May it please you!"

Ramsa Aál stepped to one side, turned half-toward Anok, and swept his arm toward him.

The great snake undulated forward, the head dropping to loom, looking down on Anok, the eyes intent and unblinking. The mouth opened more fully, the fangs, twice the length of Anok's hand, slowly unfolding from its upper jaw, glittering yellow drops of venom at their tips.

It drew back and plunged down, the tips of the fangs stabbing into the flesh on either side of his neck, just above the collarbones. He screamed as the venom filled him like liquid fire.

He was dead.

He was dead.

He was dead.

He wanted desperately to call on the Mark of Set to heal him.

It called back, through the veil of pain. "Set me free! Let us become one, in Set's name. Come to me Kamanwati! Let us be as one!"

That was it! That was the purpose of the ceremony! To force him to surrender to the Mark of Set!

I will die first!

But he did not want to die.

Help me!

I will help you, Kamanwati!

No!

The voices in his head all mixed together. He no longer knew which one was his own, which was the Mark of Set.

Help me!

Only I can help you!

But there was one other. He fought against the killing venom no more.

He let it take him.

Down into darkness.

There was no one here to help him.

There was help only in—

Dreams—

20

THE MAGIC OF the Kotabanzi swept Teferi up out of his body, and into the dreamworld. He strode across the globe, each step carrying him half a day's ride through the surface of the world, the clouds stirring like fog around his feet.

Distance had no meaning. Time had no meaning. The world was a dark void, and he could not find what he sought. *Anok, where are you?*

"Help me!" The voice was small, and far away, but it was unquestionably his friend.

It echoed through the fog. He followed those echoes, faster than any horse, faster than any eagle, the air screaming with his passage. "Brother, I am coming!"

With each step, his aspect changed, the paint of battle appearing on his face and body, the feathered headdress of the warrior, his spear on one hand, his bow in the other, his arrows upon his back. He was Zimwi-msaka now, warrior-born, scourge of the darkness. "Brother! I come!"

He burst onto a plain, to see Anok bound to a slab of stone, hanging lifeless, his head down, two streaks of blood running down his chest.

"Brother! What have they done to you!"

Even in the dreamworld, Anok was all but lifeless.

But something else was alive here.

Something evil.

He looked to the shifting clouds of mist, sometimes taking the form, for just a moment, of rocks, or trees, or mountains, before drifting away with some tiny breeze.

Something moved.

He saw a long, serpentine form. A great snake, changing as it moved, into smoke, then back again. It looked at him. "He is mine!"

Teferi stood his ground, holding up his spear. Lightning danced around the point like blue fire. "Never!"

"Then my poison will kill him. Then he will die, and you will die with his dream!"

"I will not let that happen." He thrust the spear toward the serpent without throwing it. A bolt of lightning lanced out, striking its coils.

The snake fell, writhed, turned briefly into smoke, then was whole again. "He is mine. He is *ours*!" With that last word, one voice somehow became two.

A strange mist began to flow from under the bracelet that bound Anok's left wrist. It flowed swiftly to the snake, flowing into it, joining with it, making it stronger, giving it more substance. "He will not die! He is ours! Come to us, Kamanwati!"

Anok's body began to turn to mist, and bit by bit, it was drawn into the body of the serpent. As it was, the snake began to change, changing into the shape and size of a man.

It was Anok.

It was not Anok.

He wore the scarlet robes and golden yoke of a priest of Set. A veil of scarlet was drawn across the lower half of his face, and his eyes were slitted, like those of a serpent.

"Anok!"

"Anok is dead! I am Kamanwati, son of the serpent, and I have no more use for you." He gestured, and a bolt of green fire swept out and smashed into Teferi like a wave.

He shook it off, as a dog shakes off water. "And I am Teferi, son of Kush, Zimwi-msaka. Your magic cannot harm me!"

The thing that called itself Kamanwati began to laugh. A cold, hollow laugh that made Teferi shudder. It reached for its swords, drawing forth long, curved blades that glittered in the pale light. "Then it will be two swords against none, and still you will die!"

Reluctantly, Teferi reached for his bow. Still, a ghost, a pale shadow of Anok hung on the slab. Which was his friend? What if both were? What would happen if he mortally wounded this monster?

It stepped toward him, blades dancing though the air. He had no choice.

He let fly his arrow.

Kamanwati flicked it away with his swords.

He fired again.

Again it was flicked away.

Kamanwati laughed. "Even here, nothing can best steel but steel and Zimwi-msaka do not fight with swords!"

Teferi suddenly realized that it was right. Sabé had warned him there were weaknesses in his magical immunity. Perhaps it could not protect him from some spell that simply kept him in the form he had chosen for himself. Through some trickery of Kamanwati, he was trapped in the aspect of the Zimwi-msaka, and the sword was not among their traditional weapons. Though he had used a sword most of his life, he could not wield one here.

But I know one who can!

FALLON WATCHED TENSELY as Teferi knelt before the fire. He did not move, and his eyes were closed, but she could sense something was wrong. Even in the chill of night, she could see beads of sweat on his body and face, glittering in the moonlight. His face was frozen in a scowl, and beneath his eyelids, she could see his eyes moving rapidly, frantically, as though looking for something unseen.

She leaned closer, could hear his rapid breathing, even the pounding of his heart. Closer she leaned.

Then he spoke, and her whole body jerked with surprise, her hand already on the hilt of her sword.

"Fallon!" His eyes remained closed, but his arm suddenly thrust out toward her. "If you would aid Anok, give me your arm!"

She hesitated. What madness was this? Anok was far in the desert, likely many days ride from here. How could she help him?

"Fallon!"

She was confused, but her instincts told her what to do. She put out her arm and clasped Teferi's forearm. His powerful fingers closed tightly around her arm, and it was as though he yanked her a thousand miles in an instant—

FALLON APPEARED BETWEEN Teferi and Kamanwati, instinctively fending off his attack with her sword. Teferi noted that, like him, she had adopted a warrior aspect, heavy Cimmerian clothing and armor made of leather and fur replacing the lighter Stygian garments she had more recently adopted.

Immediately compensating for his second sword, she drew a long knife from a belt scabbard. Kamanwati continued his attack, and with fierce determination she fought back.

"Fight woman! Fight with all your heart, for we battle for Anok's soul!"

Teferi looked at the rock slab, where the barest outline of Anok still hung, still and lifeless, wisps of its substance still being snatched away to become part of Kamanwati.

Fallon's bravery had bought him time, but what could he do? Though she was a fierce warrior, this demon in human form fought with all of Anok's skill, even more strength, and ten times his ferocity. They had once called him the "two-bladed devil," and now he truly was.

Steel struck steel.

Blades flashed.

The clatter of swords echoed through the shifting fog.

The sudden, horrible ripping of flesh.

A gash appeared on Fallon's arm, but she did not hesitate, did not falter. She roared her challenge and pressed the attack. Each step she pressed Kamanwati back was a triumph.

Yet Teferi could see that her opponent was only biding his time.

She will lose. Even if I had my sword, we might not win. The only person who could defeat Kamanwati was—

Sabé had told him to trust his instincts. Now they told him what he must do.

He turned to the phantom form hanging on the slab. "Brother, if you need substance, if you need strength, take mine!"

He plunged his hand into Anok's chest, felt his hand turn to smoke to be draw into the pale outline of his form, felt his very existence being drawn from his body. He felt himself fade until he was little more than an observer floating over the battle, unable to intervene or even speak. Had he made a terrible mistake?

FALLON HAD NEVER fought such an opponent. There might have been some as strong, but none so fierce, none so skilled, none so relentless.

Every stroke of her sword was met and parried. Every move countered. His twin blades flashed through the air so rapidly they seemed almost invisible. They surrounded her like a cloud of danger, closing in from all sides.

Pain! A cut across her cheek!

This foe did not seek the killing blow. He carved away at her, like a man whittling a stick. If this kept up, she would bleed to death, still fighting.

Yet . . .

Could there be a better way for a Cimmerian to die?

"Have at me, demon," she roared at him, "I will not yield!"

Kamanwati laughed. "Then you will die!"

"Step away from the woman, pretender! Step away and face your true foe!"

Fallon dared not turn to see whence the voice came, dared not take her eyes from the monster trying to kill her. But she knew the voice, though it was both familiar and strange.

"Step away!"

To her amazement, Kamanwati fended off one last attack, and did just that.

She stepped back as well, wiping blood from her mouth. She glanced at the newcomer. "Anok!"

And yet, *not Anok.* It was an Anok, younger than she had ever seen him, smooth-faced, thin and boyish, yet with eyes that were already old with experience. He wore dirt and rags in equal quantity. He held in his hands two humble and mismatched swords.

Yet there was no fear in his eyes. Only the righteous anger of the just.

She had once heard the story of how young Anok had rescued the whore's daughter Sheriti from bandits in an alley. From that, the legend of the "two-bladed devil" had been born. From that had come the Ravens, and all that followed. Could this be *that* Anok?

Kamanwati raised his swords, threw back his head, and laughed. "You are no foe! You are but a boy!"

Young Anok sneered. "I am more than that! I am what I choose to be! I am my father's son!" He glanced at Fallon. "Beautiful one, share with me your good heart. *For like you, I will not yield!*"

She felt something wet on her cheek, not blood, but a tear. "My heart is ever yours, brave warrior, my sword ever yours, my faith ever true. Do now what you must."

She stepped back, for she sensed now that this was not her fight, that she had already given all she could to save her love. Now she could only watch, and hope.

Young Anok raised his right sword in salute, then charged forward at Kamanwati, blades slicing through the air.

He seemed no match for his larger opponent, but he did not hesitate, and when they met, steel clashed with steel as they had never before.

Four swords moved like lightning, glints of steel surrounding them like a swarm of bees, the clanging and scraping of metal filling the air like terrible music.

Smaller though Anok was, they seemed evenly matched. Faster and faster the blades moved, till they were just a blur. Not even Cimmerian senses could follow them.

Still there was no end to it. Neither combatant could touch the other. No blood was drawn. Yet *something* was happening!

With each blow, Anok seemed to get larger, his face becoming more angular, the muscles of his arms beginning to bulge. Before her eyes, Anok the boy was again becoming Anok the man.

"Anok," she gasped in wonder. "My Anok has returned!"

And in the demon's eyes, there was something new as well. There was no boastful arrogance. There was only *fear.*

Back he pushed the demon. Back. Still their blades were matched, but not their force of will. Back he pushed it.

Until—

One moment of weakness. One opening. Anok jabbed forward with his right sword, plunging it deep into the center of Kamanwati's belly.

The demon screamed, then seemed to fall apart, into a flock of black things whose wings pounded the air, as they flew away into the fog.

Anok turned to face her. He smiled at her, saluted her with his sword, then turned to face his other self, still imprisoned on the stone slab.

As he did, he turned to smoke and was drawn back into the imprisoned form, which again took on substance and the aspect of a man. He looked up at her, and she felt herself falling.

TEFERI GASPED IN shock. His eyes flew open. He tumbled forward onto his knees, the Kotabanzi still in his hand. Before him, the fire still burned high, and as he looked up, he saw that the moon had not moved. It seemed like mere minutes had passed, perhaps only seconds.

He looked up at Fallon. She could barely stand. Red welts marked her arms, body, and face. Blood ran from her nose, and tears from her eyes. She looked at him with unbelieving eyes.

"Oh," he said, "it was real. That was as near to death as I ever care to be. Yet I fear it will not be the last time."

ANOK'S EYES OPENED, and he found himself hanging on the rock slab, the real one this time, still facing the great snake.

All eyes were on him, and he stared back at the huge serpent, stared until it had to turn away.

Satisfied, he strained against the bands of metal that bound him, with muscle both physical and otherwise. There was a loud report, then another, as the bands shattered, and he dropped to the platform below.

He gestured, and the great snake seemed to sense its master. It turned and swiftly crawled back into its hidden lair.

Ramsa Aál stepped toward him, eyes wide and hopeful. "Kamanwati?"

Anok looked at him, then nodded. "Yes."

But that was not what he was thinking.

Call me what you will, defiler. I will yet be the death of you!

21

TWO DAYS LATER, Teferi and Fallon sat in Sabé's parlor, telling him in detail of their dream battle with Anok's other aspect, Kamanwati. They had reported the events to him soon after they happened, but only briefly, as they wished to keep vigil when Anok returned to the world of dreams.

It did not happen. Not that day. Not that night. And while they had come away from their encounter hopeful of Anok's redemption, it had turned to dark concern.

So, it came as a complete surprise when Anok came through Sabé's front door, wearing the bloodred robes and golden yoke of a priest of Set.

Teferi sprang from his chair. His first instinct was to greet his friend joyously, but he thought better of it and reached for his sword.

Anok raised his hand, then, realizing it could be taken as a threat coming from a wizard, quickly put it behind his back. "That is not necessary, old friend. Despite my sinister finery, I remain myself, and as well as can be expected."

"It is true," said Sabé. "If he had been consumed by the Mark of Set, he would no longer be welcome here and likely would have never made it past my door alive." He leaned back in his chair. "Considering all that has happened, I had prepared myself for *any* eventuality."

Anok nodded. "You are wise, as always, Sabé."

Hearing this, Fallon ran to him and embraced him with an unbridled warmth that she would not have shown, at least not with others watching, even a week earlier.

He returned her ardor, and they held each other with a desperate intensity that spoke less of passion than of some deeper emotion. Something had transpired between them during the dream encounter that Teferi did not entirely understand, but things were clearly different between them. Teferi found himself smiling.

He waited patiently until the two lovers could tear themselves apart, then clasped his friend's arm. "Brother, we were worried. For two days I have tried to reach your dreams, without success."

"For two days, I have not slept. I am still—adjusting to what has happened to me. I do not even know if I *can* sleep anymore. It is very strange."

"Sleep will return to you," said Sabé. "You are not so different from your old self as it now seems."

He looked into Fallon's eyes. "Perhaps, in some ways, I am more like my old self than I have been in a long time. But I fear our troubles are far from over." He pulled out a chair and sat in it wearily. Despite his earlier pronouncement, Teferi wondered if he would suddenly fall asleep sitting up. "Many things have happened. Ramsa Aál now has the second Scale of Set, which had been kept in a secret temple of Ibis. He needs only the one that I carry to complete his schemes, whatever they be."

"Then," said Teferi, "we should destroy it, at once! Chase the mysteries of your past all you wish, but to keep it is to invite disaster."

Sabé shook his head. "The Scales of Set are said to be nearly eternal. They cannot be destroyed by any force of man. Forged together in magical fire, they can only be destroyed together as well."

Anok hung his head. "In any case, those two things, the secrets of my past and the fate of the third Scale are more deeply intertwined than you know, Teferi. I have found my long-lost sister."

Teferi's eyes widened. "What?"

Fallon smiled. "Anok! I am happy for you."

He frowned and shook his head. "It was a difficult reunion, a complicated reunion. My sister is a priestess of Ibis, whose duty it was to protect their Scale of Set. It was by my hand that the Scale was delivered to Ramsa Aál." He saw the look on their faces. "It was the only way to save her from torture. She is their prisoner, and now that she has seen me anointed as a priest of Set, I do not know if she will even trust me if I try to help her. In any case, she cares little for her own life. She is sworn to her duty regarding the Scale, as am I."

Fallon shook her head. "I do not understand."

He removed his father's medallion from under his robe. "My father entrusted this to me, not so that I could keep it, but so that I could give it to my sister. Until I can do that in safety, I cannot part with it."

Teferi could not help his frustration. He turned and walked away till he stopped, standing, staring into a corner. "This is madness."

"Whatever. I do not believe it will last long. All of Ramsa Aál's preparations are done. We leave for Luxur the morning after tomorrow to prepare for a great ceremony. Teferi, Fallon, if you wish to accompany me, I suggest you go pack whatever you value. I do not think we will return here again."

Teferi turned, shocked. "So soon?"

Anok laughed. "You complain at everything, brother. Soon, either the plot will be foiled and my sister will be freed, or I suspect little will matter."

"Then," said Teferi, "we should go make preparations, and you, brother, should rest."

He nodded. "Perhaps you are right." He looked at Sabé. "Scholar, you have been our friend and guide. I will miss your counsel and wisdom."

Sabé sniffed. "You will not miss it at all, for I intend to travel with you."

Anok looked surprised. "What?"

Sabé shrugged. "Whatever remaining purpose I have in my life, it is invested in your destiny, young friends. I cannot but see it through to the end. In any case, I have not seen the fabulous pyramids and temples of Luxur since I was a boy, and though I will not see them again, I would walk its streets once more and wash my feet in the waters of the mighty Styx one more time before I pass into oblivion."

Anok was silent.

"Ramsa Aál will eagerly allow me along if he thinks it might lead him to even one of my tiniest secrets. In any case, I will make my own passage if I must. You cannot stop me."

Anok considered and nodded. "We would welcome your wisdom in our dark time, great sage. The peril is great, but if I am right, there is no safety here, or anywhere."

"Then it is done. I will prepare to close this house. I must ensure that its secrets are safe, for eternity if need be. But before you go, I have one last thing for you. A gift, a reminder that you walk the narrow path between good and evil, and my faith that you will ever find its way."

He walked to a cupboard, opened the door, and removed two long bundles wrapped in oilcloth. He brought them over and placed them on the table. He took aside the smaller of the bundles and carefully unwrapped it.

Inside was a beautiful sword of moderate length. The guard and pommel were layered in gold and ornately sculpted with mystic symbols in an ancient tongue. At the top of the handle, where it joined the guard, was an eye inlaid with ivory and jade and, in the center of the pupil, a glittering black gem.

Anok picked it up, feeling the heft of it. The blade was exceptionally fine steel, the grain of the metal marbled in a

way only a few swordsmiths in the world could match. He
knew it would be strong, and hold a razor's edge. It fit well
in his hand, and was nearly the same length as his current
blades.

He looked back at Sabé. "This is a beautiful sword. I
can hardly accept such a gift."

"If it makes you feel better, it has a defect. This ancient
blade that was long ago entrusted to me is called the Sword
of Wisdom. Once it had great mystic powers, not the least
of which was that it could guide its wielder's hand to the
weakest spot of any enemy. But that magic is long since
faded, and not easily restored. Still, it is a fine and beautiful
sword." He unwrapped the second bundle, and brought forth
another sword. Unlike the Sword of Wisdom, the hilt and
guard were steel and very plain. The blade was fine, but un-
adorned in any way. "I had this sword made. It is the best
that can be made in Kheshatta, which is far from the best in
the world, but it is a decent blade. And though it looks different, in terms of weight and balance, it is the exact twin
of the other."

Also in the bundle was a pair of scabbards with a harness to wear them across the back, as was Anok's custom.
He hefted the second blade, comparing the weight and balance. They were a strange, mismatched pair, and yet the
contrast somehow seemed right to Anok. "Thank you,
Sabé. They are very fine indeed."

Anok glanced at Teferi and Fallon. "You go ahead. I
would speak with Sabé alone for just a moment, but I will
catch up."

Teferi nodded, and he and Fallon headed out into the
street.

ANOK WATCHED HIS friends go, then turned back to
Sabé, who sat with a knowing expression on his face.

"Do not worry," said Sabé, "you have them fooled."

"But not you, wise one. I was sure you would not be
deceived."

"I have been where you are, young warrior. I have stood at the edge of the pit and gazed down into the flames."

"They believe that I have come through the ceremony of priesthood unchanged, redeemed from evil. But to save myself from the venom, I had to surrender to the Mark of Set as I never have before. I have unleashed something very dark within my own soul, old one. Call it Kamanwati. Call it a demon. I know it is part of my self." He looked after his friends. "I do not wish to deceive them, but they can never understand what I have seen."

Sabé nodded. "All men have in them a capacity for ultimate evil. But most men deny it, or refuse to see it. You are different, only in that you have seen your beast face-to-face. You know the dark heart of man, as do I."

Anok shook his head. "How do you bear it?"

"Day by day, young warrior. Day by day. As must you."

22

WHEN ANOK ARRIVED at the temple in Kheshatta to begin his journey to Luxur, there was good news and bad. The good news was that Ramsa Aál and his entourage had already departed, leaving by fast chariots the previous day, and Anok would not have to suffer the priest's scrutiny during his journey.

The bad news was that the priest had taken his prisoner, Anok's sister, with him.

Anok took some comfort in the fact that Ramsa Aál seemed now to hold little interest in his sister, other than as a means to some greater end. He doubted she would be tortured or molested until it was time for her final role in Ramsa Aál's schemes, whatever they might be.

Though Luxur was north of Kheshatta, the quickest route, for those who would afford it, was to travel west to the Bakhr River, one of the Styx's few major tributaries. It was this route by which Anok and his companions traveled.

The Bakhr was, this far upstream, little more than a wide, muddy stream populated by crocodiles, and the four traveled first by small boat. As they continued, the stream became wider, if no less muddy. They stayed the nights at a series of small inns built along the banks for river travelers. Finally, after being portaged around a large waterfall, they transferred to a larger craft, a raft propelled by poles. This had accommodations aboard, though they were little more than tents on deck. Finally, at the Styx itself, they boarded a huge barge already loaded with passengers. Most of their fellow travelers were from Set, Pteion, and other points east, and nearly all seemed bound for Luxur.

Anok immediately noticed that most of the passengers wore the white robes of elders of Set, the wealthy elite of the cult, who tried desperately to buy the favor of their god. He found this curious.

Though Luxur was the most visible symbol of religious and political power in Stygia, in truth, its importance was minor in most respects. The royal palace was there, but King Ctesphon was said to be little more than a puppet of Thoth-Amon and the High Priests of Set. And though the ancient city was famed for its spectacular pyramids and devotion to the ideals of Set, Khemi was, in fact, the center of the cult's power, although other sites were considered more holy.

Finally, Anok took one of the elders, a short, balding merchant who seemed flattered to be approached by a priest of Set, and asked him where they were all going.

The merchant seemed surprised. "You are a priest of Set? How can you not know?"

Anok remained coy. "My companions and I have just returned from a long journey into a wilderness of nonbelievers, a mission for Thoth-Amon himself. I have not yet taken counsel with my superiors and am anxious to learn the news."

The merchant led Anok to a quiet spot near the railing and looked around carefully, to see who might be listening. "This is not for the ears of nonbelievers, or even for common followers of the cult. We elders have been invited only because of our—*special* station."

"I see," said Anok, trying to keep a diplomatic tone.

The priests never missed an opportunity to pander to the egos of the elders, especially if they thought it might cause them to empty their purses more thoroughly. Generally, the strategy was successful.

"There is to be a ceremony at the Great Pyramid of Set, where we will witness the coming of a living embodiment of our lord Set! All who witness this shall be granted great favor with our god and enjoy great wealth in life and great joy in the afterlife. It is a great day indeed!"

"Indeed," said Anok, trying to seem excited.

He was actually more fearful than excited. From all he had learned, he suspected that the event was not to be a ceremony to Set at all, but rather one to profane him, to steal his power. What purpose could the presence of Set's elder worshipers serve?

Later that day, they arrived in Luxur itself. Their first sight of the city was the Great Pyramid of Set, which, rather than appearing over the horizon, seemed simply to loom out of the sky's haze, like a mountain seen from afar.

Indeed, though there were many pyramids on the edge of the city, King Ctesphon's nearly complete monument being the latest, and though many were more elegant than the angular, step-sided Pyramid of Set, none was larger.

He had never been there before, but Anok was familiar with it, as there were many paintings and drawings of the pyramid adorning the walls of the two temples where he had served.

While the other pyramids were naught but tombs, the Pyramid of Set was a monument, and a temple, to the god Set. A grand entrance at its base was said to lead to many holy chambers in its interior.

Flanking the entrance were two staircases, leading to a landing above the entrance, and from this, a single wide staircase leading to the truncated top. There, at the peak of the pyramid, was a small temple unto itself, a flat roof supported by stone columns, sheltering an altar.

As their barge veered from the main channel of the river into one of the many wide canals built to bring stones for the pyramids through the city, the ziggurat loomed as a backdrop to everything. Dominating the east end of the city was the palace itself, a once-grand building marked by high walls and narrow towers of weathered yellow stone.

To the west was the black palace of Thoth-Amon, smaller than the royal palace but far more ornate and of recent construction. Even now, the distant figures of workmen building a new wing could be seen. Anok suspected the construction would never stop until it was both the largest, and the most spectacular, palace in all of Stygia.

The city itself was unlike anything Anok had ever seen. While the architecture was no less oppressive than that of any Stygian city, there were influences from the Hyborian kingdoms and the other northern lands as well. Though there were great houses and lesser ones, there were no slums here, nor anything like them. Other than the palace itself, all the buildings were neat and in good repair.

There was a sense of precision and order that he found almost disturbing, like the walled inner city of Khemi, only more so.

This is Set's city.

It was, he was sure, a city built not in the name of a cult but in the name of a *god*.

The barge was rowed in next to a long dock near the city's center, where another, similar barge was already unloading passengers and cargo. As they stepped onto the dock, they were barked at by a grim-faced official, whose tone softened as soon as he saw Anok's priestly robes.

"Apologies, lord, but your servants"—he pointed at Teferi and Fallon, ignoring Sabé, who was more obviously of Stygian blood—"will need to wear these in the city. Those without the true blood of Stygia are not often welcomed here; without these"—he produced numbered clay tags on leather neck cords—"as identification, they could otherwise be arrested and executed on sight." He looked Fallon up and down. "It would be a shame to see your property damaged."

She sneered at the official, but Anok gestured for her to remain quiet. "As I come here in the service of our lord Thoth-Amon, I would hope not. It would be an equal shame to see your 'true Stygian blood' spilled into the River Styx to feed the fishes."

The official turned pale and signaled frantically for a scribe to come over and record their names and information. "I shall include an annotation that these servants are in special service to our lord and see that the information is circulated to the guardians that patrol the streets. They will not be harmed."

"See that they are not."

As the official wandered away to tend his business with other visitors, Teferi leaned close to Anok. "What a fine city you have brought us to. I am so happy to be here!"

"Truth," said Anok, "I was looking forward to seeing the legendary city of kings. Now, I will only be glad when we can leave."

As they waited for coaches to take them to the city's temple, Anok found a quiet spot where he could recount to them his conversation with the merchant, and his puzzlement over the purpose in bringing them here.

"Perhaps," suggested Sabé, "there is some truth to the story told to the cult elders, but only a little. Perhaps we are here to witness the coming of a living servant to something, though perhaps not Set. Perhaps some demon, instead. If the wealthy and powerful could be somehow tricked into following this false god as their own . . ."

But Anok was skeptical. It seemed an elaborate ruse for such a small return, and certainly not the world-changing event they had been expecting.

Just then, Anok noticed a number of prisoners being led from the hold of the next barge. They were a dirty and tattered lot, who strained under the weight of their chains and heavy wooden yokes. Yet his eyes were drawn to the rags of their clothing, which were of fine silk, and rich colors could often be seen beneath the grime.

These were not simple slaves.

He excused himself from his companions and slipped closer. The prisoners were both men and women, mostly older, with an air of authority that translated to indignation at their current fate. Though guardians goaded them along with spears, they showed more outrage than fear. Clearly, these were people used to wielding authority.

And though their clothing was, in each case, strange to him, something of their cut and ornamentation made him think they might be priests of priestesses of gods other than Set. One man, a Shemite, bald, with a distinctive scar across his head, was familiar to him. He had seen the man many times, sitting on the steps of a Temple of Bel in Kheshatta.

This could not be coincidence. These holy men and women had been kidnapped and brought here to Luxur by Ramsa Aál. They, too, were part of his plan.

Then one of the prisoners, a smaller man, turned toward him, and he instantly recognized the face: Dao-Shuang, master of the Jade Spider Cult!

23

THE TEMPLE OF Set at Luxur was hardly a temple at all. Most of the ceremonies to Set in the city were held at the Great Pyramid.

Rather than a conventional temple, there was a large, walled compound containing many buildings. Several larger buildings served administrative functions and provided safe-keeping for sacred artifacts and the cult's treasure troves. There were also barracks for the many guardian troops posted there, stables for the animals, and blocks of apart-ments for servants and acolytes of low rank.

But most of the buildings were individual villas, some modest cottages, others nearly palaces in themselves, where priests and high-ranking acolytes lived and kept their private chambers.

Anok and his friends were quickly assigned to a medium-sized, two-story villa near the gate, and the ser-vant who showed them the way pointed out Ramsa Aál's villa, one of the largest in the compound.

Their new home was larger than their villa in Khe-shatta, and far more luxuriously furnished. Looking at the expensive but ill-matched furnishings, Anok suspected they had been selected, possibly at random, from among the tribute brought by hopeful elders.

In both size and design, it reminded Anok of his father's house in Khemi, and the thought of this brought him pain. He seemed no closer to finding his father's killer.

He blamed the Cult of Set, but he was increasingly convinced that the cult could never be looked at as a whole. It was a group of greedy and powerful men who served their god in name only, and the lust for power in fact. To damage the cult was a worthy goal, but it would never give him the satisfaction of knowing he had found his father's true murderer and served him justice.

Their belongings were delivered shortly, and they began, uneasily, to settle in. None acted as though they expected to be staying long, except Sabé, who promptly found the largest and most comfortable room and claimed it for his own. "Age has its privileges." He immediately began unpacking the boxes of scrolls he had brought with him.

Anok noted that none of them appeared to be from his trove of magical lore. Those in languages that Anok could even barely understand were plays, poetry, chronicles of heroes long dead, and a few of erotic nature. "You act as though you are on holiday, Sabé."

"The situation is dire, and my time on this world may be short. Should I not enjoy what days or hours I have left?"

Anok said nothing more. Perhaps Sabé was right. He and Teferi had been polite enough to quietly ignore that Anok and Fallon had casually moved into the same sleeping quarters.

He looked again at Sabé. "Do you know more than you are saying of what will happen?"

"You mean, do I have some prophecy, some foresight of the future? I have little belief in the former, and alas, never any talent for the latter. I have only hazy guesses.

"But Ramsa Aál has brought to this place persons who in turn have power over others. Are not the followers of most gods in turn required to bow down before their priests

and priestesses? Are not many of the elders of the Cult of
Set in turn bosses of men, kings of merchant empires,
leaders in their towns, or masters of many servants and
slaves? If a spell could be made to bind any one of them,
would its power not be increased a hundredfold? A thousand? Or more?

"Would a man who dares usurp the followers of his own
gods hesitate to do that same for others as well?"

"The Scales can do this?"

"The three Scales have not been together since before
history. I cannot say they can, but unfortunately, I cannot
deny it either."

The mention of the other priests, priestesses, and cult
masters made Anok think again of his sister. "I saw that the
other prisoners were taken to a small stockade near the
barracks, but my sister was not there. I suspect Ramsa Aál
is keeping her in his villa, but I cannot rest until I am sure."

Sabé grimaced. "It is too dangerous a thing simply to
satisfy your curiosity. There is little you can do for her now."

"Who said that was my only purpose? I will snoop,
eavesdrop if I can. Perhaps I can learn more of Ramsa
Aál's plan and how its many pieces fit together." He looked
out the window at the fading pink of the sky. "Night is
falling, and I must see what I can see."

AS ANOK MOVED through the darkness, he could smell
the dank water of the canals and night-blooming flowers in
the temple gardens. The stars were bright. There was no
moon, and the air was filled with the songs of countless
frogs, which doubtless thrived in the canals and ditches and
in the reed marshes that lined many areas of the river nearby.

Many lights were burning in the windows of Ramsa
Aál's villa, and Anok approached carefully. He was perhaps fifty paces away when he spotted the first guardian
standing watch outside. There would likely be more.

Reluctantly, he called on magic, the Walk of Shadows
spell, to hide himself from the guards. It was unlikely to

fool Ramsa Aál himself, or any priest of Set, but it should be sufficient to pass by any guardians if he was careful.

He cautiously moved around the back of the house, peering inside various windows. He only saw rich furnishings worthy of a palace, a few guards, and household servants going out their tasks. Finally, on a back corner, he spotted a shuttered window with light coming through the cracks.

As he approached and touched the shutters, he found them barred shut from the outside, a hopeful sign. He leaned close and peered through the crack.

Inside was a small room with a plain bed, a wooden chair, and a basin. Paniwi sat on the bed dressed in a simple white dress of silk. Her priestess robes hung on a hook on the door, cleaned and mended. Perhaps it was necessary to Ramsa Aál's spell that she wear them.

She looked sad, but unharmed. He studied her face, finding things that reminded him of his father, even of his own reflection. It was so strange, so sad, to have found each other this way.

I will find a way to fix this, sister. I will free you and make good my father's last wish.

He heard a door slam in the room above him and flattened himself against the wall. The window above was open, and he heard footsteps and a chair being moved.

Then he heard a voice, instantly known to him, one that sent a chill through his bones. *Thoth-Amon!*

"I am unhappy about this, priest. There can be no greater heresy against our god Set than what you plan, to steal his cult and his followers for your purposes."

"As you have done yourself, though more by cleverness than magic," the voice or Ramsa Aál answered. "You call on Set for power, as I do, but you serve him only as it serves your own interests. And what has it brought you? Dominion over a dry and fading land whose empire is long gone, whose time is long past? If we succeed, and now, how can we not, the world shall be at our feet. The followers of all gods shall be bound to follow our made-god, and in turn, he shall answer to us. Those few who do not follow some god of our thrall shall be crushed, or their priests brought and bound to the thrall of our god."

"I agreed to this mad plan only because if it fails, Set's wrath shall fall on *you,* and your minions, not I. Though I remain near, I will not be in attendance at your profane ceremony. Only if it succeeds will I come forth and take my rightful place on the throne of our new cult."

"It will succeed, my master."

"So you should hope, priest, as it is *your* life and soul that will be forfeit if it fails. Yet to even make the attempt, you still need the third Scale of Set. Where is it? You said you knew where it was!"

"The young heretic priest has it, of that I am confident."

"Your pet, Anok? I am unhappy about him. I should have killed him when I had the chance. He has so far been too effective in resisting the seductions of our cult. He never should have been allowed to come so far. Torture him, take the Scale, and be done with it."

"The three Scales must be kept apart until the critical moment. If I even knew exactly where all three were, it would attract the attention of dark and powerful forces, not to mention Parath himself. He *hungers* for the Scales, and for now, that is the only true power we hold over him. As for the heretic, fear not. Many, even I once, have joined the cult with other aims. But ultimately, all succumb to the sweet song of power. When the time comes, he will provide it to us and do so willingly, that he may share in its power."

"Then let him believe it shall be so. I don't care. But he is not to be trusted. When you have the last Scale, kill him at once."

24

ANOK SLEPT LITTLE that night.

Fearing detection by Thoth-Amon, he had left Ramsa Aál's villa soon after overhearing their conversation and without having talked to his sister. He would have liked to offer her at least some few words of reassurance that he would protect her, but the risk was too great.

Perhaps it was just as well, for the promise would likely have sounded as hollow to her as it did to him. He truly did not know what would happen or if any of them would survive.

In the morning, servants arrived at the villa to clean, make the beds, and prepare a lavish morning meal of fried river fish, elaborately seasoned rice dishes, fruit, and some strange meat that none of them immediately recognized. Anok watched the servants go about their business. They were efficient, unobtrusive, and strangely silent.

Smelling the food, he realized that he was very hungry, and the prospect of such a simple thing as sitting down to a meal with his friends offered him some small measure of cheer.

After filling his plate with more familiar items, Anok considered the bowl of fried meat. He removed a piece and sniffed it. The aroma was spicy and pleasing. He took a cautious bite, and satisfied, took a larger one. The finger-sized fried pieces looked vaguely like some kind of fowl, and tasted that way, as well. But the pieces were neither precisely legs nor wings.

The mystery was solved when Sabé picked up a piece and tasted it. He smiled in recognition as he chewed. "Ah! It has been far too long since I had frog legs!"

Teferi, who had been taking a cautious bite from one of the pieces, loudly spat it out on the table. "Frog!"

Fallon shrugged, sniffed a piece, tasted it, and added several more to her plate.

Anok laughed at Teferi. "Brother, in Odji, I often enough saw you eat *rat* when there was naught else to be had."

He looked indignant. "That was rat. Frogs are *unclean*!"

Despite his taunts, Anok passed on the frog legs, settling for a large slab of fish and a mound of aromatic rice filled with vegetables and spiced with jasmine.

As they were finishing the meal, a servant arrived and handed Anok a small scroll wrapped with ribbon. Inside was a note in Ramsa Aál's hand.

The servant was already turning to leave as Anok bid him wait. "Did Ramsa Aál give this to you personally?"

The servant only nodded.

"Is he still at the temple?"

The servant shook his head.

"Where did he go?"

The servant only frowned at him strangely.

"Speak, man? Even if you were instructed not to share such information, you can tell me that!"

The man's frown deepened.

Anok was suddenly aware that several other of the servants had stopped in their tasks and were staring at him as well.

The man opened his mouth and pointed.

He had no tongue. He made a little exhalation of air that could be barely called a noise, and Anok immediately knew it was more than that. The man's throat had been mutilated to preclude his speaking at all.

He looked around at the other servants, and knew it must be true of all of them.

"I am sorry," he said. "I did not know."

The four companions sat in silence as the table was cleared, and the servants disappeared as quickly and quietly as they had come.

"This," said Teferi, "is a terrible place. It does not look like a terrible place, and that merely makes it more terrible."

Anok looked again at the note. "I do not think we will be here long. I am to go to the Great Pyramid of Set tonight to attend an important ceremony."

"He does not have the third Scale," said Fallon. "This cannot be the spell that you all fear."

Sabé nodded thoughtfully. "But this is not a simple spell they plan to cast, and if this is as other plans conceived by Kaman Awi Urshé, it may be a plan of several steps. Tonight's could be the first."

"Well," said Anok, "I have the day then. I was unable to speak with my sister last night, but from what I overheard, Ramsa Aál has left to make preparations for the ceremony. If this first step does not involve the priests of other gods, then my sister may still be at his villa, and I may be able to contrive to speak with her now. There are things I must know, answers only she can give me."

Rather than proceeding directly to Ramsa Aál's villa, he strolled casually past the stockade. If the prisoners were gone, then likely his sister had been taken as well. He was relieved to see the little building still fully occupied.

The prisoners watched him through the barred windows and doors of the little brick building, as did a bored guard, who bowed his head in salute as Anok passed. Anok tried not to look overly interested in the prisoners, but it was hard not to stare at the ragged lot. He wished that he could talk to them, ask them if they knew why they were here, but he dared not. If there were answers, he supposed, he would have to get them from his sister.

As Anok rounded the corner of the building, he found himself looking into the face of Dao-Shuang, the Jade Spider master, who stared at him through a barred window.

As their eyes met, *something* happened. Anok found himself *elsewhere,* the hall of a great temple built in the Khitan style, with walls painted in red, white, and gold, and columns and beams covered with polished black lacquer.

Dao-Shuang was there as well, not as the miserable prisoner he had just seen, but strong, well, and dressed in his ceremonial finery, shimmering yellow silk robes embroidered with strange symbols, belted at the waist, and so long that they hid his feet and nearly brushed the floor. The long sleeves of the robes flared at the end, and long tails hung below each wrist. A small, round cap of the same shimmering silk perched on top of his head.

The sensation was familiar, and Anok realized it reminded him of when Thoth-Amon had engaged him in a War of Souls. Instantly, he was on alert for attack.

Dao-Shuang, or his avatar, held up a hand. "Have no fear, Anok Wati. This is no attack. They think me helpless, but though I am weak from their binding spells, there are still resources I can command."

"Do you know why they have brought you here?"

"I have had flashes of terrible foresight, of things that may yet come. I know that my cult is in grave danger, and it is beyond my power to help my people. All of the future hinges on you, and it is from the future I bring you this warning: To serve all gods, you must serve none."

The temple vanished, and Anok found himself again in the temple compound, looking at the stockade. Dao-Shuang looked at him, bowed his head, closing his eyes slowly as he did so, then looked at him once more and turned away, vanishing back into the prison.

A guardian stared at him curiously, and Anok continued on his way, lest he generate more suspicion. He circled the gardens as though out for a brisk stroll and headed back to-ward Ramsa Aál's villa.

Once again, he called on the Walk of Shadows spell and strolled past the house guards, who never even glanced in his direction. He walked up to the front of the house as though he had business there, stood looking in the open door for a moment, then walked along the front, peering in windows.

He saw servants, but no sign of Ramsa Aál himself. Satisfied that the priest was not at home, Anok found the shuttered window and carefully removed the bar holding it shut.

His sister was stretched out on the bed as he opened the shutters.

She sat up suddenly, and he signaled for her silence, climbing though the window and closing the shutters after him.

She sat on the edge of the bed and looked at him suspiciously.

He ignored her and focused his mind on the Walk of Shadow, extending the spell to her in such a way as to hide their speech from any potential listeners. He grunted at the effort. If the Walk of Shadows was a great expenditure of magic for little result, this spell was now far more than twice as hard.

He felt the influence of the Mark of Set, and his left hand clenched briefly without his volition. He ignored it and turned his attention to Paniwi.

"We may now talk undisturbed by your guards."

She glared at him. "Why did you come, *priest*?"

He felt suddenly self-conscious about his scarlet robes. "Despite what you have seen, I am still no true servant of Set."

"Do you serve Ibis then? Whom do you serve? Who is your god?"

He looked at her blankly. "Truly, I do not know. I thought I knew, thought I knew the god of my father, but now I find it is all a castle of lies. I need you to help me find who I am."

Her face softened, though suspicion remained. "Do you know so little of your own history? Did our father tell you nothing?"

He sighed. "Our father was killed when I was but a boy. I was cast out into the streets, fearful of his killers. I was forced to learn how to care for myself, even to trade the name of my birth for one I made up for myself."

He hesitated. It was surprisingly difficult to speak of these things. "My father revealed little of his true self to me. I thought him a simple merchant. I knew nothing of the Scale of Set, or of you. It was only in the last moments of his life that he gave me the medallion, and told me to seek you."

"So you have nothing from our father?"

"He was good to me. He passed me some of his wisdom, shared with me some of his strength, and taught me to fight well enough to survive. But of his greater secrets, nothing. I wonder now if he simply wanted to avoid burdening me with them, and if he had lived, if he would have, soon after, shared them with me as a mark of my manhood. But these answers, I will never know."

She frowned, mulling his words. "I will tell you what I know. We share a father, but as you may have guessed, not a mother.

"I was born in Nemedia, and my mother died in childbirth. When I was a baby, he gave me over to the temple of Ibis, to be raised as a priestess. But he did not forget me. Several times he came to visit me.

"On one of those visits, he told me that he had been forced to marry another woman, but that his heart still belonged to my mother, and my mother alone. Still later, he told me of you. Though there was no love for your mother, he loved you as his son and told me I should care for you as my brother."

"How did you take this news?"

She did not look at him. "I was angry. I felt betrayed. It was an honor to serve Ibis, but that my father had left me, and raised a stranger as his child—"

"My mother was Stygian, and her marriage to my father was one of convenience. He did not love her, until the end, when she died to protect me. I barely remember her. Only my father, and my father's house, until even those were taken from me."

"Then our lives have both been sad."

"Do you resent me still?"

She shook her head. "You are all I have left of my father. How can I?"

"And you are all I have left of mine. If only this could be our primary concern."

"But we have other duties, other promises," she said, "that come even before blood."

"That is why I am here. Your mission, your purpose, is clear. Mine is not. I must know, what god did our father serve?"

Her mouth opened and just hung there. She laughed. "You need ask?"

"I was told he served a lost god of Stygia called Parath."

She laughed again. "Who told you that? I have never heard of such a god. Your father served Ibis! He gave his life to Ibis. He gave his children to Ibis. What greater love can there be? He was the Keeper of the Golden Scale, as his father had been, and his father before him, and as you would have been, had fate not taken you down this strange path."

He shook his head in confusion. "You mean, my father wanted me to take the Scale to you, only so that you could return it to me as my legacy?"

She shrugged. "That may have been his intent. He knew if you came to me with the Scale, I would have taken both you and it to safety. I would have explained to you your legacy as Keeper of the Golden Scale, and you would have continued down that path."

"But now you wish to take the Scale I carry for yourself?"

She sighed. "Things are less clear now, Anok. You have placed your Golden Scale in great danger of falling to our enemies, and you have delivered my Scale to them already."

She was slow to continue. "After everything that has happened, I am not sure if you can be trusted with the Scale any longer."

Anger flared, and he felt the Mark of Set respond to it. With some difficulty, he centered himself, using the Band of Neska, and pushed the anger back into some dark corner of his mind. "I cannot see that anyone can be trusted with these Golden Scales. Why should I trust the temple of Ibis with one, much less two?"

Paniwi nodded. "Not even the temple of Ibis should have the third. Let Set keep it. It is as safe here as anywhere.

"Of all the gods that men worship, Ibis knows that power is not constant or permanent. The face of Ibis must fade to darkness before he can grace us with his glorious golden light, and even this will pass. Ibis can be trusted with two Scales, because he will not seek the third, and even those have always been kept far apart, one at a Temple of Ibis, and the other in secret by the Keeper."

"Then why are they in Stygia?"

"When I was still a small girl, agents of Set began to seek the Scales. They came very close to stealing the one in our temple, and the high priestess had a vision that the one place the followers of Set would not look for the Scales was in their own accursed land. One was taken to our secret temple there, which had remained safe for many generations, and I traveled with it. Our father took the second to Khemi, to the very heart of their cult."

"That," said Anok sarcastically, "did not work as well as your priestess predicted."

"Perhaps we do not understand the true meaning of the vision. Perhaps this was all meant to be."

"A wise friend of mine told me that he puts little faith in prophecy, and I am inclined to agree." He stood. "Do you still refuse to let me help you escape?"

"Not without the Golden Scales."

He shook his head. "Then we will see this play out. If this has all happened for some reason, then let us hope it is one we will like."

He climbed out the window, barred the shutters behind him, and was quickly gone.

A CHARIOT ARRIVED and took Anok to the pyramid at dusk.

When he got there, he found the base of the pyramid swarming with workers, guardians, acolytes, and priests. A large tent had been set up to hide the focus of their activities, but a crowd of elders and curious locals gathered, kept at some distance by a line of guardians, which parted to admit Anok's chariot.

As they passed through the crowd, he looked down and was surprised to see one person he recognized, Seti Aasi, Dejal's father, a rich merchant who had bought his son's way into acolyte training and unknowingly set him on the path to madness and death.

Anok quickly looked away and was relieved as they passed through the crowd and the guardians closed in behind them.

It was unlikely Seti Aasi knew Anok had killed his son in a magical duel. There had been no witnesses, and Anok had been less than precise even in his report to Ramsa Aál. In any case, the man was still a source of tribute, and so the priests had likely reported that his son had tragically, yet heroically, been killed in the noble service of Set.

Still, Anok had always intensely disliked the man, and wanted no contact, even if it were only the fawning attentions of an elder seeking favor in the cult.

As Anok approached the tent, he saw the long wagon Rami had described as having been made to transport the bones of Parath sitting empty nearby.

So, it is certain they intend to raise Parath.

That was confirmed as he stepped inside and was treated to a strange sight. Inside the tent were two long parallel tables, as though set for a great banquet. On one table lay the bones of Parath, and on the other, matching armor in the shape of a brass serpent, intricately articulated into individual plates to allow for the sinuous movement of a serpent.

Though the bulk had doubtless been extended by alloying it with more conventional metals, there could be no doubt this metallic shell had been forged from the melted metal of the Armor of Mocioun.

Each piece of the armor was individually bound to the table with tightly wound cords connected to hooks in the table. As he watched, he could see the brass serpent kink and shake as it struggled weakly against its bonds.

But even more strange was the transformation taking place. Starting at the tail, piece by piece, the armor was being disassembled.

Workers would first cut the cords holding one segment of the armor. It would be removed and reassembled around the skeleton of Parath. Smiths, equipped with a movable brazier, stood ready to hammer red-hot rivets, sparks arcing through the air, until each new piece was connected to the previous and again bound to the table with cords.

Anok watched in wonderment, as the brass serpent rapidly re-formed around the bones of Parath.

Parath had no skin, so they have made him one. But what of his flesh? What of his heart?

Seeing Anok, Ramsa Aál walked over, greeting him warmly.

Anok looked at him with a coldness he hoped the man could not detect.

You were plotting to kill me but last night, or have you forgotten?

But Ramsa Aál's mood was light, almost giddy, as he watched the many workers and craftsmen finish their task. Now, the back wall and far slant of the tent roof were being rolled back to expose the assembled Parath to the sun. Just beyond, he could see the entrance at the base of the pyramid, with its heavy columns supporting the landing above. If he leaned back, he could look up the long stair to the covered altar at the top.

The air was gritty with sand from the desert beyond, the great dunes always threatening to sweep around the bases of the pyramids, to swallow the narrow riverside greenbelt beyond.

"Are you not curious, priest, what it is we do here?"

"I can see," he said, "that you have made use of the Armor of Mocioun, which we claimed from the Tomb of the Lost King. But what purpose can there be in armoring the bones of some long-dead temple serpent?"

Ramsa Aál smiled coyly. "This is not one of the greater Sons of Set. This is something far older, and far more dangerous. These are the bones of Parath!"

Anok tried to look surprised. "An ancient god?"

Ramsa Aál look at him curiously. "God? No, but a powerful demon, an enemy of Ibis and—*others*."

So, he does not know of my connection to Parath! Perhaps as he plots to control the lost god, so the lost god plots against him as well!

Ramsa Aál continued. "Long banished, he will live again, in service of our cult, and our master Thoth-Amon."

Say it! And in service of yourself!

But he said nothing of the sort. Instead, he beckoned Anok and walked along the length of the brass serpent. "I hope you have remembered well the spells I taught you in Khemi."

Anok almost didn't hear him. As they walked along, he was looking at the skin of the brass serpent, which was covered with thin, overlapping plates cut in the shape of scales, scales that were, as they neared the front of the false beast, identical in both shape and size to the Scales of Set.

"Spells? Yes, I'm sure I remember them all."

"One in particular, the Ward of Anigmus?"

"The ward against demon fire? We studied it, but as acolytes we never had the power to carry it out, even in practice."

Ramsa Aál glanced down at Anok's wrist and the Mark of Set.

"Well, priest, you wield the power now, and our magic must work in unison or we will both die."

As they reached the head of the serpent, they found a priest of high rank waiting for them. Ramsa Aál introduced him as Buiku-Ra, High Priest of Luxur and his oldest friend.

Anok could hardly look at the man. He kept staring at the metal skull that had been made for Parath's bones, and the cold eyes of crystal that stared back at him blankly.

But Ramsa Aál remained focused on the task at hand. "Are you prepared with your spell, Buiku?"

The priest nodded. "The spell of summoning will bring forth the spirit of Parath to join his bones, but its completion will require a most potent blood sacrifice for its completion."

Ramsa Aál glanced casually at Anok. "Have no fear. I have prepared for this matter."

Anok's breath caught in his throat. Was *he* the sacrifice? He would be distracted by the warding spell, and his magical abilities, great as they were, would be fully engaged. Could he do all this and defend himself against Ramsa's knife as well?

"It is time," said Ramsa Aál. "Let us begin!"

25

HIGH PRIEST BUIKU-RA reached into a silk bag, and removed a handful of pungent magical herbs, dried and ground to small flakes. He tossed them into the mouth of the brass serpent and began an incantation. "Sacred messengers of the wind, bring forth from lands beyond, the spirit of the mighty one long exiled, back from the wilderness, into this great vessel."

Within the mouth of the serpent, a bluish fog began to appear, glowing weakly within its inner depths.

Anok saw, from the movement of Ramsa Aál's lips, that he was silently reciting his own spell.

He glanced at Anok. "Now, Anok! We must have the Ward of Anigmus!"

Anok held up his hands, ready to shape the forces he was about to unleash, and recited the words of the spell. They were written in an ancient tongue that he did not understand, but that made them no less effective.

Buiku looked at his friend. "Ramsa, we need the blood sacrifice soon, or the spell will fail!"

Visible as a slight distortion in the air, as though a bubble of some barely visible liquid surrounded them, energy projected out from Anok's hands. It required great concentration to shape and maintain the bubble, yet from the corner of his eye, he watched Ramsa Aál, still whispering his spell, reach for the sacrificial dagger at his belt. Anok tensed himself for the attack.

"Ramsa!" Buiku's voice was urgent.

Ramsa Aál paused his spell and smiled. "It is like old times, is it not, my friend?"

The he moved with blinding swiftness.

He uttered the final word of his spell as his blade slashed through the air, making flesh rip like ragged cloth.

A burst of orange flame appeared in the brass serpent's mouth. It seemed to ignite the blue fog and flashed explosively down the length of its body. Anok nearly lost control of the spell, which would have doomed them all.

But then his control was restored. He was able to look over and see the lifeblood of Buiku-Ra spurting from his sliced jugular vein, passing through the ward, which stopped only flame, and seemed to feed the strange fire that grew within. Ramsa Aál supported the High Priest, one hand holding the back of his robe, the other holding his head back to direct the weakening flow of blood. "I am sorry, Buiku, but the blood of a friend betrayed is a most powerful sacrifice indeed."

Within the brass serpent, the orange flames twisted and danced, almost like a living thing. Tongues of flame shot from the open mouth and smashed against his ward, shaking Anok as though someone had slammed into his body. Still, he was able to keep his focus, and they remained safe.

He felt Ramsa Aál's hand on his elbow, and he was led back away from the serpent. Finally, they stepped beyond the apparent range of the shooting flame, and he was able to drop the ward.

Anok saw now why the fabric of the tent had been rolled back. Even so, some of the poles and ropes were beginning to smoke and smolder, and wide-eyed servants stood by, waiting fearfully with buckets and jars of water to douse unwanted flames.

The brass serpent began to emit a strange hissing sound. Not the hissing of a snake, but a sound like steam escaping from a boiling pot with a tight-fitting lid. Behind the crystal eyes, a glowing, as from hot coals, appeared.

Though restrained by countless cords, a shudder passed down the length of the serpent. The long table itself twisted and bucked, its legs lifting from the ground in turn as the ripple passed down the body.

Then another spasm, more powerful. With a sound like a Khitan firework spell, the cords snapped rapidly, one after the other.

The brass serpent reared up, small puffs of steam escaping the joints in its body, its head above the level of the old canvas roof, the rear of the table collapsing under its weight.

Ramsa Aál stepped closer, his arms over his head, as though to make himself large enough to warrant the monster's attention. "Great Parath, it is I, your humble servant Ramsa Aál, who has delivered you back from your eternal exile!"

The snake looked down at him. "I *am* Parath! Behold me, and know fear!"

Anok just stood and watched as Ramsa Aál dropped to one knee and bowed his head before the false god. Then he stood and gestured toward the entrance of the pyramid. "Behold, Great Parath, the pyramid of your enemy, soon to be yours. Enter and await my coming, for tomorrow is the day of your ascension, and we must prepare!"

Parath looked at the entrance. "Yes! I will defile the pyramid of my hated enemy with my presence!" He seemed ready to move, but then looked down at the fallen and bloodied form of Buiku lying on the ground before him. He opened his mouth, and a wave of flame shot out to engulf the body.

"A funeral pyre for he who gave me his life." The great serpent began to move gracefully, but, with a soft clanking of moving plates and the low hiss of steam. "Let it never be said"—he crawled toward the darkness of the entry—"that Parath is not a generous god."

Anok watched it go in wonder. It was indeed the voice he knew as Parath, but there had been not a single word directed to him, not a single hint of recognition. Had he served his purpose? Was he now simply beneath the fallen god's notice, or had it forgotten him?

But as it crawled between the great pillars, Parath hesitated, stopped, and turned his head back.

For just a moment, Anok was sure that the glowing crystal eyes were fixed on him.

And in that moment, he felt a tugging. It was as though, for a moment, both will and ego had simply faded out, and he was directed by another force.

Then Parath turned and crawled into the shadow. Though he caught only a glimpse as it passed into darkness, Anok wondered—could a brass serpent smile?

ANOK HAD RETURNED home an hour after dusk, just as his companions were preparing to eat.

Now they sat quietly around the villa's dining table, the four of them. The evening meal was done, the table cleared, the servants gone. Around them candles burned low, and the frogs serenaded them loudly through every window. Anok had even spotted a tiny one, walking across the ceiling on sucker feet. He was gone from sight now, having found shelter in some crack or recess, but Anok could hear him still, his voice loudest of all.

"It is hard to believe," said Anok, finally. "It is—the end of the world."

Sabé made a sound of disgust. "You exaggerate. It is no such thing! The world *changes,* it does not end. Empires fall, mountains crumble, continents slide into the sea, but the world goes on."

"Your pardon, sage," said Teferi dryly, "but I do not care to be around when any of those things happens. When empires fall, people like us are crushed, and in great quantity."

"Then," said Sabé, "the empire must not fall."

Anok grunted unhappily. "You are saying, that to protect my friends, I must *aid* the Cult of Set?"

"Cults may be evil, gods may be evil, but without men, they are like Parath. Just dry bones in the desert. You must choose your greatest enemy, Anok Wati, and you must decide just what it is you wish to protect. The world is not your responsibility. What do you *care* about?"

Anok looked around the table at his friends. The world be damned. He cared about them, and yes, his sister as well, but as for the rest . . .

Yet from the kind of magic Ramsa Aál planned to unleash, there would be no escape. Not in Stygia. Not in Hyboria to the north, or the Dark Kingdoms to the south, or even across the Southern Sea.

"We will face this danger," he said. "We will face it, and we will thwart the plans of man and god, and we will leave this place, if we can, forever."

Fallon looked into his eyes. "What of your past, Anok? What of your father's killer?"

He drew a deep breath and let it out slowly. "If those things were not meant for me to know, then let them rest. I am prepared to leave them behind. Let them lie with my father in his grave, and I will accept this failure."

Sabé's mouth twisted into a curious expression, a smirk less than the aspect of a smile. "I did not tell you earlier, as I did not want it to influence your decision, but if you go to the temple tomorrow to face Parath and Ramsa Aál, the truth of your father's death will be revealed to you. No matter what else happens, for good or ill, of this thing I am certain. If you had chosen otherwise, that secret would have ever been closed to you."

There was a strange certainty in Sabé's voice that blotted

out any doubts Anok might have had in his words. "I thought, Sabé, that you did not believe in prophecy and that you had no gift of foresight."

"Just this once, in just this matter, I am certain. That is my gift to you. If you fail, you will not die in ignorance."

"That, then, is some small favor."

26

WITH THE MORNING meal, the servants delivered to
Anok a note from Ramsa Aál with instructions for the day.
He was summoned after breakfast to some gathering at the
temple gates. Anok could not imagine what this would be,
since the main ceremony, which the note called "the ceremony of joining," would be held at nightfall at the Pyramid
of Set. The name was sufficiently vague to offer little information. Who was joining what? *Perhaps,* he thought
grimly, *the joining of the three Scales.*

While eating they held a quick council, and a plan was
decided. Since the ceremony of joining was scheduled for
nightfall, Fallon and Teferi would circle around and approach the pyramid from the desert side after dark and attempt to scale the ziggurat from the back side.

"Given the prisoners, it appears there will be a sacrifice,
and that will likely take place at the altar on top of the
Pyramid of Set. It is also the place where it is most likely I
can disrupt the ceremony, but that is my concern. Do not
worry after me. Rescue my sister if you can, free the other

prisoners if you wish. If I do not come after you immediately, escape by the desert."

Teferi nodded. "This morning I will secure enough camels and provisions for the five of us to make our flight. If we must leave without you, we will leave a provisioned mount for your escape."

"For four," corrected Sabé. "I am too old and slow for such theatrics."

Fallon looked at him in shock. "Sabé, we cannot leave you here! I shudder to imagine what the Cult of Set might do to you in revenge for what we are about to do."

"I am old and slow, but I am not helpless. I will give you a few of my most precious things for safekeeping, then I will secure a boat passage to Kheshatta this afternoon. With all the travelers arriving, there are many empty boats leaving.

"Travel downstream is quite rapid, and I shall be well away before your treachery is known. When you are safe, you can send me word via any of the dealers of ancient books and scrolls in Khemi, if that is your wish. I am known to them all."

Anok nodded sadly. That would be the safest thing for the old scholar. It seemed a shame that he had come so far, for so little, but they had little control over events.

After breakfast Anok returned to his chambers to dress in his temple finery.

When he emerged a short time later and left the villa, he was surprised to find Fallon in front, brushing a great white camel.

He blinked in amazement, and Fallon grinned at him.

"Fenola! I thought you'd left her in Kheshatta!"

Fallon laughed. "I went to the camel station with the intent of selling her, but I could not bear it. Fortunately, our friend Havilah, the caravan master, and his sons were there. I was able to hire his youngest son, Moahavilah, to ride Fenola here by the quickest route possible." She looked up at the great animal with pride. "Fenola is the fastest camel in the desert, and they arrived this morning."

Anok looked around. "Is Moahavilah still here?" The young nomad had more than proven his courage and mettle when their caravan had been attacked by bandits on the way to Kheshatta, and Anok had grown to like and admire him.

"I saw him but briefly. As Sabé said, boat passage is easy to secure, and he is already on his way to meet his father and brothers in Khemi."

Anok shook his head in amazement as he walked away. Some things, some people, he thought he would never see or hear from again, and yet they reappeared.

It was good that there were such small pleasures on this dark and fearful day.

On his way to the gate, he passed the stockade, and saw the prisoners being escorted away toward the Great Pyramid. They seemed frightened, but they shuffled along beside their guards, on their way to meet their fate.

The gathering, such as it was, turned out to be mainly an entertainment for the elders, to increase their excitement for attending the actual ceremony later that evening. Anok could not figure why his presence was required, but he could hardly leave while under the watchful eyes of the local priests. Ramsa Aál was conspicuous in his absence. Anok had to wonder if it was make-work, or some kind of distraction.

Other than whipping the elders and locals into a frenzy of enthusiasm, the main function of the assembly was to introduce the newly promoted High Priest for Luxur. Anok heard amazingly few questions or comments about how this had happened, or what had become of the old High Priest. Assassination was not unknown, or even that unusual among the priesthood, but in Khemi it had always fueled lively gossip both inside and outside the temple. Not here.

Among the priests and acolytes he overheard or talked with, there was a strange mix of fear and anticipation in their voices. They all seemed to understand that something of huge consequence was about to happen, but they were too concerned about their own well-being and status to see much beyond that.

Though they did not speak directly of the sudden replacement of their High Priest, it was indirectly a topic of great concern. Regime changes often offered possibilities for promotion and advancement, and all were positioning themselves accordingly.

Overall, it was a strange and pointless experience. The elders were already excited, and responded to anyone wearing even an acolyte's robe. Any local and low-ranking priest could have presided over the ceremony with equal success. *This is not right.*

Thus, he returned to the villa after midday with a feeling of unease. As it turned out, his feelings were justified.

Teferi met him at the door. "Sabé is missing!"

Anok looked around, hoping they had misread the situation. Everything in the villa seemed neat and in order. "He said he was leaving for the docks. Perhaps he is already on a boat to safety."

"He gave me a bag of magical trinkets and some tablets, as he promised, but when I checked later, all his other belongings were still in his room."

Fallon entered through the back door. "And I was out front with Fenola all morning. I did not see him leave." She gestured at the door. "I have searched the grounds of the temple and did not find him or anyone who would admit to seeing him."

Anok walked up the stairs and checked Sabé's room. The others followed. "I see no sign of a struggle." He held out his hand, feeling the room with his mystic senses. He frowned. "There has been magic here recently, a spell of concealment, perhaps even the Walk of Shadows that I myself have used."

He turned to the others. "You were right to be worried. I think he was taken by Ramsa Aál or his agents. I was sent to this useless ceremony this morning to get me away from the villa."

Teferi frowned. "The spell might not have worked on me, but I was away buying camels and supplies."

"Or," suggested Anok, "it might have worked because it was not intended to harm you directly. Remember, Ramsa Aál knows you are Zimwi-msaka. He would have adjusted his plan accordingly."

Teferi frowned, a look of grim determination on his face. "We must find him."

Anok shook his head. "*I* must find him, and it will not be difficult. Ramsa Aál will have taken him to the pyramid, of that I am sure, perhaps for the specific purpose of ensuring I do not try to leave with the third Scale of Set."

"It is the Scale he wants," said Teferi. "Leave it with me."

"I will need the Scale to bargain for Sabé's life. We will continue with our original plan, only we will free Sabé and take him with us as well."

Fallon studied his face. "Something more is bothering you, Anok, I can tell."

"I was just thinking of what Sabé said last night. He spoke as though he'd had some vision or foresight of today's event. I think he knew this was going to happen. Perhaps that is why there was no struggle. He simply is fulfilling his own destiny."

Teferi spat on the floor in disgust. "There is no such thing. The future is not yet written!"

Anok sighed. "Until yesterday, Sabé believed the same."

WHEN ANOK ARRIVED at the Great Pyramid of Set, he found that both the tent and the long tables within were gone. Set in holes among the stones in the forecourt, and on either side of the stairway leading up to the altar, many oil lamps raised on metal stanchions had been positioned to illuminate this evening's ceremony.

There were many workers busy at preparations, and already there were a few elders milling about. Nothing about the scene suggested that it was a trap.

As Anok neared the pyramid, he realized that one of the waiting elders was Dejal's father. Again he tried to slip past, but there were few enough people there it was impossible to avoid being seen. He saw the look of recognition on Seti Aasi's face.

"Anok!" The man called after him. "Anok Wati!"

Anok walked quickly past, ignoring the man, and was soon at the entrance where several guardians stood watch. They ignored him until he asked about Ramsa Aál.

"The Priest of Needs is within the pyramid." The guardian helpfully provided directions. Apparently there were many passages within and under the structure, including an interior stair leading up to the altar.

As he traveled the pyramid's dark, stone corridors, he felt a strange tugging at his spirit, like the one he had felt when Parath had looked at him the night before. He had no doubt the false god was here somewhere, in one of the pyramid's hidden chambers. But it was Ramsa Aál he found, not the brass serpent. The priest was, as the guard had told him, meditating in a torchlit room whose walls were covered with pictograms of Set and his serpents.

He looked up as Anok entered, and smiled. "My pupil, you have come, as I knew you would." His smile faded. "The time for games is over. I need the third Scale, and I know you have it. Give it to me."

He tried to look innocent. "Master, what makes you think *I* have the third Scale of Set?"

"Because your friend Dejal swore that you did, and that if we brought you into the cult, seduced you with its power, he could obtain it from you. He was willing to wager his life on that fact."

He smiled sourly. "Unfortunately for him, that was a wager he lost. But I have always believed as he did, that you possessed the third Scale of Set. I had hoped Dejal was right on the other matter as well, that as you were welcomed into our cult, tasted the fruits of power and the aptitude for great sorcery that was already your natural gift, you would give it to us freely." His expression turned dire.

"I have no more time to wait for that." He held out his hand. "Give me the Scale!"

Anok stared at him. "No."

Ramsa Aál chuckled. "Then we will trade for it. Guards!"

A hidden panel opened in the wall behind him, and two guardians emerged, dragging the battered and bloody form of Sabé. He had clearly been beaten and tortured. They took him to the far wall of the room and chained him there.

The guardians then withdrew and stood alertly at Ramsa Aál's side.

"Your scholarly friend and I have spent an enjoyable morning together. I would have liked to have a talk, but he has been reluctant to keep up his end of the conversation. Not a wise decision for one so . . . fragile."

Sabé managed to lift his head, and laughed a weak, gurgling laugh. "I told him nothing, Anok. Do not deal with him."

"I will trade the third Scale for your elder friend's life. And if his life means as little to you as it apparently means to him, then I will have your Kushite servant and your barbarian whore arrested and brought here as well. Then we will see how you value *their* blood."

Anok still hesitated. He knew that Ramsa Aál planned to kill him once he had the Scale, and that in handing it over he would lose any leverage he had over the priest. But he could see that Sabé was badly injured. Whatever was to happen, it had to happen quickly.

He removed his father's medallion from under his robe, twisted it open, and presented the Scale to Ramsa Aál.

Ramsa Aál examined the scale. "Hidden in cold iron. I suspected it might be something that simple, but I did not need the Scale until now. In fact, having it would have complicated my dealings with Parath immensely." He glanced up at Anok. "I am grateful you have kept it safe for me."

Anok stepped back, raising his hands defensively. "I know well that you plan to kill me now that you have the Scale. You may find that task difficult. Take the Scale and leave Sabé and me alone. It will be much easier that way."

Ramsa Aál looked at him calmly and without fear. "A curious thing about the design of the pyramid. These rooms at the base of the structure, at the center, and the catacombs below, were once used to torture and imprison sorcerers. You see, magic works poorly here, if it all." The guardians drew their swords.

Anok laughed, drawing his own swords. "You think this is better for you?"

"Yes," said Ramsa Aál, "I believe it is." He casually slid his foot to one side, pressing a particular stone, which moved downward.

There was a click, and the floor opened under Anok, plunging him into darkness.

27

ANOK NICKED HIS thumb on the edge of his sword, and pulled a Jewel of the Moon from his bag. As the blood touched the stone, it immediately began to glow, revealing that he had landed on the sandy floor of a cavern running beneath the pyramid.

Fifteen feet above him, a light rectangle marked the trapdoor through which he had fallen. Ramsa Aál peered over the edge. "It's true, Thoth-Amon told me to kill you, but this is more amusing, and more fair. At least here, you have a chance of survival." He sat cross-legged at the edge of the opening and calmly began to thread the third Scale onto the chain with the other two.

"You can't use the three Scales," said Anok. "No mortal can do so and live."

"Oh," said the priest, "I'm sure I know more about the Scales of Set than you do. It's true I can't wield their full power and live, but I can carry them, and use them in a very limited way. It will be enough for my plan."

"You have thought of everything."

"Indeed. For instance, you are not alone down there in the darkness."

Anok thought he heard something move far down the cave, shuffling footsteps.

"You see," he continued, "I had my agents follow you when you traveled to the Tomb of Neska. After the tomb collapsed, they went into the rubble and found what was left of Dejal. I gave him to Kaman Awi for his surgeons and alchemists to play with. He was badly broken, but repairing him was such a challenge, they could not resist."

"Dejal is alive?"

The priest laughed. "He is no longer alive. But then, he isn't precisely *dead,* either!"

"Now," he said, standing, "I must go prepare for the ceremony. I will come back to check on you two later."

He stepped on a particular spot on the floor, and with a grinding noise the trapdoor swung shut.

The footsteps were closer now.

Anok picked his swords up from where they had fallen on the floor, putting the plain sword back in its scabbard, freeing one hand to hold the Jewel of the Moon. Anok held up the Jewel, straining his eyes into the darkness, the Sword of Wisdom at the ready.

He saw something move, a man-sized figure in a ragged acolyte's robe, hood pulled over its face, baggy sleeves hanging low at its side.

"Dejal? Is it you?"

He heard something like an angry sob. The figure tilted back its head so that the hood fell back.

It was not Dejal.

It was what was left of Dejal.

The eyes were those of his old companion, mad with rage and pain. But the face was a mutilated patchwork, stitched back together at odd angles, the skin patched with iridescent snakeskin. It opened its mouth, revealing countless needle-sharp teeth within.

Then it raised its arms, and the sleeves fell away—

In their final magical duel, Anok had caused the Rings of Neska on Dejal's fingers to explode, destroying his arms. Kaman Awi's surgeons apparently had found what they considered to be suitable replacements. They had grafted on the front parts of two great snakes, hybrids from the First Temple of Set, which writhed and hissed in anger.

"Anok," said the Dejal-thing, finally recognizing him. "Anok look what they have *done* to me!" Then the voice changed, filled with anger. "Look what *you* have done to me!"

It roared and charged at him, the snake arms whipping toward him, jaws snapping.

He dodged to one side, fending away one of the snake heads with his sword. As he did, the mouth opened, and a spray of stinging venom caught him across the face.

He cried out in pain, dropping the Jewel of the Moon, wiping the stinging fluid from his eyes with his sleeve. But so great was the agony, despite his many experiences with the venom, he could barely keep them open. In desperation, he called on the Mark of Set to heal him. It responded sluggishly, as though having been wakened from a deep slumber.

Still, it helped a little, and he opened his eyes just in time to see Dejal before him, a coiled arm striking at his neck.

His vision blurred, Anok swung his sword instinctively. The snake head was severed, sent flying into the darkness.

Dejal screamed, the headless arm suddenly coiling powerfully around Anok's waist, spewing him with warm blood, lifting his feet off the floor.

He still held his sword and desperately fended off the other arm's attacks. But his right eye had taken the brunt of the venom, and it left him with a blind spot on that side. Distracted as he was by the arm's repeated strikes, he never saw Dejal's biting attack, only felt the crocodile teeth as they clamped down on his shoulder with crushing force.

He screamed. Dejal had clamped down on him with the tenacity of a snapping turtle and could not be pulled free.

But Dejal was distracted as well. The undamaged arm, until now in constant motion, hovered before him for a moment, mouth open.

He thrust forward the Sword of Wisdom, deep into the serpent mouth and out the back of the head. It whipped away, yanking the sword from his hand.

He felt Dejal's body jerk in pain, but still his teeth dug into Anok's flesh. He reached for his dagger blindly, found it with his fingers, and, in one motion, pulled it and stabbed it deep into Dejal's back.

The Dejal creature stumbled back, bellowing in pain. He swung his less-damaged arm, Anok's sword still embedded in it, at him. Anok ducked, just as the point of the blade nearly found his neck.

He pulled his second sword, holding it in both hands, his damaged eyes seeking the shadowy form of Dejal. He saw the outline of his body. Unsure if he was striking at Dejal or his shadow, Anok drove his sword forward with all his strength.

There was a wet crunch, a sting in his gripping hands, as the sword plunged deep into flesh. Warm blood spattered him, drenching the Mark of Set, whose energies seems suddenly revitalized. Anok could feel it beginning to work at his bleeding shoulder, damaged eyes, and the blisters across his face.

The Dejal-creature stood there, looking down at the sword rammed through its body. Then it looked up at Anok. "Brother," it said, "it is like old times."

Then it fell back, the body lifeless, the arms still twitching weakly.

Even with such a rich blood sacrifice to feast on, the Mark of Set was weakening already. For that, Anok was grateful. The blood of a friend twice-betrayed was powerful and evil magic indeed, and keeping the Mark of Set in check would have been difficult otherwise.

He recovered his blades and staggered over to lean against the cool rock wall. Even with the healing magic, he hurt everywhere, especially his shoulder, and his vision was only now clearing.

He was still trapped in this cave, and his sister and Sabé were still prisoners in the pyramid above.

"Anok Wati!"

The voice came from above him, and he did not immediately recognize it, only that it was neither Ramsa Aál nor one of his friends. He was aware there was light coming from above as well, and he squinted upward.

At some point, the trapdoor had been reopened. It could have happened at any point during the fight, and it was doubtful he would have noticed.

He saw movement at the lip of the trap and a knotted rope tumbled down to hang a few paces away. He grabbed the rope, and slowly, painfully, was able to climb up it. As he neared the top, hands reached down and helped pull him the rest of the way.

As he rolled over onto the floor to lie on his back, he looked up and his eyes focused on a white robe. The figure turned away from him and looked down into the pit.

"Anok Wati," the voice was suddenly familiar, though he could not yet identify it, "look at what I have done."

The man turned away from the pit, and Anok saw his face clearly for the first time.

Seti Aasi! Dejal's father!

Anok reached for his dagger, but there was no anger in the man's voice. He seemed sad and broken. "Now his body is finally at rest, but my son was lost to me long ago. I thought for a while he might be restored to me, but I was mistaken." He shook his head. "My fault, all my fault."

His heart pounding, Anok jumped to his feet with renewed energy, grabbed the man, twisting his arm behind him and putting the point of his dagger to his throat.

Seta Aasi seemed genuinely terrified, no evil mastermind.

"What are you?" Anok growled. "Whom do you serve?"

"I am——" He swallowed, and seemed to force his voice to work. "I am only a loyal and humble worshiper of Set. It has always been so. I tried to gain the favor of the cult, of the priests like Ramsa Aál. I never suspected that the masters I served were—*heretics*—who would *betray* our god. I never understood."

Anok released him and pushed him away, quickly replacing the dagger in his hand with his sword.

"I only wanted to destroy the Ibis worshipers who rotted Khemi within. I took it on myself to kill them——"

"*You* killed my father!"

The man was childlike in his lack of guilt. He spoke as though he had killed only a few annoying flies. "They served Ibis. *I had no choice.*"

His face was a mask of confusion. "I never understood why the priests were so angry, never understood what your father had that they could want. They kept saying, 'the Scale, the Scale,' but it meant nothing to me. Then we learned you had escaped, and I was ordered to find you. I tricked my son into joining you, to gain your trust and aid you in coming to manhood."

"You killed my father before your masters found the Golden Scale they suspected my father kept. My father's death was for nothing more than your misguided faith in an empty god!"

There was more contempt than rage in his heart. It was as though his father had been killed by a falling stone: useless and without meaning.

But there *was* someone at fault.

Anok pointed into the pit. "Look at your son!"

The man complied sadly.

"Look on him, know what you have done, and let that be the last sight you see, before you begin your journey to the pits of fire!"

He drove his sword deep into the man's chest, twisting the blade to be certain the wound was mortal. Blood showered over him as he pulled the blade free.

Seta Aasi toppled like a felled tree and landed below

with a thud. Anok looked down, and saw him draped across his son's lifeless body.

"Now, at least, you are together, father and son. That is more than I shall ever be able to say."

He turned and walked away from the pit, fresh blood tingling as it ran down his left wrist.

He found the hidden switch Ramsa Aál had used and watched as the trapdoor swung shut.

28

SABÉ HUNG SO still in his chains that Anok thought he might already be dead. Only as he touched the old man's face did he stir and, with difficulty, lift his head.

Sabé smiled weakly. "Anok, is it you? I was just talking to Teferi. He is coming here, you know—"

Though his magic was weak, with considerable effort, Anok was able to release the locks on Sabé's chains. He lowered the old man to the floor and leaned him against the wall. Wet streaks of blood marked where he had slid down.

"Yes, Sabé, I know. I will take you to him, and you will be away from this evil place."

Sabé coughed weakly, and a pink froth appeared on his lips. He reached up and grabbed Anok's wrist, his fingers still surprisingly strong. "Anok, I did not tell you the full truth about the sword I gave you. It's magic is faded, yes, but the Sword of Wisdom can be restored—" He coughed. "It can be restored, only if it is bathed in the living heart blood of a wise and just man."

"What are you saying?"

He laughed. "Listen to my words, Anok! With my last breath I flatter myself! But I am already dead. You cannot save me. Let my death mean something."

"No! I will not do it."

"You don't have a choice, Anok. You will need the Sword of Wisdom's power. Neither of us has a choice. But, if you cannot kill me, then kill the serpent." He reached up and ripped away the cloth wrappings over his face, uncovering the cold, hateful eyes of a reptile.

"Heretic!" Sabé called, in a voice not his own. "The heretic must die!" He swung his arm, knocking Anok backward with shocking force.

He was, Anok realized, making no attempt to restrain the evil creature with which he had coexisted these centuries. The old man was weak and broken, but the beast was still strong.

Sabé leapt to his feet, and Anok realized he had a dagger in his hand. He felt for his own scabbard, and found it empty. Sabé had stolen his blade as he knocked him away.

He rolled to his feet, pulling his swords as he did.

"Sabé! Stop this! I do not wish to harm you."

But Sabé charged with shocking swiftness, the dagger outstretched in his hand.

Instinctively, Anok stabbed his sword out defensively.

Sabé threw himself onto the Sword of Wisdom, running himself through until he struck the guard and fell against Anok's chest.

Sabé looked up, the life fading from his now-human eyes.

The old man smiled at him. "I see you—as you are—for the first time. I wish—you were my son."

Then he was gone.

Anok pulled back his blood-soaked blade and lowered him gently to the floor. He reached down and closed the old man's eyes. They were brown, he noticed.

He stood, and as he did, he realized that the sword felt different in his hand. He looked at it. The blood coating the blade began to glow with a strange, nebulous fire, then seemed to be drawn into the metal.

The grip became hot in his hand, and the gemstone eye below the hilt changed, becoming wet, almost lifelike. Then, suddenly, golden eyelids snapped shut over the eye, and the handle cooled.

But the sword was still different. It seemed to tingle and vibrate as he moved it, resisting travel in one direction but not another, as though guided by some unseen hand. "Sabé, my friend. You are gone, but your spirit still guides me, does it not?"

ANOK PULLED DOWN several of the lamps from the walls, doused Sabé's body with oil, and set it aflame. It was both the only funeral the old man was likely to have and a useful distraction, as Anok began to make his way through the interior of the pyramid.

As he moved away from the heart of the pyramid, he felt the magic return to him, and with it, a growing unease.

The Mark of Set paced through his mind like a cat in a cage, restless and ever seeking escape. It had tasted powerful blood this day, several times over, and he had many times called on its power.

He still did not feel recovered from the priesthood ceremony, and he was beginning to think he never would be. There was no "getting better." He was changed, and he would have to live with that for the rest of his days. The Kamenwati was now attached to him like his own shadow.

He wandered through a series of passages, hitting several blind alleys. He thought he might be hopelessly lost, when from down a hallway he heard a familiar noise: a clanking of metal plates, a hissing of steam, a soft roar of flame.

The brass serpent!

He slipped into an alcove and flattened himself against the cold stone of the wall.

The noise grew louder, and he heard footsteps and voices as well. Two priests, dressed in long, ceremonial robes, walked past, and following them, Parath.

They must be going to the ceremony of joining.

The priests did not see him, but as it passed, the great metal snake turned and briefly looked directly at him.

Anok felt a warmth flow through him, a sense of purpose and belonging. Then the snake looked away, and it was gone, fading so that within a few seconds, he could hardly remember the feeling.

What was that?

He shook his head to clear it, then peered around the corner after the strange procession. As he did, he saw the tip of the brass serpent's tail vanish around a corner. Knowing they would be headed for the ceremony, he followed.

As he had hoped, he found himself in a series of inclined corridors climbing up through the pyramid. There were no side passages, no way to get lost.

He was headed for the altar of Set, and his destiny.

He moved slowly and carefully, allowing the priests and Parath to remain well ahead of him. He could tell they were nearing the top because he could hear the cheering and chanting of thousands of voices.

The ceremony had begun.

"Set, Set, Set," they chanted, again and again, "glorious Set!"

Then the chanting collapsed, as though in surprise, and they broke into a mad cheering.

They have seen the brass serpent.

Above him, the ramp opened, and he could see the light of many lamps shining on a stone ceiling twenty or more feet above. The cheering was quite loud.

Cautiously, he poked his head about the lip of the opening.

The ramp emerged at the rear of the platform. In front of him was a row of stone pillars, with one of the captive priests or priestesses bound to each one. Their chains were all engraved with mystic symbols, a binding spell to prevent them from using their own sorcery. He looked for his sister and saw her chained to the farthest post to his left.

Beyond the captives, he could see Parath, Ramsa Aál, and a group of other priests and acolytes in ceremonial garb. Finally, at the front of the platform stood the sacrificial altar. Next to it waited a wooden table draped with a red silk cloth, and on its top, a row of shining sacrificial knives, one for each prisoner.

As he turned, Anok now saw that Ramsa Aál openly wore the Scales of Set over his robe. Then he turned away, and while keeping the chain around his neck, held up the Scales so that those assembled below could see.

Again, they cheered. He held his arms up and waited for them to quiet. "For the first time in recorded time, the Scales of Set are reunited, their power now in service of your cult! Soon all shall turn their backs on their lesser gods and worship as you do! Behold, the instrument of our god that we have created! Tremble before its power! Worship it as the embodiment of your god!"

In his hiding place Anok sneered.

Fools! You know not what god you worship.

"And now," shouted Ramsa Aál, "is the ceremony of joining. It is the night of ascension!" He turned and looked up at Parath looming over him.

The great snake bowed before him, but only to expose the three blank spots on his forehead, where the Scales of Set would fit. "Now, my servant, give me the Scales!"

Ramsa Aál made a signal with his hand, and several of the acolytes began chanting a spell. Suddenly, the sounds of the crowd were silenced, and it became eerily quiet.

Anok could hear the groaning of the prisoners, the wind as it whistled past the stone columns.

He could clearly hear Ramsa Aál, as he said, "No."

The brass serpent reared back. "So, you renege on our bargain?"

Ramsa Aál laughed. "As would you have, if you had the Scales. You would have made yourself god of all the world and would have had no use for such as I. I cannot summon the power of the Scales of Set to rule all men, but I can use enough of it to rule *you,* and through me you can use the greater power to rule men. Have comfort. You might have no use for me in your plan, but at least I have use for you in mine!"

The great snake hissed, and a puff of fire emerged from its mouth and curled around its head. "I should slay you!"

Ramsa Aál laughed again. He spread his arms, taunting Parath. "Try!"

He stood thusly for a moment, but Parath did nothing. Again Ramsa Aál laughed. "You see? You will be their god, and I will be *yours*!"

Again Parath hissed his anger. But then he seemed, to relax. "I knew you would betray me. I have been betrayed by gods, little man. Did you not think I would prepare?" He raised his voice. "My servant! Come forth and destroy the priest!"

No one was more surprised than Anok when, through no will of his own, he stepped suddenly from the shadows, the Sword of Wisdom in his hand.

"Come to me, my servant," said Parath. "Come to me, my Kamenwati!"

29

THERE WAS A stairway up the back side of the Pyramid of Set as well, though it had been unused for centuries, and was in poor repair.

Often, in the darkness, Teferi and Fallon stepped into holes created by missing stones, or had loose stones crumble and fall away beneath them.

Several times they had held their breath as blocks of sandstone tumbled loudly away into the darkness below, sure that the noise would bring the guardians down upon them. But in every case, the cheering and chanting of the masses assembled on the far side of the structure had saved them.

They were startled when, with the torches of the upper temple just a few dozen paces above them, the crowd suddenly fell silent.

Fallon grabbed Teferi's arm, and they stood, motionless, waiting for something to happen. When it did not, she leaned close to his ear and whispered, "What could have happened?"

"This is not natural," he whispered back. "Such a large assembly cannot be silent. It is not possible. We would hear them breathing. If they had been killed, we would hear them fall. This is magic at work, I am sure of it."

Then they heard voices from above, and were just able to make out what was going on. As Parath called Kamenwati as his servant, Fallon could not help but let out a tiny gasp of shock.

Teferi frowned grimly. "If our brother is fallen, it falls to us to prevent the ascension of Parath, and to free his sister."

But Fallon found herself trembling in a most un-Cimmerian fashion. "If we can," she said.

ANOK STEPPED BOLDLY forward, even as guardians and priests closed protectively around Ramsa Aál. He felt strange, as though a passenger in the chariot of his own body. But for the moment, Parath's wishes and his own were the same.

Kill Ramsa Aál. Take the Scales.

The guardians were the first to charge.

In his mind, Anok heard the Mark of Set shriek with delight, as he waved his right hand forcefully.

The first wave of four soldiers were thrown backward through the air, over the edge of the platform, to land far down the side of the pyramid.

The second wave charged, swords held high.

He sliced his hand through the air, and they were sliced in half at the waist, their torsos flopping to the floor, spurting blood, their severed lower bodies toppling more slowly.

He smiled. He laughed.

No! Not him!

It was someone else—some*thing* else—that exulted in the carnage.

"You see," said Parath, "he is bound to the power of the Scales, as soon will you all be. But you are bound by your worship of Set. Not this heretic. For he, and only he, once believed in *me!* Part of him still does. The Kamenwati!"

He saw fear in the acolytes' faces as they closed in front

of Ramsa Aál. One called up a spell, and a blue bolt of lightning shot out from his hands.

Anok swatted it away with the sword.

The sword has other powers!

More spells were cast, and he deftly deflected them, as he would have blows from a blade.

The Sword of Wisdom is defense against magic. Sabé has delivered this weapon into the hand of our enemy, as have I!

Yet even as he thought that, it seemed wrong. Sabé had known much of what would happen today. Could he have made such a dire mistake without some good cause?

I must have the sword for a reason.

He struggled to regain control of himself, but it was as though his mind was gripped in bands of iron. He watched, helplessly, as he waved his hand, and one of the acolytes was ripped to pieces, arms, legs, flying in all directions.

He was striking at the Cult of Set, destroying its servants. Wasn't that what he wanted?

Another acolyte stared at him, eyes wide with fear, then turned to run.

He waved his hand, and the man burst into flames. Engulfed in them, he ran over the edge of the temple and fell out of sight.

He looked at the other acolytes. The Spell of Silence collapsed, and he could again hear those watching below. What he heard were gasps, moans, the occasional scream of fear or hysteria.

He gestured. Their skin shriveled, fell in on their bones, turning them into dried mummies before they could hit the stones of the floor.

One of the priests clutched at his chest and fell dead, not from magic, but from fear. Another tried to crawl away, sobbing, begging mercy. A third simply stood, eyes closed, waiting to die.

Parath watched approvingly.

Ramsa Aál stood, his hands clutched around the Scales of Set, his face white, backed against the altar. "Stay back," he said. "Stay back! Obey me! Stay back!"

Anok reached out with his free hand and grabbed the priest by the throat, lifting him into the air, then slamming him down upon the altar, his head landing with a crack, so that he lay still.

Anok picked up the first sacrificial knife and drew it swiftly across his throat, hot blood spurting into his face.

He took the chain in his hand, snapped it from around the dead priest's neck, then turned and walked with the Scales to where Parath waited.

He removed the chain, and snapped the three scales into the gap in Parath's forehead.

The great brass serpent reared back. "Yes! The power of the Golden Scales is mine! By this fool priest's blood, all who worship Set belong to me! Bow now to your new god!"

Then, as one, the throngs assembled below bowed down, as did the surviving priests. They moved like puppets.

They move like me!

"Next shall be the worshipers of my hated enemy, Ibis!" Parath turned toward the prisoners. "Go to the priestess, my Kamenwati! Kill her in my name!"

Anok returned to the altar, selected a fresh blade, and walked toward the pillar where his sister was bound. As he walked, he struggled to control even some small part of his actions, without success.

Is this how we are all to live our days, puppets of a false god?

He stood before his sister, the knife in one hand, the Sword of Wisdom in the other.

Paniwi looked at him, her eyes pleading. "Anok, do not do this! This is not what our father died for!"

He raised the knife, held it poised over her heart.

His arm tensed.

His hand trembled.

TEFERI STOOD AT the back of the temple, as yet unseen, his bow drawn back, his arrow aimed at Anok's heart.

His body shook with tension. What was he to do? Was his brother already dead? Would this be a mercy?

The bowstring slipped from his fingers.

ANOK STRUGGLED WITH all his will, all his soul, and knew it would not be enough.

Then the arrow struck.

It glanced off the blade of the knife, sending it flying from his stinging hand, flying away to clatter in the darkness far down the pyramid.

He growled (*it* growled) and unleashed a mighty death spell at his new attacker.

A bolt of light shot from his hand, and swept over Teferi, who leaned back as though hit by a sudden gust of wind. Then the giant Kushite planted his feet and drew back another arrow.

"The sacrifice," called Parath. "I will deal with him! Complete the sacrifice!"

The great serpent suddenly lunged at Teferi, who turned and loosed his arrow.

There was a clank, as the metal tip bounced off Parath's metal scales.

Anok lifted the Sword of Wisdom to complete the sacrifice.

But as he raised the blade into his field of vision, the eye on the handle suddenly sprung open.

"Anok Wati!" Sabé's voice suddenly spoke in his head. *"Who are you? Whom do you serve?"*

He stopped, remembering Dao-Shuang's words—

To serve all gods, you must serve none!

His body shuddered as though waking from a dream.

He looked up and saw Fallon standing behind his sister, her sword at the ready. He looked into her eyes.

She swung her sword a mighty blow, and Paniwi's chains parted.

He turned to Parath. The brass serpent stood over his

friend, who was desperately trying to hold it at bay with his sword.

He found his voice. "Parath! Hear me! I am—*not* Kamenwati!"

At first he struggled with each word, but with each word, he felt stronger. "I am born *Sekhemar,* and I have given myself the name Anok Wati!

"I am a heretic. I *renounce* the false god Parath. I renounce *all* gods! I renounce all sorcery, save this blade in my hand!"

The sword seemed to move itself, pointing toward the brass serpent.

Anok lowered his head like an angry bull, looking up at Parath through narrowed eyes. "Yield to me, demon, or be sent back to the pits from which you came!"

"Fool!" The great snake turned on him. "I will kill you myself!"

Anok drew his other sword. The plain, undecorated metal felt *right* in his hand. On the Sword of Wisdom, the eye closed, but still it felt guided by some invisible hand.

"Teferi," he yelled, "Fallon, free the prisoners!"

He ran toward the serpent, swords at the ready.

The great head shot down at him.

He rolled to one side, flames from the serpent's mouth singeing his arm.

He came to his feet running, trying to get behind the serpent, keeping it turning so it would be more difficult for it to strike.

Parath came after him, one of its coils crushing a still-prostrate priest of Set, who did not even scream as he died.

There was a shifting of heavy stone, and one of the pillars that had until moments before held a prisoner, toppled and smashed the serpent's tail. As it fell, Teferi could be seen behind it, his rippling muscles speeding its fall.

A scream of flame poured from Parath's mouth, and it turned on its new attacker.

Then something—*someone*—flew through the air past Anok.

Dao-Shuang of the Jade Spiders landed at the side of the beast, both fists glowing orange, like hot coals. He slammed them down like hammers against Parath's body.

Sparks flew, and a dent appeared in the metal.

Parath's body twitched toward the Khitan master, sending him flying to one side. He rolled to safety, coming to his feet.

"If you have magics," Dao-Shuang yelled to the other freed prisoners, "it would be best you used them now!"

Several of the others stepped forward: a priest of Yogah, priestesses of Ishtar, a savage-looking acolyte of Ajuju the Dark One, and more.

Teferi and Fallon fell on Parath with their swords, hacking away as a woodsman would at a tree, leaving creases in its metal back. They struck from all sides, like ants on a caterpillar, torturing it with their stings.

Parath whipped its head from side to side, unsure where to strike first.

As the head whipped past, Anok thrust his plain sword into the roof of its mouth, shoving his arm past the flames, so that the hilt of it caught in its lower jaw.

He fell back as Parath reared, its jaw propped open.

Anok ran past the huge head, returning the Sword of Wisdom to its scabbard on his back. Reversing direction, he leapt into the air, wrapping his arms and legs around Parath's neck.

The metal was hot beneath his limbs, and burned where bare skin touched it. He ignored the pain, shinnying up the snake's neck, struggling to maintain his position.

At last he climbed over the top of Parath's head as it swung from side to side, trying desperately to throw him off.

He reached down, grabbing hold of the Scales of Set, then let the serpent shake him off.

He landed painfully on the hard floor, rolled, and slid to a stop against one of the pillars at the edge of the temple roof.

He scrambled to his knees, only to see Parath slithering after him.

He smiled grimly, clutching the Scales tighter in his hand. He did not run *from* the great serpent. He ran *at* it.

It lunged at him.

He twisted his body, dived past. As he did, he threw the Scales, as hard as he could, into the flames of Parath's open mouth.

It screamed.

The head flailed from side to side, until Anok's sword popped free.

Still Parath screamed, whipping its head up and down. Bursts of flame shot from its mouth, until at last the Scales of Set flew out and landed on the stone floor, the metal melting into a puddle on the stone, its golden color turning to black.

Below them, from a thousand throats, came a mournful cry of anguish. The surviving priests jerked into motion, sobbing or crawling for safety.

The followers of Set were free!

Parath cried with them.

Cried at them.

"No! No! I am Parath! I am god above all other gods! Follow me! Worship me! Fear me!

"Love me!"

Anok again drew the Sword of Wisdom, felt it guiding his hand. He charged straight at Parath, launching himself through the air.

Parath turned, *and the tiniest gap opened in the plates of its neck!*

The sword struck hard, driven home by the full weight of Anok's body, stabbing deep into Parath's body. Flame shot out around the edge of the wound, but he held on as the great snake flailed.

The blade struck bone, the solid column of Parath's spine. It jerked to one side, and Anok's body shifted.

The blade scraped, as Parath's backbone snapped and parted at the joint.

Anok was thrown clear, the Sword of Wisdom still clutched in his hand. He landed on one knee and looked up in time to see Parath reel backward, then fall over the altar, down the front of the pyramid.

He ran forward to see. It tumbled, loose and lifeless, down the steps, leaking flame and smoke as it smashed down the stairs. Faster and faster it bounced, until at last it landed at the bottom with a crash, and shattered.

Plates of metal flew in all directions, mixed with bits of bone, accompanied by a cloud of rapidly dying flame.

When at last the smoke cleared, there was nothing of the false god but broken and scorched pieces. The life had even been extinguished from the metal of his body, which lay still upon the pyramid's forecourt below.

Parath was dead.

Anok picked up his second sword, nicked and scorched, still warm from Parath's flames, and shoved it home in its scabbard. He glanced at the Sword of Wisdom, then placed it upon his back as well.

Teferi stepped up to him, clasped his arm, and smiled. "Brother, are we done here?"

Fallon ran to him, throwing herself on him with such force that he nearly fell over, smothering him with her kisses.

"Good lady," he said. "Lend me your heart."

She beamed at him. "I already have," she answered.

FOUR CAMELS RODE swiftly across the trackless desert of Stygia, losing themselves in the vast wilderness.

"I do not recall," said Anok, "inviting you along."

Paniwi looked at him with a curious half smile. "You did not, but I came anyway."

"It seems as though every worshiper of Set in all of Stygia is still in a daze and will be for some time to come. You could have easily stolen a boat, as the other prisoners did. You could be across the Styx and on your way home to Nemedia by now."

She shrugged. "With the Scales destroyed, my sworn duty to Ibis is done. Now I must find a new task in his name.

"The Great Temple of Ibis here in Stygia is gone. It will

take us years to establish another, but it must be done, if Stygia is ever to be free of the curse of Set."

"Gods," said Anok, sourly. "One is as bad as the other."

Paniwi pointedly ignored his words. "Until then, I would come to know my lost brother. Perhaps you need me to look after you."

He frowned. "You could have been more helpful against Parath."

"Not all gods grant their followers spells of power. I used my counterspells to keep you from cooking your arm when you thrust the sword into its mouth."

He flexed his arm, the skin pink and peeling. "It still hurts," he said.

"It is still attached," she said dryly.

Fallon looked at the arm with concern. "It isn't healing," she said.

"Nor will it," said Anok, "except in its time. I meant my words. I have sworn off spells. I have sworn off this cursed mark. Let me hurt as other men hurt. Let me fight as other men fight."

Paniwi looked at him skeptically. "It is not so easy to swear off the temptation of dark magic. Mark my words, Anok, you cannot do it alone. You must pledge yourself to some god. If not Ibis, then some other."

"Gods!" He shook his head. "No good comes when they meddle in the affairs of men."

"But sometimes," said Fallon, "good comes when men meddle in the affairs of gods."

He looked again at Paniwi, his eyebrows raised. "You think I must have a god?"

She nodded.

He turned back to Fallon. "Tell me," he said, "about Crom."